# Whipped, Not Beaten

by Melissa Westemeier

Cornerstone Press
University of Wisconsin-Stevens Point

Copyright © 2011 by Melissa Westemeier

Printing, collating, and binding
made possible by a generous contribution from
Worzalla Publishing
3535 Jefferson St.
Stevens Point, WI 54481-0307

Library of Congress Control Number: 2011940685
ISBN: 978-0-9846739-0-2

Cover design by Cassy Kollock
Cover image © iStockphoto.com/Burke Vector

Cornerstone Press
University of Wisconsin-Stevens Point
Stevens Point, WI
www.uwsp.edu/cornerstone

# I am grateful to:

Doug, for all the support in the world, making me laugh and pushing me when I wanted to quit.

Mariana Damon, Marni Graff, Nina Romano & Lauren Small; the dearest Screw Iowa Writers who give the most brutally honest and brilliant advice on writing and life.

Sarah Ogden, my BFF whose encouragement never flags.

The Bumble Book Club, whose monthly conversations about what makes good reading inspire me to write more and better.

My girlfriends, those who invite me to home parties and those who don't, thank you for including me at your tables and in your lives.

Dr. Cherney, who granted permission for me to attend the 2004 Iowa Summer Writing Festival four weeks before my due date.

Mitchell S. Waters, who saw something in the early draft of this novel and helped me refine it.

Wisconsin Public Radio, for daily talking about issues that matter to me.

# Contents

# Whipped, Not Beaten

# Chapter One

**"Make money, make friends, have fun!"**
*—Coddled Cuisine recruitment brochure*

I feel like I'm caught in a chase scene out of a movie—but instead of crashing to a stop after a couple of minutes, I spend my entire life rushing in a panic to get somewhere or do something before time runs out: pay my bills before they're due, track down a guest for the radio show before we go live, stay up with the latest news and trends. Right now I'm ten minutes late to meet my friends downtown. I give up trying to smooth the cowlick at the back of my head and start applying concealer to a trio of pimples erupting between my eyebrows when I hear Tom Jones croon my mom's ringtone, "She's a Lady."

"Sadie! How are you!" My mother's commanding pitch fills my right ear. I cap the concealer and reach for lipstick.

"Fine, Mom. What's up?"

"I'm so glad I caught you before you head out for the night." My mother has a very exaggerated view of my life in Madison—she thinks it's all concerts, nightclubs, and wild Halloween parties. To be fair, things are always crazy in a city housing a huge university (and a disproportionate amount of graduate degrees), Capitol politics, big money bio-tech, granola-crunching fringe element, and conservative Midwestern stock. "I need to brief you before this weekend."

"This weekend?" I rack my brain to remember.

"You're going to Jane's party, right?"

Jane's party. My older sister lives on a rambling farmette in the hills, forty minutes west of Madison, where she raises Samantha, Davis, and Olivia on organically grown vegetables and free-range chickens. My brother-in-law, Erich, works as a computer programmer in Madison and commutes back and forth to their twenty-acre kingdom. This weekend Jane has invited me, our mother, and everybody else she knows to one of those despised home parties where stay-at-home moms peddle everything from candles to cosmetics. In a moment of great duress, I had agreed to attend.

"I almost forgot."

"Bring comfortable shoes. We're going to an estate sale on Sunday. I think it would be appropriate for you to bring something nice for your sister. A hostess gift of some sort: wine, flowers, you'll think of something. There was something else." A long silence fills the air between us while I wait for my mother to remember. My mother has a sharp tongue and mind, which she now applies to various volunteer positions in her retirement.

She's made it both a career and hobby to boss people around.

"Damn, I can't remember. When I think of it I'll let you know."

"Okay, Mom."

"I won't keep you. Have a good night. Love you."

"I love you, too."

Mom hangs up and I hold the phone receiver while thinking about the weekend ahead. Thanks to my friends and co-workers, I've sat in various living rooms and compliantly purchased eye shadows and glass platters, apple-scented candles, and plastic storage containers. My sister called apologetically a month ago to tell me that her friend, Sydney, had started selling cooking utensils and she'd agreed to hostess a party for her. Jane called in favors from everyone she knew, family included, in support of this venture.

But I honestly don't mind this small favor for my only sibling. A weekend at the farm is always relaxing. After letting me sleep as late as I want, the kids greet their favorite aunt with a sticky breakfast of caramel rolls and juice. Then we stroll through the woods before heading back to a shaded hammock to read the newspaper. Jane will create some gourmet extravaganza for dinner before we begin heated contests of Monopoly or Pictionary. Returning to my life as a singleton after these weekends feels depressing, even though my Madison life seems relatively glamorous and free compared to Jane's family.

Speaking of glamorous Madison nightlife, now I'm *twenty* minutes late.

One good thing about Brothers, besides being one of the few affordable downtown taverns not completely overtaken by Madison's college crowd, is that they play their stereo loud enough to distinguish Neil Diamond from Dave Matthews, but soft enough to hear people talking three feet away from your face. I can bitch about my boss without fearing that someone might overhear me.

"Why? Why, why, why do you put up with it, Sadie? You need to produce a series of flops to reveal what a fraud he is. You're like a ventriloquist and he's your dummy!" Molly slaps her hands against the glossy round table in a rhythmic beat.

"Can't you propose a show for yourself?" Kara asks. "I mean, if it's all your work already, wouldn't they save a bundle if they fired him and gave you even half of his salary?"

Ben shakes his head and orders another round of drinks. "Face it girls, it's a man's world out there." He leans back, his muscular chest stretching the Badgers logo printed across his tight grey T-shirt.

"Only when you maintain your position as oppressor," Molly tells Ben.

"You're right. I need to get a spine." I run my hands through my short blonde curls and exhale. "Enough about my crappy day, tell us about Rhonda."

Ben leans forward to report the latest on his new conquest, a former Miss Iowa he hired to tend bar at his restaurant on Monroe Street. Ever since I met Ben three years ago during my waitressing gig at his restaurant, he's had women dripping from each arm. I'm about the only woman on the planet, other than Kara (lesbian) and Molly (too angry and political), he does not know carnally.

Ben's a stud—hot like Bradley Cooper. Ben's charm could stop an angry marching feminist in her tracks. He's also the breed of male that either loves a woman like a sister or tries getting her straight into bed. Any bed: theirs, his, even the back seat of his Explorer will do. They ought to have pictures of guys like Ben on the sides of beer cans in the way there are pictures of criminals at the post office, only below Ben's photo it should read "Warning: Womanizing Bastard!" Yet, despite the hundreds of women who have offered up their hearts to be stomped on, Ben's reputation isn't enough to keep them away from him. If anything, it makes him an even more exciting conquest. I thank God he feels brotherly toward me. The trade-off for him, I've always believed, is gaining insight on the female brain during our weekly happy hour rendezvous.

"We're going to Chicago next weekend. I have Bulls tickets lined up…" Ben looks up and winks at the waitress bringing a tray of drinks to the table. Dark beer by New Glarus for Molly, Cosmopolitan for Kara, Jack Daniels and Coke for Ben and light beer on tap for me.

"Let's get a pitcher of margaritas next!" Kara interjects while Ben wraps up his glorious description of the upcoming weekend in Chicago.

"Oh, Kara, I've got an early morning." And no money—only five dollars to last until Thursday; my share of a margarita pitcher would rule out both morning coffees. I hate to ruin my friends' fun by being poor.

"Come on, Sadie! Let that old blowhard manage things on his own for a change. You deserve a little fun!" Ben nudges me with his elbow while scanning the bar. "Besides, this place is full of plenty of fresh meat." He touches the back of his hair, gelled stiffly enough to withstand gale force winds.

Molly leans forward and nods at the booth directly behind our table. "Plenty of rotten meat, too." She shoves her empty beer bottle towards the center of the table.

Simultaneously we swivel to look in the direction of Molly's nod. There in a corner booth sat Dr. Scott Vale. An assistant professor of anthropology at the university, he and Molly met while doing field research. She now works in an office three doors down from his.

Scott's nuzzling the neck of a young blonde thing in a halter—she could still be jail bait—when he glances up and spies the daggers shooting at him from across the room. Averting his gaze, he murmurs something into the blonde's ear and signals for the check at the same time.

"Bastard!" Molly spits this out before grabbing her fresh bottle of beer and chugging it while the rest of us exchange a grimace.

"You pick 'em, Molly. They sure as hell don't pick you," Ben smirks.

"He's not worth your hate," Kara turns around to face us and pulls her Kate Spade handbag onto the table. "Look, I've got a book full of eligible bachelors, all more worthy of you."

Ben leans over Kara's cashmere clad shoulder and peers at the tiny screen on Kara's iPhone. "Any eligible women seeking men?"

"What about Rhonda?" Kara asks.

"You girls know you can't count chickens before they hatch."

Molly grunts an obscenity before finishing the dregs of her beer. Scott's treatment of Molly was shabby at best. Her constant suspicions of his fidelity were confirmed one month ago when she showed up at Scott's office early for a lunch date. Like something off of a *Lifetime* movie, she found him and his "research assistant" working on paperwork. But they weren't working on a research grant; they were on the paperwork sprawled half-naked across the top of his desk.

Scott tries to get past our table to reach the exit while Kara describes the attributes of an imaginary male. "Bill, he lives two doors down from me and plays tennis." She stops and freezes Scott in his tracks with her shrieking voice. "Well, if it isn't Scott Vale!"

"Good evening," he smiles politely at us. "Good to see you out and about, Mol."

Molly scowls behind her wire-rimmed glasses and raises her middle finger at him.

"Hardly surprising to see you out and about, Scott. Sadly predictable," Kara remarks coolly before turning away from him to smile at Molly. "Where *is* Bill planning to take you next weekend?"

Molly looks over at her, confusion widening her brown eyes.

Ben catches on more quickly than Molly and picks up the thread of imaginary conversation. "Galena, right Molly? Galena's great. Is it true Bill was drafted by the Brewers?"

I chime in, gushing, "Bill sounds like an absolute *dream*. Too bad about this recurring nightmare..." I glare at Scott. He clears his throat.

"Well...uh...I guess I'll see you around..."

The blonde appears just then at his elbow and looks at our group, her pretty eyebrows raised in what is probably a constant expression of cluelessness. "Scotty? Who are these people?"

"Er...just a few acquaintances. Sheri this is Ben, Kara, Sadie, and Molly."

Eyebrows still raised within an inch of her hairline, Sheri nods and looks up at Scott. "Well? Are we, like, going to leave?"

Taking her by the elbow, Scott leads Sheri away like an obedient lapdog while Ben and I snicker.

Kara shakes her head and Molly slumps hers over her empty bottle of beer. "I need something stronger than this. Like a shot of Jack Daniels."

"No girlfriend, you need to try better taste in men!" Kara tells her.

As Kara continues to lecture poor Molly, I feel relief that no one feels sorry for me anymore. I can do just fine feeling sorry for myself now that Henry's been my ex for approximately one year, two months, and five days.

## Chapter Two

**"Does self-employment appeal to you?"**
*—Coddled Cuisine recruitment brochure*

I roll over and realize the sun is up. My eyes focus enough to discover I've hit the snooze button three times, making me seriously late for work. "Shit!" I race for the shower, peeling off my underwear along the way. Skin still damp, I run a glob of mousse through my curls before spackling the zits between my eyebrows with cover-up. Is that a fourth one erupting on my chin?

In my bedroom, chaotic with clothes and boxes piled up to the ceiling, I yank on black dress pants and a pink cardigan with a lacy tank top underneath and jam my feet into black ballet flats. My head aches, my mouth feels dry and disgusting despite a thorough brushing and two rinses with mouthwash. In the bathroom cabinet I find one lonely Tylenol in the bottle and curse myself for not keeping a running shopping list so I don't have this sort of problem. I toss the little white capsule into the back

9

of my throat, praying for it to have the strength of three pills, and lean into the sink to drink straight out of the tap. The faucet leaks onto the sleeve of my sweater and streaks down the side of my cheek.

Twenty-three minutes, a new record. Passing the kitchen, I grab an apple and a breakfast bar while wishing for a greasy helping of fried eggs and bacon to absorb the hangover. "I'm so late," I hiss while jogging down my building's front steps. The brightness of the day forces me to grope for sunglasses, the headache shooting between my eyes like a nail hammered into a two-by-four.

Two blocks later, I run out into the crosswalk as a white minivan turns the corner toward me. My face melts to a dull red as the heavyset soccer mom rolls down her window to screech at me. "Watch it, you moron!"

I know that everyone for a city mile can see me backtrack onto the curb, knocking over a shopping bag resting next to a tall elderly gentleman waiting for the bus. A box of Saltines and a bag of oranges tumble around his shoes as I apologize, trying to gather his spilled groceries.

"Slow down," he snaps, his freckled hand reaching out to set the bag upright.

Ignoring the stares from two teenaged boys slouching behind the man, I flee into the crosswalk once more.

*I need water and I need coffee.* I recite this mantra while banging through the double doors of Wisconsin Public Radio and jogging down the tile hallway. Unfortunately, these two hangover remedies will have to wait until I contact this morning's guest, review the transcript with Dean, and make sure the show starts out smoothly.

Maybe then, after they break for the news and weather, I'll sneak out for hydration and caffeine.

I freeze in the doorway of my office at the sound of Dean's voice coming from behind me like an air horn. "Where have you been?" he demands, his voice causing heads to glance up from phones and computer screens.

"Sorry, I'll be right there." I duck into my office with Dean on my heels like some deranged Great Dane.

"Do you realize we start the show in less than ten minutes? We need to review these notes!"

Inhaling deeply, I force focused thoughts through the muddy cloud of my hung-over brain. Finally, I croak a reply. "We reviewed the show yesterday. I need to get our guest on the phone, so if you'll excuse me—"

"Don't give me attitude, Sadie!"

I look Dean right in the eyes. Actually, I crane my neck to look *up* into his beady pig eyes. "I'm just stating facts. I need to get our guest on the phone."

Dean responds by shrugging and turning around, glancing over his shoulder to bellow a final threat. "This show *better* run smoothly."

As I rush down the hall to the studio, Evelyn catches up to me, striding on long legs beside me. "Anything I can do?"

Sweet and helpful Evelyn became my best friend at the office within my first month at the radio station. We worked phones together during the fall fund drive and discovered we shared more than just a common work-place, which is surprising since Evelyn's twice my age, staunchly conservative, and married with children and a dozen grandchildren.

"Oh, Evelyn! I overslept and I have to get Senator Toole on the phone in the next minute and—"

"Say no more, dear." Evelyn disappears around a corner. I enter the studio and, in my rush, misdial the senator's phone number twice before finally getting the phone to ring.

Impatiently tapping my pen on the Formica desktop, I look at the clock above the door and watch the second hand swiftly pass the numbers. Twenty-nine seconds later, the phone stops ringing.

"Senator Toole's office."

"Hi, this is Sadie Davis from *Idea Exchange*. We arranged for an interview this morning."

"Oh. Oh dear. The senator is at a committee meeting this morning…" the young woman's voice on the other line trails off.

Shit! My mind frantically spins at this unexpected turn of events. "Do you have his cell number?"

"Well, I can't really—"

"Listen, the senator is up for re-election this year. *Idea Exchange* has offered him a free format to discuss his education legislation and, in turn, given him an opportunity to connect with his voting public. I think the person who might be unhappy if he misses this show would be the intern who forgot to book it properly in his schedule." I tap my foot faster.

"555-1224" the voice responds promptly.

I hang up and dial the new number. As I listen to the phone ring once more, the studio door opens. Evelyn tiptoes in and sets a Styrofoam cup of coffee and a bagel on the desk next to the phone.

"Evelyn, you're the best," I whisper to her retreating back. Shaking her head, Evelyn closes the door with a soft click as the phone stops ringing with a loud roar in my right ear.

"What!"

"Senator Toole?"

"Yes. Who is this?"

"Sir, this is Sadie Davis from *Idea Exchange*. You agreed to an interview this morning with Dean LaRoche to discuss your education legislation—"

"Damn!"

Please don't let this fall through, I pray silently while I listen to the muffled sound of voices on the other line. A minute later Senator Toole returns. "How long will this take?"

"Well, we can have you off the air within forty-five minutes if absolutely necessary. The show usually runs an hour but..." I want to persuade him to do the show, and he really can't be finished in forty-five minutes, but once he's on we can deal with that problem—fifty-three minutes from now.

"Okay. Let's get it over with."

My headache recedes as I run through the details of the show with the senator and prepare him for the live interview. He seems to mellow after his initial explosion, and my shoulders drop a full three inches when I glance at the clock. Two minutes to spare.

Dean thunders into the room and whips his chair back from his desk with a clatter. "Well?"

I motion to him with open hands, indicating that all is well. Dean nods and reaches across my desk, grabbing my bagel with one hand and my coffee with the other. Before I can stop him, he takes a huge bite out of the probably dry and stale cafeteria bagel and washes it back with a swig of the steaming coffee.

"In the future, remember that I only like to drink Steep and Brew's Amaretto French Roast," he tells me around a mouthful of bagel before leaning back in his leather swivel chair.

Bastard. I watch my breakfast disappear and the throb in the back of my neck wraps more tightly around my temples and forehead. While the senator explains the highlights of his proposed legislation, I watch Dean eat two more bites of the bagel and toss the remaining half into the trash. My stomach growls in response while I try to focus.

After the show I head straight for the ladies' room. He's such a bastard! I check my mascara in the mirror and swipe a wad of toilet paper beneath my eyes, where it streaked a bit. This is ridiculous. That overgrown, underdeveloped Cro-Magnon man shouldn't make me feel this miserable! Pushing down the cowlick above my left eyebrow, I declare to my reflection, "Guess what, Sadie? We're starting over! So get over it!" Affirmed, I return to my office vowing to stick up for myself from here on out.

At noon, I pick through my desk drawers in my office to discover a SlimFast bar and two packages of crackers crushed beneath a Spanish-English dictionary. Depressed and dragging after the initial rush of the morning, I glance at the time. I've done little besides stare at a computer screen and shuffle the same two files for an hour now.

"Screw it," I mutter to the screen, the files, and the world at large. I check e-mails one final time and note the agonized subject line of Molly's "Men Suck!" Opening it, I read Molly's repeated bashing of all men everywhere, especially Scott. "Oh Molly, move on already!" I groan, disgusted at my friend for not getting over a total scumbag who's hardly worth the time or effort spent hating him. What is with women and the sick torture they inflict upon themselves (and their friends) by obsessing over the most horrible types of men? And an even worse thought: how often did my own friends wonder the very same thing about Henry and me? That's too horrible to even contemplate.

Deleting an offer for enlarging male genitalia, I click on the confirmation response for tomorrow's show from Dr. Brian West—a major coup, in my opinion, since research scientists are reluctant to spend their time doing radio interviews. I trash Molly's latest rant before shutting down my computer. I grab my bag, sending the Post-it notes stuck all over my desk and bookcase fluttering in the breeze of my exit.

On my way out of the office I pause at the front desk and look for any sign of Ron, our station manager. His Creepiness not lurking nearby, I decide to leave word with our receptionist. "Lottie, I'll be out the rest of the afternoon."

Lottie never looks up from her computer screen, where she's shopping online for maternity clothes from

Old Navy. I'm not sure how to take her nonchalance—am I so unimportant that she doesn't try to hide her improper use of office computers or does she think I'm cool enough not to say anything? It's hard to tell with Lottie.

Leaving the building, I realize something else: Lottie thinks I'm going to the library or someplace to continue work on the show. A free afternoon and no penalty attached. The day feels lighter, and my body seems less ill as I retrace my route home at a slower pace than this morning.

My block is very quiet in the early afternoon. I check my mailbox and trudge upstairs. Ahhh. I kick off my shoes and peel off my wrinkled pants and top. Slipping into cotton shorts and an old Camp WeHaKee T-shirt from my counselor days, I grimace at my red, throbbing feet and collapse on the couch.

I debate the merits of taking more Tylenol. I figure it can't hurt, and I go to pop two more down my throat with a glass of cold water. The ache is dull and constant now and my eyes burn. Opening the jar, I remember I swallowed the last one before leaving for work this morning. Resigning myself to ice water, I lie down on the couch again, draping one forearm over my eyes to block the sunlight blazing through the huge window across the room. I have to get blinds or something…my thoughts slow down.

*"Miss Davis, they're ready to see you now."*
*I look up from the files on my giant mahogany desk*
*and stand, smoothing the front of my charcoal pinstriped*

*blazer. Three-inch suede heels make me taller and more intimidating. Checking my lipstick in the mirror and brushing a blonde curl from my forehead, I ask, "Is security in place?"*

*"Yes, Miss Davis."*

*"Bring 'em in." I cross to the floor-to-ceiling windows overlooking Lake Mendota. The lake looks still from up here, as calm as I feel at this moment.*

*I hear the voices outside the door and the suits enter the room, taking their spots behind the giant leather chairs surrounding the conference table. I turn and smile at Henry, who pales at the sight of me. He begins to sweat the moment he recognizes me.*

*"Good afternoon, gentlemen. Please take a seat." I remain standing while Henry blanches, hands visibly trembling as he sits. "As you know, I've recently acquired Masterson Inc. and, as the new owner, I think it's time to make some changes in leadership." I meet Henry's eyes. Shady bastard. He looks up, side-to-side, and then down at his hands, clasped together tightly in front of him. Look who can't make eye contact now.*

*"We'll be keeping everyone on board with just a couple of exceptions." I pause and watch the suits hold their breath, anxious to learn where the axe will fall. "Henry Kendall and Dean LaRoche, you have ten minutes to clear out your offices. Security will assist you on your way out."*

*Henry bursts into tears, begging to stay, pleading for his job. Dean lunges for me across the boardroom table and is held back by two of the middle-aged men seated beside him. "You bitch!"*

*"Sorry fellas, that's the way it goes sometimes." I nod at the man closest to the door and he opens it for me. The uniformed security officers come in to manhandle my ex-boyfriend and tyrannical boss, and I add, "Guess I just need some space."*

*"Sadie! Please don't do this! I'll do anything!" Henry struggles against the two officers guiding him towards the door. "I was wrong!"*

I emerge from my revenge fantasy and scavenge in my kitchen for dinner, trying to ignore a plastic package of Totino's Pizza Rolls, promising tangy pepperoni wrapped in an oven-crisped crust, and grab a Yoplait instead.

A pile of unpacked boxes looms in the middle of the living room. For the first night in ages I'm home with the intention of getting after them. And I do—until the ten o'clock news comes on in a mighty rush of dramatic music. I wad up tape and paper and walk across the room to turn off the television (Henry got the remote control, quite fitting when I consider how much time he spent fondling it instead of me when we were together). A yawn nearly splits my head in two on my way to the bathroom, where I examine my complexion while I floss. Adult acne is a real bitch. Snapping off the light, I take five steps and trip over a box of sweaters I'd shoved to the foot of my bed.

"Damn it!" I swipe a kick at the box and miss it in the darkness, snagging my little toe on my metal bed frame. I fall over, clutching my left foot. Pain throbs up my leg. Switching on the bedside lamp, I see blood oozing out of the ripped toenail.

My medicine cabinet has tampons and dental floss, and even some cruddy bright blue eye shadow I bought back in junior high, but no bandages. I'm forced to piece together a homemade version out of toilet paper and scotch tape. Call me Ms. MacGyver.

Tears well up when I confront the state of affairs I'm in. I'm twenty-eight, single, and three dollars from flat broke. Not exactly a huge success story so far. Living on my own hasn't improved my financial situation, but fantasies of elegant dinner parties and retro cocktail hours, hosted by yours truly, swam in my mind while I scanned the classified section months ago. I envisioned myself a modern-day Holly Golightly, surrounded by handsome bachelors and my swinging girlfriends, holding bright bubbly drinks in tall glasses and conversing in an obtuse way with intellectual equals. In reality, I can barely afford decent groceries, let alone funky cocktail napkins or a great stereo system.

A year, two months, and six days ago I could have. That's when Henry and I were still living together in one of the decent apartment complexes in Madison. That's when my biggest concern was whether I should stay at the radio station or move on to something more lucrative. Radio's good work, regular hours, mentally stimulating, and my working conditions are even pretty tolerable, except for my show's host and my minimal salary. And it beats retail, waitressing, or working the front counter at the Holiday Inn. Unfortunately, a four-year degree from a small liberal arts college coupled with Peace Corps experience makes me unqualified for conventional work. According to my résumé, I can teach English to Spanish-speaking schoolchildren and train third world farmers in modern agricultural practices.

Living with Henry was the best part of adulthood for me: it lasted eighteen months and eleven days. We kissed before heading out to work each morning, came home to share take-out food and some television at night. We spent our weekends together in premarital bliss, enjoying love, sex, and all the great culture Madison has to offer. Then, when I anticipated an engagement ring to seal the deal, he came home one Thursday night declaring that he "needed space." Just like that.

"I just think we should feel free to see other people," he told me, his handsome face all earnest except for his brown eyes looking around the living room, refusing to make contact with mine.

"Excuse me?" Fearing where this conversation was headed, I remember studying a pimple near his neck, concentrating on its redness sprouting in the stubble of his beard like a warning beacon.

"I mean, we should really just be sure about this before we take things a step further."

I'm a person who sees the world in two colors and two colors only: black and white, not grey. Henry needed grey.

"I don't think so, Henry." My voice quavered and my mouth dried despite my attempts to maintain my composure. Crimson rage and betrayal blurred my vision, melting his full lips and goatee into a dark shadow. "You don't spend this much time with someone, move in with them, and live with them for a *year* and *then* decide you want to go backward in the process. No. You should have decided to see other people when we were dating. Not now, damn you!"

"It's not that I don't love you—" he reached across the couch for my hand. The compassionate break-up attempt. How insulting!

I jerked away from him, shaking with fury. "Don't try to get off the hook here. Either shit or get off the pot."

"Sadie, you're asking for more than I can give just now."

Tears, tantrums, and a slap to Henry's face ended that chapter of my life. I might have handled the whole thing with more grace and dignity, but damn it! I deserved better treatment than that! Within twenty-four hours, I hauled out my belongings (and a few of Henry's) and the television set I'd paid half of. In the heat of screaming obscenities at Henry, I left behind the remote control and my favorite sweatshirt. I hate getting up to change channels during commercial breaks.

After a week of calling in sick to work, the numbness eroded and, with the helpful support of my friends and Häagen-Dazs, I emerged from Ben's apartment to see the world looked pretty much the same despite my broken heart. Puffy eyes notwithstanding, I knew I had to move on; I cramped Ben's style. He couldn't bring his dates home to me, a grief-stricken woman surrounded by crumpled tissues, sniffling on his couch.

"He's a bastard anyway," Kara repeated, emptying a box of tissues into my clenched hands. "You'll find someone who really deserves you."

"I never liked him from the start," Molly declared as she ground a cigarette into smithereens, "he had shifty eyes."

"Men are pigs." Oddly this last bit came from Ben, who acted like the greatest hog of them all for the trail of broken hearts he'd left in *his* wake.

A month later I read in the newspaper of Henry's engagement to a cocktail waitress I vaguely recognized from a dance club downtown. I crumpled up the newspaper, wiped the newsprint from my fingertips, and moved into the spare room at Molly's. The scars of Henry hardened and eventually blurred around the edges.

At Wisconsin Public Radio, I worked my way into a new title and a private workspace off to the side of the cubicles reserved for "underlings." Job security and minor prestige were all mine. I only have to endure Dean LaRoche. At six feet (actually six feet two inches, if you added the height of his pompadour), Dean's flamboyantly grandiose. He's more diva than Mariah Carey, J-Lo and Barbara Streisand combined. His radio audience recognizes his voice, low and polished, and his public appearance reinforces this persona. Armed with a pipe and wool jackets with patched elbows, he seems every inch an engaging intellectual. In reality, his actual IQ hovers in double digits and my job is to feed him the questions and commentary he parrots each morning on his daily show, *Idea Exchange*.

"What's this?" he'll demand, striding into my office to lean across my desk in a cloud of cologne and poke his well-manicured finger at the transcripts I carefully prepare for him each afternoon. "What's a NAFTA?

Some new rock band? Why am I asking Senator Grey about a rock band?"

Each afternoon I provide thorough tutorials to prepare Dean for the next day's show. I like to think of myself as CliffsNotes on current events. This, in addition to phonetic spelling, practiced pronunciation of key words like *gubernatorial* before each show, and standing by to jot down new questions or remarks should the conversation take a turn I haven't planned on. Grinding my teeth to mere stubs, I listen Monday through Friday in the studio as Dean takes calls and, consequently, praise in response to *my* work.

"Great show, Dean. I love your guest…"

"I love your show, Dean, and I'm excited that you're bringing awareness to this topic…"

"I'm a long-time listener, first-time caller, and your questions are right on the money…"

Post show, he grabs his coat and leaves to spend the bulk of the day at lunch and at some trendy fitness club downtown. Dean LaRoche has a great deal worked out: come in and talk live for two hours, take a four hour break, and return to review the notes with me for the next day's show before beating the rush hour traffic home.

Meanwhile, I prepare the show each day by researching and developing discussion topics that have Madison and much of the state buzzing. This requires reading no fewer than three daily newspapers, four weekly journals, and dozens of websites in order to keep one step ahead of political and cultural developments, both locally and internationally. *And* I'm accountable to Ron, our station manager—the arrogant troll who has a gift for making me feel like the Invisible Woman, since he's never made eye contact with me.

The score stands: love life and career a big, fat zero.

# Chapter Three

**"The home party industry continues to grow"**
*—Coddled Cuisine recruitment brochure*

Kara's ringtone ("I Kissed a Girl" by Katy Perry) interrupts a lovely dream involving George Clooney, a beach, and me. I wake up breathlessly aware of what George was about to do to me while we played in the sand, and find my hangover has receded. My fingers search the coffee table for my phone. "Hello? What time is it?"

"I'm your wake up call. It's six. Girlfriend, we have to help Molly." Kara, as usual, trying to manage everyone's life for them. She's a younger, gayer version of my mother.

"I assume you got her e-mail, too?"

"She's pathetic, Sadie. What on earth are we going to do with her?"

"Excellent question." I know Kara has the answer from her tone.

"It is. I've been thinking, we need to introduce her to somebody new, somebody to take her mind off of Scott."

"What a marvelous idea. What*ever* made you come up with that?"

"I don't need your sarcasm, I need your help. I've hired a new accountant. I'm throwing a dinner party next Thursday night and you need to come with a date so they're the only two single people there. It will practically *push* them into each other's arms." Kara sounds triumphant.

"Great plan Kara, just one thing."

"What's that?"

"I have no date."

"Honestly Sadie, I think you could come up with *some-body* to bring to a party. Tell them it's purely platonic."

"Wouldn't it be easier for me to not come? Then you'd have all couples."

"But we need you for moral support, if not for any other reason."

"I'll get back to you."

"You're not getting out of this. You owe it to Molly, to me, to yourself."

"I'll get back to you," I promise before hanging up. Where will I find an escort for a dinner party? I'd ask Ben, but he has Rhonda now. The only single man at the station besides Dean, I grimace at the sadistic thought, is Leroy Smullton. He's no dream date; he's fifty, flannel-clad, and specializes in environmental topics. There's the guy in my apartment building I've passed in the lobby a few times. I peeked at his mailbox to discover that A.

Martinson indeed lives alone. A. Martinson is tall, dark, and ruggedly handsome, in a *GQ* cover kind of way. Can I ask him out and not come off as desperate?

Great. I have to prepare for the weekend, figure a way to meet and ask A. Martinson to accompany me to Kara's party, and manage to make enough money to afford the little luxuries in life, like pitchers of margaritas and coffees. The sheer enormity of this to-do list sends me deeper into the couch cushions. Why don't I just add running a marathon, getting a doctoral degree, and ending world hunger?

At least my headache and hangover are gone. Rome wasn't built in a day, so I resolve to tackle one small chore at a time. I haul my ass off the couch. Getting to the office early will be one way to start.

# Chapter Four

**"How to become a Coddled Cuisine consultant!"**
*—Coddled Cuisine recruitment brochure*

I breeze into work half of an hour early, greeting everyone in my path with a cheerful smile. My outfit is adorable. My skin is pimple-free. I even discovered a ten dollar bill in my jacket pocket. On my way to the office, I treated myself to a large coffee and muffin at Bakers Too, leaving me over five dollars to spare. Today's show is ready to roll. All this grand success can only mean one thing: asking A. Martinson to accompany me to a dinner party will result in a confirmed date.

Setting my coffee beside my Aaron Rodgers bobblehead doll, I fire up my computer. I feel in control. This must be the mental state of truly accomplished women, like Ellen DeGeneres and Sandra Day O'Connor. Their lives are no doubt smooth and placid lakes of competency. Surely I can achieve the same effect; I'm feeling invincible.

*Idea Exchange* is planned into next month, adding another layer of self-satisfaction. I reach for Dr. West's file and, armed with folder and coffee, I stroll to the studio. Coming to work early and prepared feels good; why don't I do this more often?

"Good morning, Sadie. Do you feel better today?" Evelyn joins me in the soundproofed studio, closing the door behind her. I like the red scarf she has tied around her neck, a bright touch against her black dress.

"Yeah. I love your scarf!"

"Thanks. I heard yesterday's show went okay." Evelyn tugs at the ends of the silk scarf, pulling the knot tighter.

"It did. I had to bully some poor intern in the process, but I tracked down Senator Toole."

"Where were you yesterday afternoon? I stopped by your office and you were gone."

"I took the afternoon off. It was weird. I told Lottie I was taking the afternoon off and she just said 'okay.' Maybe she thought I was going to do research somewhere." I shrug and pull out the questions for Dean. "Why were you looking for me?"

"I wanted the story on why you were hung-over." She smiles in anticipation and I hate to tell her the whole boring truth of it.

"I wish there was more of a story," I tell her. "Same old friends, new pitcher of margaritas. Molly ran into Dr. Vale and his new girlfriend and Ben left early for a poker party."

Her face falls and she shakes her head. "How disappointing."

It kills me that she cares so much about my social life.

"Tell me about it," I tell her.

"I'll let you get back to work then. Good luck with the show. I'm off to do some fact-checking!" Evelyn waves goodbye, leaving me alone to phone Dr. West.

On the second ring, he answers.

"Hi, this is Sadie Davis from *Idea Exchange…*"

"Right."

A long silence follows before I move right into my canned speech about the show's format and time allotment.

"Shall I just hold while the show gets under way?"

"Yes, that'll be fine," I tell him.

Dean storms in at that moment, raging about finding a parking space and why can't he expect to find his production assistant in the same spot each morning.

"Good morning to you, too."

Grunting, he sits at his desk and stares at the file. "What's this?"

"Today's show," I reply sweetly.

"I thought we were doing movie reviews today."

"We're not. Artificial intelligence. I left a copy of the file on your desk." I knew he wouldn't return yesterday to look it over.

"I can't do this!" he yells, his face turning the same shade of red as Evelyn's scarf.

"I guess we can just ask Ron to run a repeat show or something. I have our guest on the line already…" I trail off knowing he will run with it, regardless of his lack of preparation. He'll bluster through and risk embarrassment before admitting failure to Ron.

Grabbing the phone, he slaps the desk hard enough to make his framed certificates on the wall rattle. I'm sadistically pleased to have kept my cool.

"Dean LaRoche here."

Moments later, the show is under way and I sip my coffee.

"We have with us today Dr. Brian West from the University of Wisconsin–Madison to discuss the future applications of artificial intelligence. Thank you for joining us, Dr. West, and welcome to the show." Dean shoots a final glare at me.

Dr. West's response is dead air, the most dreaded taboo in radio business. Hurriedly, Dean speaks up again. "You've worked at the University of Wisconsin–Madison for two years now. What is your background before coming here?"

"Undergrad at Penn State, graduate and doctoral work at Columbia."

Another long pause.

"I see…then you've been researching?"

"Yes."

Dean waits a beat and asks the next question on the list I've given him.

"Could you explain your current work to our listeners?"

"I'm examining the possibilities of using artificial intelligence for processing laboratory tests in medical clinics." He ends this curtly, each syllable precisely clipped, sounding like a robot himself.

"I see…" Dean scowls fiercely at me, his carefully groomed eyebrows meet dead center above his nose, creating an unfortunate unibrow effect. He's used to guests who start out by stroking his feathers, telling him how much they enjoy *his* work, *his* show. Dr. West doesn't compliment him—he doesn't even come across as cordial or conversational. I close my eyes and concentrate on breathing slowly through my nose, cursing myself for selecting such a horribly anti-social scientist for a radio *talk show*, for God's sake!

"Well, Dr. West, let's open our lines to callers so they might join in our discussion right away." Dean shrugs and rolls his eyes in exaggerated exasperation at Ron, who's standing at the window, pointing at his watch. We don't take calls until halfway through the program to avoid the risk of too few callers to fill the hour. But normally the guest would have more to say, and Ron's threatening glares through the soundproof glass aren't exactly helping the situation.

Dean glowers at me while I scrawl a question on a legal pad for him to ask. Time is ticking by and someone has to fill the static silence. Dr. West isn't going to pick up the slack.

"I'd like to know what kind of plastic you use to make artificial intelligence," Dean finally says.

My pen clatters to the floor.

"Er…I'm not sure what you mean." Dr. West is dumbfounded by Dean's inane question.

"You make *artificial* intelligence, which means it comes from some manmade source. I assume you use some sort of manmade material to make it." Dean leans back in his chair, arms crossing his chest, proud for coming up with a difficult question.

I bend down and grab the pen while listening to Dr. West fumble for an explanation.

"The computers we use have plastic in them, and I guess some metal, too…"

I frantically finish writing and shove the legal pad in front of Dean who picks it up, wanting to strangle his guest by the look on his face.

"Here's another question for you," he begins to read off my notes, "What type of laboratory work could your research affect? How might people benefit from your work?"

As Dr. West starts to answer this question, warmth and excitement infuse his voice and he becomes almost human to our ears. He describes the inaccuracies of lab testing and processing, arguing that human error causes unnecessary pain and suffering. "I can only imagine the frustration a person must feel when diagnosed with a disease. And then they get a second opinion only to hear a completely opposite result from the same battery of tests. By increasing the accuracy of information processing, we save not only time and money, but we improve the quality of people's lives."

He talks on and on. Dean looks at Ron through the window, nodding in satisfaction since he's finally free to drink his coffee. Ron nods briefly and walks down the hall. The tension knotting my shoulders drips away and my stomach stops rolling. Nothing's worse than a talk show that forces Dean to talk and think on his feet. Except for the reticent guest who refuses to engage in a discussion due to fright or a lack of social skill, the latter plainly being Dr. West's dilemma.

Back at my desk an hour later, I check my phone and read a text from Kara:

> Find escort, pay if must but
> **DO NOT COME ALONE!**

I glance up to see Ron scuttling past cubicles, obviously heading for my office. I pull up the file for tomorrow's show. Ron's battered tennis shoes step through the doorway when my phone rings. Relieved at having an obvious excuse to avoid a discussion with him, I grab the receiver and yank it to my ear.

"Hello?" I answer gladly.

"Sadie! What the hell is this about a dinner party at Kara's?"

Molly! Ron stops directly in front of my desk, leans his knobbly knuckles on its surface, and stares over his glasses and down his nose at me while I smile apologetically.

"Thank you for returning my call—" I begin as Molly blares again into my ear.

"I mean *really*! You know this is just another lame attempt to introduce me to some guy she met and thinks would be just *perfect* for me. Who the hell does she think she is, setting me up in front of all my friends like this?" Molly fumes.

"I see. I think that your concerns are certainly valid," I motion to Ron, rearranging my expression to look concerned and serious about the caller's problems.

"Later," he snaps, his pale eyes seeming to look right through me before he stalks away.

"You might be grateful for a night out and a free meal." I slouch back in my chair and mutter into the receiver, "What makes you think this is about *you*?"

"You mean it's not?"

"I don't know, she just called me and invited me last night." Omission isn't really a sin, I figure. It's more an act of divine intervention.

"Oh." Molly sounds subdued now. "I thought she was trying one of those 'invite all couples and then the spare single people will wind up together' kind of party. I'm turning into a paranoid freak, aren't I?"

"Scott just killed a little of your faith in people, that's all. I'm sure it's a temporary condition."

"I'm starting to wonder." A wet sniffle fills my ear and I know she's been crying.

"Molly? You okay? Want me to stay with you for a while? You know, keep you company?" I hold my breath. I'd rather get my new place settled alone, and I can hardly afford to pay rent on a place I'm not living in.

"Would you?" Relief warms her voice. "Oh Sadie, you're a good friend."

"Of course I would, Molly," I squeak through my tight throat. "Listen, Ron needs to yell at me about something, so I gotta go. Call later, okay?" I hang up, feeling my stomach curl at the thought of staying with Molly and talking to Ron. Happy thoughts, I remind myself. I've unpacked two rooms in my new apartment and I'll figure out a way to make Molly happy without moving back in with her. And I'll figure out a way to make more money and get a date for Kara's party. Perhaps some unknown wealthy relative will die, bequeathing their entire estate to me.

I brace myself for Ron and stand, smoothing my skirt, preparing myself for whatever may come.

Out of nowhere, Delaine Andrews from Human Resources appears in my doorway, bearing a plastic bag labeled "Sadie Davis" in green marker.

"Hellooo Sadie! I have your stuff from the party already!"

Bustling toward me, she holds the bag like it's the Holy Grail. "Did you know I ended up with over a thousand dollars in sales at that party?"

Delaine invited me, along with all of our other female co-workers, and a battalion of aunts, sister-in-laws, cousins, and neighbor women to a candle party two weeks ago. I sat wedged between a plump, middle-aged aunt who whispered her praises of the Cozy Times Candle Company the entire evening, and Evelyn, who politely nodded and stuffed her mouth full of cheese spread and crackers during the entire presentation. The aunt won a door prize for her astounding knowledge of candles and home decorating. My only other impression of that evening was the high-pressure presentation by the saleslady who, every five minutes, reminded us of how to become a Cozy Times Candle Company consultant.

"Thanks, Delaine." I open the bag. What did I order?

"I see you ordered the cranberry votives. They smell so good, don't they? My whole car smells like candles after driving around with them in my back seat. Are you going to Lottie's scrapbooking party next week?"

"Lottie's party? Oh, right." The invitation is buried somewhere on my desk. Lottie's having an album-making party. I haven't been to one of those yet.

"I still have to double-check my calendar." I slide a couple of files around, making a show of finding the invitation. There it is, cheerful blue balloon letters inviting me to "store the memories of the past for the generations of the future." Just the thing for a single gal with no kids.

"I can't wait for her party," Delaine chatters on. "I have so many friends who make these albums and they turn out just *darling*. I know I want to order the starter kit and some of the camping stickers. I think my first one will be of all our family vacations."

"I'm sure it will be fun," I agree diplomatically. "Thanks for reminding me. I'll go tell Lottie that I'll be there."

"You get a prize if you bring a friend. I'm bringing my sister-in-law, Patty. Remember? She was at my party."

"Right," I lie.

"Must get moving. I have more candles to deliver. Have a great day, Sadie!" As cheerful as the bright flowers on her blouse, Delaine waggles her fingers at me and bustles back out of my office.

I peek in the bag again and take a delicate sniff. They actually smell pretty good; the warm, spicy aroma reminds me of fall holidays. Pulling the receipt out, I read that I ordered two boxes of cranberry votives and one box of vanilla tapers. Thirty-five eighty-seven, including tax, shipping, and handling. I have to start keeping track of the gifts I keep buying for people at these parties. I rarely like anything for myself, so I justify my purchases by thinking they'll be for other people. Then they get stashed somewhere and forgotten until another year has passed. I've probably spent hundreds of dollars on gifts for my mother alone, yet none have made it as far as a gift bag.

I pull a spiral memo pad out of my desk drawer and flip it open to a blank page. I print at the top: *Holiday Gifts Purchased*. Hmmm. I actually may keep the candles. I consider this for a moment and then write on the top line: *Mom—one box cranberry votive candles*. There. Then at Lottie's party I'll add to this. Oh yeah, and at Jane's party I'll add to it, too. I don't know whether to laugh or cry at the fact that another sixty dollars will continue the vicious cycle of these damn home parties.

Remembering that my presence is wanted in Ron's office, I take one last vigorous sniff out of the bag of candles before setting it next to my purse. Cozy Times aromatherapy. I straighten my shoulders to face my gnarled-up gnome of a boss.

I knock twice on his door and wait until he barks, "Enter!"

"Sit down, Sadie." Before the backs of my thighs make contact with the seat of the olive green chair cushion, he continues, "Not our best show this morning, was it?"

Ron makes his criticism sound like the other person's idea, no question coming out of his mouth without some sort of hidden agenda. It's always best to keep answers short when talking with him and let him do as much of the talking as possible. I nod.

"Who's to blame?" He looks over his glasses and down his nose toward me. His small, grey eyes look through me again. I'm so insignificant that he can't even look *at* me.

I want to yell, "*Dean* is, you idiot! He's a raging idiot who doesn't know the difference between a right-wing conservative and a bleeding heart liberal! He thinks that United Way is some New Age religious movement!" But Dean is the star of the show, a show that has been picked up by three stations out of state, and his book based on the series, *The Idea Exchange* (co-authored of course), is already on its second printing. "I guess Dr. West came across as more engaging in print than in person."

"Sadie, your job is to pull in guests to *discuss* timely topics on our show. I don't care if they've won a Pulitzer Prize—if they can't talk, they don't belong on radio!" He spins his chair around and starts digging in a desk drawer.

"I understand, Ron."

"How do you plan to prevent this sort of problem in the future?" Aha. Here's the part where I'm in charge and then he can hold me to whatever I choose to say.

"I guess I should talk to the guests at some point before they come on the show, and then I'll get a sense of whether they are appropriate for radio. I just hadn't with Dr. West because he was traveling and I—"

"Sadie, I think that's a wonderful solution." He pulls out a file folder and glances up at me. "From now on you will talk to each guest before they come on the show, and then we won't have this problem in the future."

Ron's also a big one for repeating what you say. I swear he was a first grade teacher in a previous life. I nod, lips pressed together so tightly they hurt. I fight back the overwhelming urge to kick him in the shin.

"I thank you, Sadie, for taking the time to discuss this with me." He stands, indicating that he is ready for me to leave.

Every time Ron talks to me I want to cry. I feel the same way my ninth grade biology teacher made me feel. Mr. Sternway would ask people questions in a slow voice and respond in this loud, amazed tone when they got the right answer. I remember sitting in the third row in the far left aisle of the room, and he'd pat my head whenever passing my desk. "Congratulations, Miss Davis, it looks like you're figuring it out!" A lot of people really liked him as a teacher and would tell me how much they learned and how great he was. I privately thought he wouldn't know his ass from his armpit without the teacher's edition in his hands. I look at Ron the same way. If he wasn't station manager, would he have any greater knowledge or authority than anyone else?

# Chapter Five

**"Meet new people, make new friends"**
—*Coddled Cuisine recruitment brochure*

After lunch I call Molly from my office, praying her state of mind has improved. "Hey Mol, how're you doing?"

"Okay." She treats me to a loud and drippy sounding sniff.

I gulp a lungful of air and begin my rehearsed speech. "Why don't you come over tonight? You can sleep on the couch and then tomorrow come to Jane's with me for the weekend. She's having some sort of party on Saturday and I know she wouldn't mind if I brought you along. I think a weekend at the farm would be just the thing to clear your head." Whew, that left me winded.

Molly doesn't answer.

"You still there, Molly? What do you think?"

"I don't know."

"Come on, you need to get away from your apartment and your work and get some fresh perspective. This'll be perfect!" I try to sound positive and punchy.

"Well…"

"Molly, I insist. Allow me to take you away from it all. I mean it." I cannot allow myself to stay in her apartment again.

"I don't know. I just want to stay home. I don't really feel like being around people right now."

"For Christ's sake, Molly! This is exactly what you need! Enough wallowing in self-pity. You're coming over tonight and you're coming with me to Jane's!"

"Okay. You're a good friend, Sadie. I really appreciate this."

"Don't mention it. I'll be home by six, so I'll see you then?"

"Okay."

As much as I hate to share my weekend at Jane's, this will provide me with someone to sit by while watching Sydney demonstrate cooking utensils and explain how to become a Coddled Cuisine consultant. I should have taken Kara's advice and never agreed to go to the first party. People see you at one and they invite you to every home party they hold; there is no way off the mailing list once you're on it. They practically send around the sign-up sheet for the next party before you leave the one you're attending. At this rate I'll have sat through a hundred parties by the time I'm forty.

Staying at Molly's seemed so ideal after I broke up with Henry, or rather after he broke up with me. I couldn't stay at Ben's forever; the couch was too hard and narrow to sleep on, it was like spending the night on a two-by-four. His refrigerator only held beer, wine, and the occasional box of leftover pizza or Chinese take-out. By contrast, Molly's place was clean, spacious, and had a spare room she offered to rent me. The smooth wood floors, sunny window seat, and flowers in terra cotta pots on the front porch charmed me. Even though I ended up staying there for nearly a year, it only took a month to know it was a bad move, literally.

But I averted the disaster of moving back to Molly's. She's a great friend, the best, but friendship and living together are totally different concepts. Since living in my new place, I appreciate the truth of that even more.

Molly's particular. A throw rug half an inch out of place, a slightly off-center stack of magazines in the living room, a dirty glass in the sink instead of in the dishwasher (God forbid!) are all cause for snappish lecturing. I huddled in my bedroom to stay safe from her fury.

The cheap rent was terrific, but between the ocean of difference in our housekeeping standards and her hippie friends who came over all weekend to talk philosophy and politics while drinking black beer and eating tofu, I just couldn't handle it. I hated feeling like some yuppie sell-out each time her friend Rapha raged against "The System" or Bonita extolled the virtues of buying only fair-trade goods. Their lists of products and places under boycott were so long that I shudder to think what they eat or wear. No fur, no meat, only organic food, and stay away from anything made in most of Asia! Honestly, who lives like that? I found their strict principles pretty harsh, even by Madison's standards.

When I began apartment hunting during my lunch hour, I wondered why I kept it from her. Then the whole Scott thing happened and I put off moving into an adorable condo on the west side of town so I could lend her moral support. When she again had the energy to bitch constantly about leaving the toilet lid down and shutting off every light when you leave a room, even if you're just getting the phone or going to the bathroom, I figured she was back in her groove. I was obviously very wrong.

It's okay though, it'll probably be fun to have Molly stay over and come to Jane's for the weekend. Which reminds me, I should call and let her know I'm bringing a guest.

I e-mail tomorrow's guest, an expert in lawn and garden care slated to discuss alternative landscaping, and grab my supplies to head to the library. I have to find a copy of a former governor's autobiography, just released this past Friday.

On my way out, I stop by Lottie's desk where she's checking out baby layettes on her computer screen.

"Lottie, I'll be at the public library. If anyone needs me, they can call my cell."

"Okay, Sadie." Lottie barely glances at me before lowering her crisply hairsprayed head once more to look at baby clothes.

As I walk the eight blocks to the public library, I call Jane.

"Jane, Molly is having a bit of a crisis—"

"The Dr. Scott Vale sort?"

"Sadly, yes. Anyway, I invited her along this weekend, is that okay?"

"Oh my gosh, yes! The more the merrier! Did you mention the party?"

"Sort of. I left out the specifics about it being a *home* party," I add.

"That's okay, I just don't want her to feel ambushed when you bring her into a living room filled with women watching a cooking demonstration."

"I don't think it will matter anyway. Can I bring anything?"

"Is this Mom telling you to bring me a hostess present?" Jane asks.

"How did you guess?"

Jane snorts. "If it'll make you feel better, bring something. Otherwise, I think there's a bottle of wine somewhere around here that Erich got from a client. It might even be gift wrapped. I can leave it in the mailbox for you to pick up on your way to the house."

I really don't have the cash to spend on a present just to impress my mom, and Jane knows this but doesn't say it in so many words. She is the best sister.

"That'd be great. I don't think I'd have time to get you something, unless I pick up an air freshener or magazine at a gas station on the way there."

"Say no more. I'll have Erich stash it there after Mom comes so you can grab it on your way up the drive."

"I have to get back to work. Thanks a lot, Jane."

"No problem! We'll see you and Molly tomorrow night."

I hang up smiling. Jane always makes me feel loved and completely understood. For an older sister, she is awesome. Even as a teenager, she never was embarrassed by me and always offered up wisdom without sounding preachy. When she was a junior in high school and I was a sniveling and pimply seventh grader, Jane let me hang out with her friends whenever they came over. She drove me everywhere after she got her license, did stuff with me, like take me to movies and the mall—things no one's older sister ever did. She'd watch me try on sweater after sweater at The Gap, never buying anything for herself, but stood by while I burned through my allowance.

I remember Jane's high school graduation as being surrounded by big hair and blue eye shadow. Jane stood solidly in Birkenstocks, hair comparably flat and face freshly scrubbed. Kitty Cavarotti, the head cheerleader and homecoming queen, had run straight toward Jane and gave her a huge hug, telling my sister "you're the coolest girl in our class and I'll miss you so much!" I remember that moment so clearly because in my mind, at that same moment, I was thinking, how can I become just like Kitty? Jane never thought like that. She just concentrated on becoming herself and following her own path. People liked her despite that or because of that. I envied her but couldn't help caring what other people thought about me.

Rather than discover who I was, I wasted middle school, high school, college, and even most of my adult life copying someone else's model of who to be. I constantly watch people and compare myself. At a party, I'll spend half the night obsessing about the thinnest, best looking and best dressed women there. I'm always trying to figure out how to look like somebody else, what their secret is. If I channeled all that energy into just having fun and enjoying myself, I'd probably be a happier person. And in the face of my obsessive worrying and wishing, Jane smiles, listens, and hands me a plate of cookies or homemade bread. She makes me feel absolutely okay in spite of my dysfunctional self-image.

In the library I scout the reading room before approaching the front desk to ask about the book. The grim-faced librarian gets the autobiography for me, covered in shiny plastic and practically untouched.

"Now, this is on reserve for someone. If they come in while you're looking at it, I'll have to get it back from you," she informs me.

"I understand, thank you."

She watches me take my seat across the room. I open the cover and hear the binding crack slightly. For some reason, I feel very pleased to be the first to read this book. I inhale the crisp scent of fresh paper and ink.

I gloss over the first few chapters and, before I know it, a shadow stretches across the table where I'm sitting. The sun has sunk behind the trees. I glance at the clock on the wall above me. Five-thirty! Where did the afternoon go?

Hurrying to beat Molly to my place, I slide everything into my bag and leave the book at the front desk. As I bump through the security gate, my stomach growls, reminding me that I have to figure out plans for dinner, too. Ugh!

I merge into the flow of people on the sidewalk outside, looking at the buildings for some sort of inspiration for supper. I have about six dollars and Molly will not eat red meat, so burgers are out of the question.

Two blocks later, I narrowly avoid collision with a green-mohawked skateboarder and duck into Kabul, my favorite Mediterranean restaurant on State Street, and study their take-out menu. Barely, and I mean barely, I pay for chicken kabobs and a side order of burani and an iced tea for the road. The fragrant bag clutched against my chest, I push the door open and a man bursts inside, squashing the entire package against my pretty blouse, sending my iced tea streaming down my neck and across my chest. With my breasts now soaked in freezing liquid, I could win some kind of perverse wet T-shirt contest. The flimsy fabric, I notice as I pull the bag back from my chest to survey the damage, barely conceals me and clings to my bra, every lacy detail as clear as day. Even my belly button stands out in bas-relief.

"God damn it!" I screech. That's right, call even more attention to myself. I can only think about how embarrassing it will be to walk the remaining five blocks home. Now I'm late. Molly will be waiting in the hall outside my apartment and I have no money to buy another dinner, so she's going to have to eat processed, chemically-laced, antibiotic-laden pepperoni Pizza Rolls or starve to death.

I see the man behind the counter staring at me and the two cooks behind him ogling from the window of the kitchen. The man who ran into me is bent in half before me, picking up the carton of rice that fell from the bag and apologizing over and over.

"I'm sorry. I'm so, so sorry," he tells me as he scrapes up the rice and straightens up to look at me, his face deep red.

I catch my breath: it's A. Martinson.

His eyes never make it to my face. He's staring at my shirt. He's staring through my shirt probably, and I jerk the ripped and soggy paper bag back against my front, uncertain which nipple I should cover.

"Let me get you some napkins," he mumbles and turns to the counter, leaving me awkwardly hugging my food. Forget the napkins—what about my dinner? A moment later he returns and hands them to me. A dim recognition creeps across his expression.

"I'm sorry, do I know you from somewhere?" he asks, looking at my face more closely now.

"I'm not sure," I frown slightly and purse my lips so I appear deep in concentrated thought.

"You look familiar somehow…"

I shake my head. I don't want to look like I recognize him; it would mean I've paid attention to him as he has come in and out of our building. I don't imagine too many women forget him, however.

"I'm Adam Martinson. I'm so sorry for running into you." He holds out his hand for me to shake.

"I'm Sadie Davis. I forgive you." I take his hand while keeping my left arm crossed strategically in front of me.

He smiles a great gleam of bright teeth and my knees feel as flimsy as my blouse.

"Please let me buy you a new dinner," he offers.

"Oh no, that's really not necessary."

"I insist."

Actually it is necessary, but it would be rude to say so. Humbly I tell him, "That's very kind of you. I had just ordered a couple of kabobs with rice and an iced tea."

He nods and I follow him to the counter where he places the order and adds on an Abdul special while pulling out his wallet.

Awkwardly, we stand next to each other and wait for the food. I feel like an idiot still holding a bag of smashed and dripping food against my chest, but the only alternative is looking like a porn star.

"So, do you eat here often?" he asks.

"Ummm, sometimes." I shift the bag slightly as it has begun to drip onto my sandal.

"Oh! I'm sorry!" He suddenly walks out of the restaurant, leaving me standing there.

What on earth? Adam Martinson may be handsome, but so rude! Why on earth would someone just walk out like that? What a clod! I glance around the restaurant and, with relief, notice only three tables are occupied and no one is paying any attention to the drama by the counter anymore. Suddenly the door swings open again and Adam Martinson approaches me, carrying a copy of the *Capitol Times*. He had to suddenly leave to get a newspaper? I stare at him in disbelief.

"I'll trade you." He hands me the newspaper and reaches for the bag of crushed food.

"Thank you." Oh, he *is* gallant. Gratefully, I replace the bag with the newspaper and smile a sheepish apology for all my distrustful thoughts.

"Sorry I didn't think of that sooner," he tells me, leaning forward. He smells faintly of lavender and something very clean.

At that moment, our food is ready and he hands me my order. I thank him while he protests my gratitude.

"It's the least I can do. I ruined your dinner and your blouse, after all."

"Thanks anyway."

He pushes the door open and stands aside for me to pass. I smile at him, I hope winningly, and begin to walk home knowing he'll be in my wake. Sure enough, I hear quick steps as he catches up to me.

"I'm headed this way, too," he tells me. I note that my head reaches his shoulder. He's my ideal height for a man.

"I live over on Orchard," I nod.

His eyebrows raise and he responds, astonished, "Me too! I live in the big white house with the porch across from Menona Heights."

"No way!"

"Do you know it?"

"I live there, too!" I shake my head, acting surprised at this amazing coincidence. "Looks like we're neighbors."

"I can't believe I've never run into you before."

"I must say I'm rather glad." I gesture to my still soaked blouse.

"I'm glad you have a sense of humor. So, do you live there alone?"

"Just moved there a month ago. Great location." I'll let him share about himself without my help. I don't want to seem like I'm desperately looking for another single guy, which of course I am, but he doesn't need to know that.

"Isn't it though?"

We walk along silently for a bit, and I enjoy feeling like we belong with one another, and I notice more than a few women glance twice at him. They probably think we're together and I savor their envy. As we pass an import shop, I glance in the window and admire the reflection of us together. Adam is so tall and dark next to my short, blonde image in the window. He pauses midstride, noticing me looking at the glass.

"Do you see something you like?"

I stop walking and look into the window for an answer. "Ummm, I saw a pair of earrings last week. I was wondering if they were still there."

"Did you want to go in to look?" He sounds as if he would willingly join me, wait for me, accompany me.

"No, that's all right. I really don't need another pair, anyway."

He shrugs at that. "Okay. I don't mind, you know."

As I begin to walk again, I ask, "So, do you work downtown then?"

"Yes, at O'Leary, Overland, and Krauss."

"Aha. A lawyer?" Oh my mom would be so impressed!

"Please hold the shark jokes."

I smile.

He continues, "I just joined the firm two years ago and even now I'm amazed that I'm actually a lawyer. It still feels weird to say."

"Did you go to law school here?"

He shakes his head. "Minnesota."

"What kind of law do you practice?"

"Mainly real estate. Hardly the high drama you see on TV. I do some estate planning, but mostly I deal with paperwork for developers. I don't make grand speeches in a courtroom."

"Is that what you dreamed of doing in law school?"

"My father is a lawyer, the same kind, and I knew pretty much what I was getting into. My roommate went into prosecution though, and from the sound of it, it's very stressful."

"I can imagine."

"So, Sadie Davis, what do you do?"

"You mean besides order take-out at Kabul?"

He grins. Oh those white, white teeth—he could advertise for toothbrushes or dental floss for a living!

"I work as a production assistant for public radio."

"Have your own show?"

"I'm the gal behind *Idea Exchange*."

"No kidding! I love that show! That must be why your name sounds familiar."

"Thanks. Dean does mention me at the very end of each hour." So, I guess he's not such a big shit after all.

"What's it like working with Dean LaRoche?"

Adam seems to be a fan, so I refrain from the whole truth. "It's an experience." That's partly accurate.

"I bet! You have the most incredible guests and topics. I loved the program about property rights you ran two weeks ago."

"That was actually one of my better shows. I suppose a topic like that is right up your alley."

"It gave me some new perspective, which is always helpful in my line of work."

We turn off State Street and head down a narrow path toward the lake. Our building looms ahead of us, marking the end of this happy walk home. I kick my brain into overdrive trying to figure out how to invite him to Kara's party. Consequently, my brain stalls in this gear and I can't think of a single way to ask him without sounding like an idiot.

We walk the three blocks way too quickly and there we stand on the porch outside. I glance around for signs of Molly, but she's nowhere in sight. Thank God.

He holds the front door for me and, as I pass under his arm, I check my mailbox. I dawdle, thumbing through a Pottery Barn catalog, an electric bill, and a Coddled Cuisine postcard reminding me of Jane's party.

Adam removes two long envelopes from his mailbox and slides them into the side pocket of his briefcase. Then he turns to me.

"It was really nice to meet you, Sadie. Would you like to get together some time for coffee or beer or maybe a bite to eat?"

"That would be nice," I nod. Okay, this is my opening, why am I not taking it?

"I'm sorry about your shirt. See you." He turns to climb the staircase along the left side of the lobby.

"Would you like to come with me to a dinner party next Thursday night? A friend of mine is hosting one and I'm supposed to come with a date. It doesn't have to be a date actually, we're trying to surround another friend with couples so she can get set-up with this guy my friend knows from work. You see, she was brutally dumped and everyone's working together to get her confidence back." I realize I am blabbering and sound idiotic.

"Quite a party," he smiles. "I'd love to come along."

"Great!" Relief surges through my body and out of my mouth, "Why don't I meet you here in the lobby at six. Is that okay?"

"No."

No? Before I can speak, he clears his throat.

"My mother raised four sons to be gentlemen. If you tell me your apartment number, I would much rather pick you up there."

"Seven."

"I'll see you Thursday," he lifts his bag of food in a kind of salute and disappears up the stairs.

Breathing a huge thanks heavenward, I race up the opposite staircase and let myself in, wanting to scream out loud that I have a date with Adam Martinson! I kick off my shoes. I'll window shop in the Pottery Barn catalog later; I toss it on the couch and rip the bill open. Another stroke of good fortune! Less than I had anticipated. Evidently, never being home translates into lower utility bills. Feeling absolutely buoyant, I sail into my bedroom to change. I peel off the wet blouse and bra and nearly have redressed in sweats and a tank top when I hear knocking at the door.

I throw the door open to Molly, looking lonely and pathetic with her backpack drooping behind her right shoulder.

"Hey," she mumbles and slinks into my living room and flops onto the couch, backpack sliding to land between her scuffed-up Birkenstocks and socks.

"I got us some take-out from Kabul—" I stop, suddenly realizing I can't very well share the great news about Adam Martinson because Molly is in a state of rejected depression and to do so would be like rubbing salt into a wound; the fact that I have a date for Kara's dinner party is supposed to be sort of a secret.

"Swell."

I imagine Tigger had a better time partying with Eeyore than I'll have tonight with Molly. No big deal, I'll let her sulk it off. Maybe a good movie and some wine will help cheer her up. I head back to the kitchen and open the cupboard above the sink. I have stashed up there next to my two cookbooks three bottles of wine Jane gave me last Christmas. I pull one down and carry it hopefully back to the couch.

"How does a little Domaine du Sac sound? I think this will go well with kabobs and rice!" I hold the wine out against my right forearm and wiggle my eyebrows at her. "Two-thousand-nine. That was a good year." I display its burgundy splendor and read from the back, "With overtones of raspberries and bing cherries. The finish has a touch of oak and rosemary."

Molly smirks.

"Ah! A yes," I return to the kitchen to load up on plates, forks, and glasses.

"I'm only sorry I haven't any Häagen-Dazs to offer you!" I call to her.

"That's okay."

Balancing the bag of food on top of the plates and forks, carrying two wineglasses laced between my fingers, I sit on the floor on the other side of the coffee table. She slides the bag of food off the plates and begins emptying it while I arrange the dishes.

"Scott and I ate at Kabul once," she comments, her mouth pathetically turned down.

"This is unacceptable." I stand. Actually I have to go get the corkscrew, but the action punctuates my comment. "No Scott talk! I don't want to hear it. By the powers vested in me, I declare this apartment officially a Scott-free zone."

Molly's mouth reverses its course, even revealing for a second the dimple on her right cheek, and I leave her to get the corkscrew. There. Step one in breakup recovery is not admitting the problem, it's *forgetting* the problem. In this case, the problem is Scott.

I sit again on the carpet in front of Molly and grab the bottle while she gets busy divvying up the food.

"I love kabobs. What do I owe you?"

"Nada. My treat."

"Really? Thanks, Sadie."

"Don't mention it. I was thinking we could watch a movie tonight."

"What one?"

"Your call. We can drown ourselves in the raw humor of *The Hangover* or refine ourselves by watching *Pride and Prejudice*."

"Hmmm. I'm rather leaning toward drowning myself at this point."

"We'll watch *The Hangover!*" I generously pour out two glasses of wine and raise mine.

We clink our glasses. From the way Molly attacks her food, I think she'll be okay.

Two hours later, I untangle myself from an old crocheted afghan and stand to pop out the DVD while Molly takes dibs on the bathroom. I'll let her soak in the tub while I load up a couple of garbage bags with my dirty laundry to take to Jane's. As I pick up my soggy tea-stained blouse, I pause to picture Adam. Maybe my life is turning around. It takes all of my willpower not to share every bit of this afternoon's exchange with Molly. I'm dying to tell somebody. That's the bad thing about secrets: the minute you have one, you feel like you're about to burst with telling it.

I shove the blouse into the second bag and tie it off. Already my bedroom looks much neater, and I admire the dark blue carpet I have uncovered. I listen for Molly and only hear the radio. Since she isn't draining the tub yet, I tackle the box labeled *sweaters*. My efforts reward me with four more square feet of floor space—not a bad investment for my time. I nearly finish straightening up the row of shoes on my closet floor when the phone rings.

I fall across my bed and lift the receiver of the white princess phone I got on my sixteenth birthday. "Hello?"

"Sadie?"

"Hi, Mom."

"Glad I could catch you. I remembered what I needed to tell you the other evening. Your Uncle Bert is coming in from Boston and needs someone to pick him up and bring him to his hotel."

Uncle Bert is my magician uncle, Mom's younger brother. Eccentric does not even begin to describe him, but he is lovable in a Mickey Rooney kind of way.

"I take it he's flying in to Madison?"

"Yes, you'll want to call the airport to confirm this, but he's coming in next Thursday at four o' clock, flight 8769, Midwest Express. He's staying at the Radisson and attending some magic convention."

Thursday. Kara's party is later. Adam's picking me up at six. I should make it if there aren't any delays. I jot down the flight information on the back of a Canterbury Bookstore receipt for a *Vanity Fair* and an Oprah Book Club pick I never read.

"Sure, Mom, I'll pick him up."

"Splendid. Thank you, Sadie! See you Saturday."

As she hangs up I shake my head, thinking of Uncle Bert. My earliest childhood memories involve coins appearing in my ears, mouth, and nose. He could levitate furniture, make any card in the deck turn up at will, and create rabbits and pigeons out of thin air. Uncle Bert never married. Instead, he followed his "dream" of becoming a great magician in the tradition of Houdini and David Copperfield. When he wasn't working in a pet store, he toured around performing at festivals, children's birthday parties, and the occasional grand opening of a store.

Uncle Bert lived with us for several months when I was about eight years old. To this day, I'm not sure why he moved in, but it was so cool to have a magician living in our house. I brought every one of my friends over to show off, begging for one more card trick, one more rabbit out of the hat. I'm sure his presence made my parents nuts. They constantly nagged us: "Leave Uncle Bert's swords alone! He'll need them tonight for his show! Don't touch the wands, you don't know what's inside of them! Quit messing around with his cards! No, you may not saw your sister in half!"

But we all loved him. Jane and I idolized him, Mom indulged him, and Dad envied him, I'm sure. He and Uncle Bert would spend hours working out tricks together. After Bert left, Dad told Mom, "Boy, does he have the life or what? Just roaming around, chasing his dream." I remember the wistful look on his face as he said it, and for the first time in my life, I looked at my dad as another human being with dreams and longings, not just some automaton there to tickle us, dole out weekly allowances, and occasionally punish us. I wondered what his dream might have been, but I never asked. By the time I reached the age of twenty-four, when we could have talks about such things, he died of a heart attack and left his three girls to pick up the pieces and grieve over the empty place at the table each holiday.

The loud gurgling from the bathroom jolts me back to the present and I finish arranging my shoes. One red wedge-heeled sandal remained, mysterious in its solitude. In the living room I tuck a sheet over the couch cushions and leave a pillow from my bed and a quilt for Molly to sleep with. I turn off the kitchen light and check the deadbolt on the front door as she emerges from the bathroom in a cloud of steam.

"Feel clean?" I ask her, grinning at her red and puffy face.

"Yes, I soaked all my cares away, right down the drain."

"Good for you. The couch is all set up. I have to get up at seven. Do you want me to come get you?"

"Yeah," she squints her eyes, blind without her glasses, "what time is it now?"

"About quarter past ten."

"Yeah, if I'm not up when you wake up, give me a shake."

She shuffles into the living room and curls up on the couch. Molly has an amazing ability to drop off to sleep. She never needs to toss and turn and flop into slumber the way I do. She can just lay down, close her eyes, and that's that.

I fall into my bed fifteen minutes later and, at last glance, see ten-thirty glowing green next to me on the bedside table. What keeps me awake, rolling from side-to-side, an hour after I hit the sheets? It's the memory of tall and ruggedly handsome Adam Martinson, lawyer and neighbor, casually walking alongside me down State Street. How can any girl drift right off to sleep after so much excitement in a single day?

# Chapter Six

**"Coddled Cuisine makes cooking easy and fun"**
*–Coddled Cuisine winter catalog*

I hate mornings when I can't wake up in a leisurely fashion, stretching a bit, letting my muscles warm-up before walking around. I prefer the slow adjustment to daylight, first letting my eyelids filter the brightness to my closed eyes. If I had a nine o' clock job I could savor the morning: eat cereal and toast, drink coffee, watch the news, maybe even head out for a morning jog. In reality, I'd probably just sleep in later and waste more of the day. I've never been a morning person, but thanks to caffeine, I can at least function like one.

Punching my alarm off, I stagger into the bathroom. Fortunately my cowlicks are again working in my favor and I don't spend an hour fretting with my hair and wishing hats were "in style." Adequately made-up, shaved, and sprayed, I find Molly in the living room, drinking coffee out of one of my twelve red public radio coffee mugs leftover from a fund drive.

"You have a coffee maker!" she exclaims when she sees me.

"I know it. Can you believe my kitchen?" I have not yet used the coffee maker, but just unpacked it brand new from the box it came in last Christmas. Molly must have found one of the sample packages of coffee stashed in a drawer.

"This Kona Blend isn't bad."

"Thanks." I fill another station mug and, after the first sip, I instantly feel calmer and centered. Ahhh.

"Bathroom's all yours," I inform Molly.

"Thanks, can I get you a bagel on the way to work this morning?"

"Only if we're out of here by seven. Otherwise I'll be late and I have to get a chef from this new restaurant in Milwaukee on the line for today's show."

"What's the topic?"

"Raw foods." I know she'll love this one. I wrinkle up my nose while she smiles at my disgust.

"Cool."

A small part of me misses living with Molly. I liked the company of a girlfriend during parts of the day. I enjoy the camaraderie, someone to share breakfast with, to watch a movie with, to talk to about my day at work. We stroll down the block together, two career gals on their way to work on a Friday, like Carrie and Miranda.

"Thanks for the bagel. I'll see you after work. Have fun in the anthropology lab." I wave at Molly as she crosses the street to the bus stop.

"See you later!" She raises her hand and salutes before merging into the crowd of college kids and professional adults headed down University Avenue.

The morning's show went tremendously well. Our guest, Pierre Soirette, was enthusiastic about the new rage in cooking (actually, not cooking) and we didn't get to all the callers. Dean slaps my shoulder as we leave the studio.

"Great show today, wasn't it?" He grins into my face, his hand still heavy on my shoulder.

"It sure was."

"I'm off. I'll meet you at two to go over Monday's show?"

"Two it is."

Dean walks off and I head back to my office to find Evelyn perched on the edge of my desk. I can feel in the air that her visit is not benign.

"Good morning, Sadie!"

"What's up?" I ask her.

"You know that I have a sister in Arizona." She cuts right to the chase.

"Yes."

"Her son is coming to Madison next weekend for a conference and I thought to myself, who better to show him the sights and sounds of Madison than my young friend, Sadie!" Evelyn rearranges the pens on my desk, trying to appear casual.

Oh, no—a set up! My face falls in dismay and Evelyn waves her hands anxiously, shaking her head.

"No! No! No! I'm not trying to set you up! I promise! I just don't think Todd would have much fun trailing along with his old Aunt Evelyn. I thought it might be nice for him to spend a night on the town with someone closer to his own age."

"I don't know, Evelyn. You're an awful lot of fun."

"You flatter me, dear. You really do. David and I are already taking Todd out for dinner on Wednesday, and he has plans for Thursday. What I need is someone to occupy him for a while on Friday or Saturday."

"I guess I *could* bring him out and about one of those nights."

"Wonderful! Actually, I have tickets to a hockey game. You can bring him to that. Saturday night."

I look Evelyn in the eye. Her expression appears innocent enough. She gazes back at me, her blue eyes clear and calm. She raises her eyebrows and clears her throat.

"You have hockey tickets?"

"Of course! I could hardly expect you to just drag him up and down State Street, pointing out drunk frat boys and tattooed rockers! I thought you could get a bite to eat and go to the game and then bring him back to his hotel."

"I *suppose* that could work out..." I should know better than to go out with her nephew.

"Fantastic! He's a fine young man, you'll have a wonderful time with him."

"I thought this wasn't a set-up."

"It's not, but Sadie," she winks as a smile spreads across her thin lips, "when opportunity knocks, you really should answer the door."

I snort as she stands up and heads out, maternally patting my shoulder on her way out. "Thank you dear, I really appreciate it."

When it rains it pours, and suddenly it seems to be raining men in my long-range forecast.

In the cavernous underground parking garage my car's engine starts up right away and I exhale with relief. I only drive once a week or so, and car maintenance never crosses my mind until it's too late. I back out of my parking spot and carefully round the corners.

After circling the block three times, I find a spot across the street from my apartment. I clamber out and wave at Molly, who sits reading a book on the steps of the porch. She stands, buries the book in her backpack and waves back. Next to her is a huge army-issue duffel bag. It looks like she packed for a summer in Brazil rather than a weekend at Jane's.

"All set?" I ask her.

"Yep. You?"

"No, go ahead and put your stuff in the trunk and then you can help me carry my stuff down." I toss her the keys.

She looks at my key chain and then back at me. "How will you get in your apartment?"

"Good point." I catch the keys she throws back to me. "Want to come up with me?"

"I'll wait here. Will you be long?"

"I'll hurry." It'll probably only take me five minutes to stuff a backpack full of toiletries and a change of clothes.

I race up the stairs two at a time and burst in the door. Despite the party on Saturday, I'm really looking forward to this weekend. I slide my cosmetic pouch, toothbrush, and hair supplies off the back of the sink and into the bottom of my backpack. I add a razor and my tube of Clearasil and rush to my bedroom. I stuff the last pair of clean underwear, socks, jeans, and zip the pack. What's missing? Shoes. I shove a pair of sneakers and an extra T-shirt into the side pocket. Backpack on my shoulders and a garbage bag of dirty laundry in each fist, I back out of my apartment and wrestle the locks shut.

I feel like a beast of burden with my bags scraping the walls on both sides of the stairwell and I stop at my mailbox. The same moment I drop the garbage bags to get my mail, the front door swishes open and in walks Adam Martinson. POP! The left garbage bag bursts. My dirty laundry slides onto the floor out of a huge rip up the side of the bag.

"Heading to the laundromat?" Adam Martinson bends over to help gather my clothes, holding his tie back with his left hand. He picks up a lace bra and hands it to me.

Yes, nothing like a woman's filthy laundry to turn a man on. The stench from workout clothes I wore jogging a month ago hits me. I have to lean back, gagging as I snatch a pair of particularly stained underwear and stuff them back into the bag, which rips even further, sending a bra and sweat socks cascading dangerously toward his outreached hand.

"Maybe I could get you another bag? It doesn't look like that one is going to make it." Adam stands, frowning at either the mess or the smell, I'm not sure.

"Thanks." My cheeks steam so red I can probably melt ice cubes off of them. Huddling my body over the mess so he can't see or smell the worst of what's probably still in there, I look up at him bravely.

"I'll be right back."

The second he disappears, I jump up and clang open my mailbox. I yank out the mail, stuff it in my backpack and return to the floor. I dig around to find the smelliest clothes and hide them underneath the pile. Can a person die of embarrassment?

He returns down the stairs as I am wadding up a bra.

"Here. This should do the trick." He whips open a huge yellow garbage bag and I begin dumping my laundry into it while giving him a grateful smile.

"Thanks."

"You're welcome."

"Guess you can tell laundry isn't the top of my to-do list."

I pick the last of my wardrobe up off the floor as tenant number three, Mrs. Jeffries, walks past, pausing to watch me scrabbling around at Adam's feet like some vagabond. Her eyes, distant behind bifocals, emit disapproval and she continues out the door.

"Good day, Mrs. Jeffries!" Adam calls after her.

"Do you know her?" I ask, standing once again.

"She lives next door to me."

"Has she ever spoken to you?"

"Nope, never." His eyes crease as he laughs. "I just figure I'll kill her with kindness. It's become kind of a game actually, to be obnoxiously friendly toward her until she finally cracks."

A rapping on the glass of the front door pulls my attention away to Molly, standing on the front porch giving me a look.

"I'm sorry, that's my friend. We're about to go to my sister's for the weekend."

"Need any help carrying all that?" He looks down at the baggage by my feet.

"No. Thanks for the bag, though."

"You're welcome. I'll see you Thursday then."

"Until Thursday," I reply, leaning down to grab my laundry. I try to make a graceful exit, despite the heavy bags knocking into my legs with every step I take. Outside, Molly leans into me with the subtlety of a mafia hit man.

"So who was that?"

"My neighbor. Cute, isn't he?"

"Yeah. If you like that type. What's he do? Sell cars?"

"Actually, he's a lawyer." I see she's slightly impressed by this. I open the trunk and heft my bags into the back. "All set?"

"Just waiting on you."

"Let's roll then."

I carefully negotiate my way out of a very tight parking spot. Two inches from my rear bumper is a Volvo, and I have about four inches between the Ford Expedition and me parked ahead. So much for rushing out of town for the weekend. It takes me three minutes to wiggle back and forth out of the spot; I've spent less time squeezing into nylons and my tightest black dress.

Finally, after taking some liberties with the bumpers on either end, I pull into the narrow street and whiz down it, expertly merging into the traffic on University Avenue. I glance triumphantly at Molly, who shakes her head at me.

"So what's all going on at your sister's this weekend?"

"Nothing much. Just a little party tomorrow afternoon—"

"A party?" She narrows her eyes at this. "Right, you said something yesterday. What kind of a party? Do I have to go?"

"A, well, sort of a cooking party." I lie to her, full of good intentions. "And yes, you have to go! It's not a big deal. One of Jane's friends is having a Coddled Cuisine party. After that we're free to do as we wish. I was leaning toward catching up on some reading."

"What's a Coddled Cuisine party?" Molly has every right to sound suspicious.

"Ummm...I believe it's one of those home parties where they sell things. In this case, it's kitchen stuff." I try to sound casual.

She sniffs at this. Not wanting to continue any vein of conversation with Molly, I turn up the stereo a bit more and begin singing along.

Dave Matthews Band proves irresistible to Molly; eventually she's tapping her fingers along and nodding her head to the beat.

Forty minutes later, I turn off the two-lane highway and onto the narrow road leading to Jane's driveway.

Heavy still with last year's dead leaves, the trees block what little light remains in the sky. My headlights lead me to the driveway, their dim light reaching to the gigantic lilac bushes bordering the front yard. I pull up alongside the mailbox and instruct Molly, "There's a bottle of wine in there. Grab it, will you?"

"Why?"

"Mom believes in gifts for the hostess. Jane planted my gift so I wouldn't have to go buy one."

"I see." She holds the bottle carefully in her lap as I negotiate the bumpy dirt driveway. Between random children's toys and the occasional stray chicken or cat, it's an obstacle course.

"Okay, here we are. Home sweet home! For the weekend, anyway."

Molly hands me the bottle of wine and I shove it under my arm. We unpack the trunk and approach the front porch. Olivia has already spied us and charges out of the front door, racing up to collide into a gigantic hug. I drop my bags and wrap my arms around her tiny neck.

"Sadie!"

"How's my favorite niece?"

"I'm good. I want to show you my new bunny. I named him Jumpy."

"I can't wait to see him."

She scampers beside us toward the house, chattering every step of the way. "I have to warn you that Samantha's in a real *mood*. Davis took her favorite T-shirt and used it to paint in. She's still mad at him. I found a caterpillar yesterday and we put it in a jar. Do you know what caterpillars eat? They eat leaves. Davis tried to eat a leaf too, but he spit it out. Mom made two pies today. I helped her. Do you like cherry pie?"

I'm breathless as I try to keep up with her steady stream of info. I nod and let her finish her story.

"Jumpy is sad because he misses his family. I told him we are his new family. Davis says we can't be a bunny's family, but I told him he's wrong."

We reach the house where Jane opens the door for us and tells Olivia, "Scoot! You'll have your Aunt Sadie to yourself in a little while. How are you?" Her arms, tanned and muscular, reach out to squeeze me. "Hi, Molly. We're glad you could come this weekend. And Sadie, you've brought a lovely bottle of wine!"

Huge winks flash all around while she takes it from me and sends us stomping upstairs with our bags. Our feet echo on the clean pine boards and I show Molly around the guest room we'll share. Two twin beds with colorful quilts separated by a rag rug greet us in a chaotic blend of colors. A wooden chair and a chest of drawers (already full of off-season clothes) and what looks to be a castle made of Legos and a half-assembled paper mache blob with four legs round out the ensemble. I look out the window. This room has the best view; a Burr Oak all but blocks the windows, making it feel like a tree house. I sleep here with the windows open in every season, lulled by the rustling of the leaves.

"Nice," Molly says, admiring the castle, an intricate network of red, white, and black Lego bits.

"I assume that's Davis' handiwork."

"So where's your mom?" Molly asks.

"Probably down in the living room. She likes to play cards with Erich because no one else knows how to play Sheepshead. Just put your stuff there and we'll head back down."

Molly sets her backpack next to the dresser and leans over to take off her Doc Martens. I settle my bags into a corner by the window and, again, enjoy the view outside.

We tromp back downstairs and find her seated across from Erich, the cards piled between them on the coffee table.

"Aunt Sadie!" Davis looks up from his television program.

"Hey buddy! Meet Molly. Molly, this is Davis, Lord of the Legos."

"Great castle." Molly tells him.

"Thanks. Took me over a week because somebody," he narrows his eyes as he meaningfully looks at Olivia, "kept *helping* me."

"Sadie, come and see the bunnies now!" I'm tugged away to the barn, escaping my mother with a wave and a shrug. She nods approvingly over her silver-framed glasses before taking another card from the deck.

Having avoided my mother right away, I know my weekend will be charmed.

# Chapter Seven

**"To become a consultant"**
*—Coddled Cuisine recruitment brochure*

It's still dark out Saturday morning when the rustle of leaves rouses me. I slide quietly out of bed and head downstairs. Molly will probably sleep until noon, giving me plenty of time to share the fabulous news of Adam Martinson with Jane. My feet smack across the warm pine steps and I inhale the rich scent of coffee and something bread-like baking.

Jane is at her kitchen table, leaning over the *Wisconsin State Journal* with a cup of coffee cupped in both palms. She looks up smiling and brushes a lock of hair out of her eyes. "Good morning! Sleep well?"

"I did, thanks. Where's Mom?" I scan the room for traces of our matriarch.

"She went down to the creek with Samantha this morning. I convinced her that no one was better suited to collect and identify insects for her school project."

I chuckle and pour myself coffee before sitting across from Jane.

"So, tell me what's really new in your single-girl city world."

I grin and plunge ahead.

"Adam Martinson."

Her eyebrows rise a full inch. "Hmmm. He sounds respectable. A professional, I'm guessing accountant. Tall, blonde, enjoys Woody Allen films, football, and long, romantic walks in the moonlight." She sighs and pats her hand on her heart.

"Nearly smack on. He's a lawyer, tall, dark, and I know he enjoys Indian food."

"How did you meet?"

"Actually, we met at Kabul, but he lives in my building."

"Oh! And how was your first date?"

"I'll tell you when it's over."

"You haven't gone out with him?"

"Thursday. Dinner party at Kara's."

"I'll expect a phone call by ten if he's awful, two if he's glorious."

"And nine the next morning if he's pure heaven," I shoot back with a wicked glance.

"You're a naughty girl, Sadie."

Olivia interrupts us just then by clambering onto Jane's lap, rubbing her eyes and leaning against Jane's chest. "I'm hungry, Mama. What do we have to eat?"

Jane ruffles her hair before squeezing her shoulders. "I baked some apple bread and we have granola and yogurt, too."

"I want all of those."

"Me too, Jane."

Jane smiles at me and slides Olivia off her lap.

I feel a hundred and fifty-seven times better to have finally gotten the news of Adam Martinson out. Which reminds me. "By the way, Jane? Don't mention our conversation to Molly."

"Why not?"

"It's complicated. She's suffering some serious man-hate right now, so I don't want to rub her nose in it."

"Gotcha."

Hours later, I'm dozing off in the sunny spot I've captured by the front window. My head jerks back and I open my eyes to catch my mother glaring at me from across the room full of women. Sighing, I try to follow the thread of what Sydney is doing at the island in the center of Jane's kitchen. Something to do with Cheesy Crab Canapés. She swiftly mashes shredded cheese, cream cheese, and artificial crab together in some clear plastic contraption. Jane's neighbor remarks to Molly, "Oh, the chopper is wonderful. I use mine all the time."

With the island counter full of prepared appetizers and a gigantic chocolate chip cookie freshly baked in a skillet, Sydney invites everyone to start eating. "I'll be in the living room to take any orders." She whips off her navy blue apron and briskly picks up an accordion file folder and briefcase.

Molly cocks an eyebrow at me and I shrug. What the hell? I load up a small paper plate with a generous hunk of the cookie and some Cheesy Crab Canapés. "Mmmm. They taste marvelous." Molly takes a canapé off my plate.

"How are they?" she asks.

"Excellent."

She stuffs it whole into her mouth and nods in agreement. Food still in her mouth, she keeps talking to me. "You ordering anything?"

"Ummm, I don't know. I'm sort of looking at the measuring cup and spoons."

"I'm going to get the food chopper and the Sensational Salad Spinner."

"You don't have to order anything, you know. Jane doesn't expect you to."

"I know. I want to. This stuff is actually pretty cool."

I flip to the back of the catalog and glance at huge letters:

> **Become a Coddled Cuisine consultant yourself! Create your own hours! Earn extra money! Be part of the Coddled Cuisine success story! For $90 you can purchase $150 worth of Coddled Cuisine products and start your own business.**

For some strange reason, this actually sounds tempting to me. I could sell this kitchen stuff. Did Sydney sneak something into the canapés? I find myself mentally calculating the potential in this offer. A couple of nights a week and I could earn enough to pay my rent. Lord knows I don't do much at night, anyway. It would be a great way to meet people and—

I'm interrupted by Molly, who sounds a little irritated.

"I said, do you want to go place your order now?"

"Okay, okay." I push the chair back and stand, bracing myself for the decision I know I will make. We go to Sydney, sitting professionally at the edge of the couch, surrounded by a calculator, money bag, briefcase, and file folders.

She efficiently takes orders from the women in line, one by one, and soon I'm at the head of the line.

"You're Jane's sister, right?" She smiles at me with expectation.

"That's right."

"And what do you want to order today?" Her pen is poised over an order form.

"Actually," I inhale my last deep breath of free air before saying the words that will seal my fate. "I'd like to know more about becoming a Coddled Cuisine consultant."

Enthusiasm nearly bubbles right out of the top of Sydney's dark curls as her lips stretch even wider. "Really? That's fabulous! I'll be glad to help you get started!"

I feel very conscious of Jane's eyes on me while I take a huge folder from Sydney.

"You're going to have so much fun doing this! There aren't many consultants in the Madison area, so you'll have *lots* of opportunities. How does next Wednesday look for you? We can get together after you get done with work and go over this information together. You can pay me then and I'll have all your stuff ready so you can get started."

"Okay." My hands actually tremble a little as I nod in agreement.

"You live downtown, right? I can come by your place, if you'd like."

"Sure, let me write directions for you."

"And I'll drop Molly's things with you, too. You'll see her sometime after Wednesday, right?"

"Oh, yes, Thursday night actually."

"I'm so excited for you! You're going to love doing this!" Sydney claps her hands like an enthusiastic cheerleader.

When I rejoin Molly in the kitchen she jerks her chin at the folder clutched in my sweaty hands.

"What's that?"

"Oh, nothing. I just decided I'd try selling Coddled Cuisine in my spare time."

The expression on Molly's face as her jaw drops, like a dead bird out of the sky, makes this consultant stuff already quite fun. Mom, standing nearby, overhears us and begins shaking her head.


"Are you sure this is a good idea, dear? I mean, one does not want to spread oneself too thin, you know," Mom says while we get out of Jane's car. Cars and trucks line the road for a quarter mile and we have a good hike up to the estate sale.

"I know, Mom, I know."

"And if you spend all your free time doing this, how will you find time to relax?"

"Mom, I have tons of time to relax. In fact, if I use some of my relaxing time to make some extra money, my relaxing time will be even better!"

My mother's nostrils flare slightly as she sighs. "You'll do as you please, Sadie. You always do."

"Mom…" I begin.

"Yes?"

"Nothing." Sometimes, no matter how badly you want to say something, you just can't find the words that say exactly what you want. My mother is like Mount Everest. I look at her like one might look at the long climb up that mountain. It's much easier to just turn around and buy a photo of the view from the tourist shop at its base.

"I think it's a great idea!" Jane bubbles. "I can hardly wait to hear how it goes."

"I don't suppose you'll hostess a party for me, too?"

"I'd love to!"

"You're sweet, but I can't expect you to invite all those people again for a replay of the last party you had."

"Why not?"

"I'll have a party for you, Sadie," Molly offers.

I look at Molly in surprise. "You will?" This is totally out of character for her. The only parties Molly has are book groups and political rallies.

"Sure. I read in the catalog that I can get tons of free stuff if I hostess a party and you need to get started somewhere, so why not? I'll invite some people from work, some of my book club members, it'll be great!"

"Thanks Molly, that means a lot."

Jane throws her arm around my shoulders and shakes me. "This is going to be so much fun!"

My mom finally stops questioning me somewhere in the middle of the estate sale Sunday afternoon when her attention is taken by an antique typewriter in mint condition. Her purchase puts her in a rare form as she reminisces about her career as secretary to the bank president and how technology hasn't really made anyone's job that much easier than it was back in her day. Molly and I stroll through the barn, half listening to her commentary.

Later, over loose meat sandwiches and chips at a picnic table at the far end of the auction barn, my mother still doesn't bring up Coddled Cuisine. I feel grateful for this small favor and think how it ended up being a peaceful and eventful weekend after all. Even Molly looks calmer as she eats potato chips out of a bag, licking her fingers after each one. Her shoulders look lower on her body and her lips have relaxed into a loose smile. In more ways than one, this weekend has turned out just fine. It's next week I'm worried about.

# Chapter Eight

**"Booking parties is easy and fun"**
*—Coddled Cuisine training manual*

I skip into work Monday morning, my news ready to spout out of my mouth. I look for Evelyn on the way to my office. Where is she? I have two parties all but booked and I know Evelyn will hostess my third; it's the least she can do in return for entertaining her nephew.

I turn on my computer, check my messages, and grab the file for the day's show. All set. I return back down the hall, looking left and right for Evelyn's short silver hair and trademark scarf at the neck.

Finally I spot her coming out of the newsroom. "Hey, Evelyn! How was your weekend?"

"Oh, fine. Yours?"

"Great! I went to Jane's, you know, and she had one of those Coddled Cuisine parties."

"And let me guess, you booked your own party off hers so she could get some free kitchen do-hickey?"

"Actually, no. I decided to become a Coddled Cuisine consultant."

Evelyn stops in her tracks and turns to face me. "You're kidding, right?"

"No. I'm going to do it. I need the extra money and besides, it will get me out of my apartment a couple times a week."

"Good for you, dear." She hesitates for a nanosecond before repeating more firmly, "Good for you. I suppose you would like *me* to hostess a party for you."

"How ever did you guess?"

Evelyn chuckles. "Been around the home party block more than once. Just tell me when and I'll do it."

"Super! Next month."

"You've got it."

I hate to cut her off, but time waits for no one in the radio business. "I have to go before Dean pitches a fit, let's meet up for lunch."

"Sounds great. I need to catch up with three reporters and tell them some bad news. I'll see you later." Evelyn stalks off in the general direction of her cubicle as I double-check my file folder. All good. I square my shoulders and head in to face Dean and today's guest.


After we wrap up the show, Dean slides his coffee mug across the table, presumably for me to tend to, and glances at his watch.

"Sadie, I'm going to have to meet with you a little earlier today to go over tomorrow's show. I'll see you at twelve."

"That's my lunch hour, Dean."

"Super. Then we'll meet at noon." He pushes back his chair and strides out to the hallway before I can utter another word, his cell phone already clamped to his right ear. Great. I now get to spend my lunch hour, technically my time off, with old Dean-o. I sulk back to my office and check out a text from Kara:

**Hope you have a date lined up for Thursday!**

I absently punch in the numbers of Kara's work extension with my left hand while scrolling down on my computer keyboard with my right. Kara answers on the first ring.

"So, who's coming to dinner?"

"Lucky for you I have managed to find an escort." I feel inexplicably prissy towards her. She's only trying to help Molly, I remind myself, trying for a kinder tone of voice.

"And your escort would be…?"

"One Adam Martinson, Esquire. Ever hear of him?"

"Martinson…Martinson…nope. I'm coming up empty. Is he local?"

"No. That is, not native."

"I see. Is he handsome?"

"Excessively."

"Outstanding. Give our little Benny Boy a run for his money. Could be fun to see the two alpha males strutting it out around the table."

"I don't think he's the pissing-in-corners type, Kara."

"Trust me, they all are. Especially the handsome ones."

"And speaking of Ben, how was his weekend of romancing Rhonda?"

"Nauseatingly naughty, according to him, of course."

"Of course." Ben's a great one for kissing, telling, and embellishing.

"He let slip a new use for the complimentary bottles of hair conditioner."

I close my eyes and shake my head. "I don't even want to know."

Kara snickers. "I have to go, I have a new artist coming in. Guess she's a real diva."

"Good luck with your diva. I'll see you Thursday."

"Thursday then. Ta ta."

Kara was my roommate in college by assignment; she came from serious money. So serious that instead of moving her things into our dorm room like other parents did, her parents sent professional movers ahead with their daughter's stuff. Kara's the only person I ever met with a trust fund, something I thought only existed in movies and soap operas. College was sort of a hobby for her, needless to say. She wasn't in training for any particular career, just immersing herself in a relatively useless four-year liberal arts program to soak up the atmosphere and "find herself," as she put it. After five years, she graduated and opened an art gallery in downtown Madison. Kara put to good use all the art classes she took, however has had little opportunity to apply the Greek and Comparative Literature minors she worked so hard on finishing, save for a month she spent on a yacht hopping about the Mediterranean.

Kara experimented sexually, which is easy to do in Madison, and declared herself a full-fledged lesbian her junior year. For the past two years, she's lived with Elizabeth, a medical student working on her residency. Kara's parents accepted Elizabeth with considerable enthusiasm; they had met Melissa Etheridge at Sundance and decided being a lesbian was not only harmless, but trendy, too. While Elizabeth saves lives in the ER, Kara spends her life in pursuit of amusement, whether by arranging her friends' lives, taking on new artists in her gallery, or heading to all the nether reaches of the planet for a new adventure. She's a poster child for *Lifestyles of the Rich and Famous*.

Returning to my work, I e-mail confirmations to the next week's guests, including a poet from Guam, a political analyst from Oregon set to discuss foreign policy with China, and a woman working on becoming a Buddhist monk. One thing I aim for in my work: variety.

The pile on my desk quickly dwindles in the swells of my enthusiasm; Coddled Cuisine has the effects of adrenaline coursing through my veins. By noon, I have much of Tuesday's work under way, and consider heading to Big Mike's Subs with Evelyn for lunch when Dean casts his hulking shadow across my desk. I look up and remember in despair our meeting scheduled earlier. Ugh. I'll have to call her and cancel lunch. Maybe we can do happy hour after work.

"Is it noon already?" I try to replace the irritation in my voice with a friendlier tone as his eyes slide around the room. No doubt he's making sure I don't have a single perk in my office that isn't already in his.

He juts his chin in the direction of my bookcase in the corner, sagging under the weight of files, reference books, and a great photo of me on the edge of Lake Mendota (Henry cut out and replaced by a *People* photo of Taye Diggs). "Where did you get the encyclopedias?"

Trust Dean to come down with encyclopedia envy. Incredulous and knowing his literacy limitations, I reply, "I bought them at the public library's used book sale last fall. They're from 1987, but I figured they would be helpful for the more basic sorts of questions I might have."

"You spend station money on those?"

Nosy bastard! Like it's any of his business! "As a matter of fact, yes. I did. Ron approved the expenditure several months ago."

His nose seems to pinch itself shut as he raises it another notch into the air. "You ready?"

"Are we going to work here?"

"Did you have a better idea?"

I do, but I am not going to tell him that, so I motion to the chair across from my desk and he perches his tweed-covered ass on the edge of it.

"Okay then, Rabbi Lovitz is our guest, he'll be part of our series on religion in the twenty-first century..." Resigned, I begin the tedious task of bringing Dean up to speed on how Jews are different from Christians, knowing he'll be asking that soon enough.


Even hitting happy hour with Evelyn didn't kill enough time, and I'm pacing in my apartment by seven o'clock, working off the remains of a Cosmopolitan-induced buzz. Tomorrow night I learn the secret art of scrapbooking at Lottie's party and two days until Sydney will change my life by handing me the supplies to become a Coddled Cuisine consultant. Three days until my official first date with Adam. How's a girl expected to keep calm under these circumstances? I feel as twitchy as I used to the night before the first day of school.

My mother has a solution for nervous energy: cleaning. That probably explains why her home is more sterile than many surgical tables. I wash the dishes piled in my kitchen sink, then tackle bathroom grout with an old toothbrush. I've pitched all my old lipsticks and gummy nail polishes into the trash and even organized my medicine cabinet by symptoms: top shelf, sinus and stuffy nose; second shelf, headaches and cramps; third shelf, flu and cold; fourth shelf, stomach aches and acne.

Taking a final swipe along the edge of the sink with the old sock I'm using as a rag, I drop it into the wastebasket. I have earned myself a long, hot bath. I'll study and soak. I'm becoming a goddess of efficiency: the Mata Hari of multi-tasking.

I turn to "Baker Buddies" on page twenty-four of the spring catalog and close my eyes to imagine myself expertly demonstrating the Quick-Stir Batter Bowl and the Super Spatula to a group of rapt women. They ooh and aah with each whisk of my arm as the cookie dough takes shape for baking. My crisp blue apron never has so much as a speck of flour on it; I wear it with style and panache for my shows. After the cookies come out of the oven, browned to perfection along the edges, I slide them onto the Serving in Style Platter without breaking a single one. Passing around the plate, I smile benevolently

91

and promise, "With Coddled Cuisine products, every one of your cookies will come out perfectly, every single time." The women can't get their checkbooks out fast enough. I calmly process order, after order, after order...

My reverie is shattered like a Serving in Style Platter against a concrete floor when I hear a knock at my door. I glance at the clock on the microwave. Who might be visiting me at eight o'clock on a Tuesday night? Not coming up with anyone off the top of my head, I go to the door and peer through the peephole. As my eyeball focuses, Adam's tall, dark, and knee-jelling handsome form takes shape.

"Hello, Adam," I sing, flinging the door open. In my enthusiasm to greet him I forget that I'm wearing a horribly stained T-shirt and had washed off my make up to apply wrinkle-fighting eye cream after getting home from work. I reach up to smear the remaining cream away and make the pretense of smoothing the T-shirt.

"Hi, Sadie. I hope it isn't too late to bother you, but I was baking cookies tonight." Holding forth a paper plate, he looks me up and down. I can't read from his expression whether he is disgusted or intrigued.

"You bake cookies?" I consider this new line from a man.

"On occasion. It's an old family recipe and tomorrow is one of the partner's birthdays. We have a tradition at the firm of bringing snacks to celebrate other people's birthdays, not our own, so I baked a batch and thought you'd like some, too."

"That's very nice of you, thanks. Would you like to come in?"

"Thanks." He steps through the door, filling the room with his manly shoulders and the warm buttery smell of freshly baked cookies. Handing me the plate, he looks around approvingly and nods. "Nice apartment."

"Thank you. I just got it settled," I say. He'll never realize how just *just* means.

"Mine needs a woman's touch desperately. I even asked my mom to come spend a weekend to help me out. She hasn't been able to clear her calendar yet."

"I can't imagine letting my mom decorate my place. If she did, I'd be perched on a plastic slipcover right now looking at a bowl of fake plastic fruit. Do you want to sit down?" I'm new at this asking-a-guy-into-my-apartment thing. On television women seem controlled and sophisticated. "I only have yogurt and diet soda."

"No, thanks."

I watch Adam sit just slightly on the edge of the center of the couch. Do I sit very close to him? Grab the armchair as my territory? Perhaps the more important question is, what do I intend to have happen this evening? Buying time to decide this, I motion to the cookies and tell him, "I'll put these in the kitchen."

He's really, really hot. He seems like a nice enough guy. I don't know why I'm trying to convince myself. As I glance at my reflection on my way to shut off the tub faucet, I realize there's still a healthy glob of eye cream near the top of my right cheekbone. I smear it in and return to the living room to sit next to him on the couch.

"Coddled Cuisine. What's this?" He pages through my catalog.

"Oh, it's a home sales company. Cooking supplies."

"Are they any good?"

"I think so. My sister had a party last weekend and that's where I first saw them."

"My mom is really into cooking, she even goes to weekend cooking school events sometimes. Quite the gourmet cook, I guess you'd say. She'd like this stuff."

"You're welcome to the catalog if you'd like it."

"Really? Thanks. Hate to shop, so this might solve the problem of what to get for her birthday next month. Anything you'd particularly suggest?"

"I hear great things about the food chopper."

"What about these skillets?" He points an elegant and tan finger to the Coddled Cookware on page thirty-two.

"Very nice. At that price, you can imagine."

He pulls the catalog closer to his face to study the description. "Scratch-proof, coated, steel bottoms, oven-safe… wow, these are pretty fancy."

"Yes, they are."

"How do I order this stuff?"

"You can just tell me and I can order it for you."

"Great. Mom will love these. Why don't you put me down for the skillet and medium-sized pot. I'll bring you a check Thursday, when I pick you up."

"Sure." Calculating my cut of this in my head, my commission will be about fifty dollars, and I didn't even have a party.

Adam sets the catalog back on the coffee table and leans back. "So, what's it like working with Dean LaRoche? He seems like he'd be an interesting guy."

I have no doubt Ron would can Dean faster than a tomato in the middle of August if he knew what a useless slug he was, but I know nothing good comes from trash-talking your boss, so I'm careful. "Probably like working for any other mid-level celebrity."

"Meaning?"

"He thinks he deserves diva treatment—you know, the right brand of bottled water, no late hours, and guests who always agree with him."

"Really? I had no idea. He seems so…capable on-air."

"Yes, yes he does. And in many ways he is quite capable," of award-winning stupidity, I finish in my head.

Adam sits quietly for a moment, studying his hands clasped loosely together in his lap, and I finally break the thickening silence.

"Shall I tell you about some of the people who will be at the party on Thursday?"

"Oh yeah, that would be helpful."

"To start, Kara is having the party. She's a friend of mine from college and runs an art gallery downtown. Her partner's name is Elizabeth." I add.

"Right, Kara and Elizabeth." He nods, frowning slightly in concentration.

"Then there's Ben, my former boss when I worked at Paisan's—a complete male slut, but genuinely kind if you haven't yet slept with him. He's probably bringing Rhonda, the flavor of the week, unless he's met someone new since we last spoke."

"Okay, Ben and maybe Rhonda."

"Molly—you met her the other day when I dropped my laundry—is getting over a failed love affair. She's the one Kara's having the party for. She's very political, teaches at the University, extremely liberal."

"I see, so no discussing my affiliations with the NRA or the Right to Life Council?"

I see the smile play at the edge of his lips. "That's almost funny if you didn't know how fierce she can be."

He chuckles. "I'll behave, don't worry. My mother trained me to stay clear of discussing politics, religion, and sex at a dinner party."

"That's too bad."

"It is?"

"I mean about the sex part." Terribly bold, but I'm getting a little nervous about this guy. Between the multiple references to his mother and the fact that he cooks for a hobby, I have to know if this is going anywhere. I mean, Madison is like the San Francisco of the Midwest, for crying out loud!

Relief sweeps over me as Adam leans toward me the slightest bit and responds in a deeper and huskier voice, "It would be, but I think those conversations should take place in a more ... intimate setting."

Somewhere deep inside I feel a liquid swoon, not entirely unlike the hot rush remaining from my George Clooney beach dream. I can only nod as Adam slowly leans his perfectly proportioned torso further across the couch, sliding his arm around my shoulders to pull me into his firmly muscled arm. I close my eyes, barely able to breathe, and wait expectantly for the kiss that arrives... just ... about... ahhh.

Moments later, when we come up for air, I feel dizzy as he reaches out to touch my cheek with his hand.

"I've been dying to kiss you since we met the other day."

My voice is not entirely trustworthy at the moment, so I nod dumbly at him. This seems okay as he begins to kiss me once more, and I open my lips to receive those kisses like precious nectar. Oh, he is good, I think, my inner voice foggy with desire.

Eventually he pulls away again and looks at me, his eyes dark with the same desire melting through my thighs like ice cream spilled on hot asphalt. "I really should go."

How reasonable of him, the better part of my conscience responds. The worst part of my conscience simply begs my mouth to say, "No, stay," and reach up to pull him back down. But I haven't even gone on a first date with him, and this fact squelches any lustful urgings. No one wants to put out before a first date. No one wants to be a slut, right?

I close my eyes and silence the inner voices while nodding. "Right."

We both stand and I follow him to the door.

As he opens the door to let himself out, he pauses a moment.

"See you Thursday?"

"At six." He smiles and walks out. I lean against the door after it closes and sigh deeply. Oh my, oh my, oh my.

# Chapter Nine

**"Use this helpful checklist to ensure the best possible experience for your party hostess and guests"**
*—Coddled Cuisine training manual*

After work Tuesday, I grab a burrito and hop on the bus to the Kennedy Avenue neighborhood where Lottie and her family live. I manage to spill only twice on the front of my white shirt, leaving two sizeable brown stains and a streak across the sleeve of my jacket. By the time I get off the bus, my hands feel disgustingly greasy and I'm burping up the sickly sweet aftertaste of diet soda.

I dig through my purse to find the invitation from Lottie. Okay, five-fifteen Kennedy Avenue. I look at the nearest house and read that I'm on the seven hundred block, so a short walk until I'm there. I pass twenty identical ranch-style houses before I get to Lottie's, notable only for the mallard ducks painted across the garage door and the Green Bay Packers helmet posing as a mailbox. The driveway is full of cars and there are more parked down the street. I recognize Delaine's van and Evelyn's Honda, making me feel a little better about going inside. I hate going to parties where I don't know anyone else. It's so uncomfortable to make small talk with strangers you'll probably never see again. And it really feels awkward to be the odd person out when the rest of the party is well-acquainted already as neighbors or family.

I ring the doorbell and a small girl in pigtails and a Disney Princess T-shirt answers the door. "Hi. The party's back here. I'll take your coat."

I hand her my jacket and she trots it back to a bedroom while I hear Lottie bellow down the hall, "Anna, make sure you ask to take their coat!"

"I did, Mom!" The girl's voice echoes back down the hall. A moment later, she comes out and stands in front of me.

"Follow me." Anna guides me around a curio cabinet filled to bursting with Precious Moments figurines, through the corner of the kitchen to where Lottie stands in front of a punch bowl, pouring in a liter of ginger ale, and to a doorway leading to the basement.

"Sadie! Glad you could come." Lottie sets down the ginger ale and looks at me with more interest than she's expressed in the three years I have known her.

"Thanks, Lottie. I'm assuming the party's downstairs?"

"Yes, we're going to get started in just a few minutes."

"Can I help you carry anything down?"

She hands me a huge plastic container full of potato chips and a smaller bowl full of dip. "I'll be right down."

I carefully climb down the steep shag-carpeted steps

and nearly make it without incident when something warm and hard slams into my stomach and the bowl of chips goes flying, leaving me to stand at the bottom of the steps surrounded by debris, holding the dip in my right hand.

"Tommy! You're it!" A boy about seven years old stands up from the floor, where he landed upon impact with me and scowls. Without any apology, he runs up the steps past me, followed by another boy who jostles me with his elbow on the second step, sending the dip soaring into the air and *splooch!* onto the shag carpeting. I follow the trail of chips and dip with my eyes and then look up at twenty women sitting on folding chairs at card tables, all staring back at me.

"Um, are they both Lottie's?" I ask, completely at a loss for anything else to say. The pounding of feet on the floor above leads me to assume the game has continued and I'm left cleaning the mess on my own.

"Tommy is my son. It's a wonder he didn't get hurt, running into you the way he did!" A fat woman with very big hair and bright pink lips snaps at me. I gape at her in astonishment.

"Excuse me?" I decide right now that I hate everyone at this party.

Evelyn stands up from a table set up in the back of the room, right in front of a wood-paneled bar. "I'll help pick that up, Sadie. Don't worry." She squeezes past another table full of women and kneels on the carpet, scooping chips back into the plastic bowl. "Nothing's broken, nobody got arrested, it's not the end of the world."

I kneel next to her and begin grabbing at chip bits with greasy fingers. "Apparently Lottie's friends don't believe in babysitters," Evelyn tells me under her breath, while the chatter of the tables starts up again. "Those two brats have been terrorizing the room since I got here and no one feels compelled to tell them to stop—or leave."

"It does inspire one to use birth control, anyway," I mutter back and Evelyn grins.

"I've saved you a spot at our table with Delaine and Bernadette."

"Bernadette's here?"

"Didn't you know she was coming?"

Bernadette Hill is the hostess of the morning show that's on right after Dean, the most gracious and classy woman I've ever met and, while she could legitimately pull diva stunts all day long, she never ever does. I'd gladly work for her rather than Dean any day.

"She's going to have to vacuum the rest of this up. That's the curse of shag carpets." Evelyn stands and brushes off her hands. "I'll go upstairs for a rag to wipe up that dip. You just go back to the table."

"Actually, I need to use the bathroom before we get started."

"Follow me."

After scrubbing my hands, I return to the party. I edge around the landing and, immediately, a huge Golden Retriever bounds up to me and shoves its snout in the general area of my crotch.

I pat the dog on its head and try to edge away from it, all the while pushing at its skull. The room silently stares until Lottie calls out, "Here, Copper! Here boy!"

I look at the dog. Surely it has been well trained and will run to its owner. "Good dog, good dog." I stand straight and wait for it to leave me alone. Instead, I'm nearly knocked over for the second time tonight as the dog again thrusts its nose firmly between my legs and sniffs around. I try edging around it and the thing follows me, its face still buried.

"Copper's friendly. He's just getting to know you," Lottie tells me.

"Great!" I smile in my most polite expression. "I can't say too many men have gotten to know me so well so quickly!"

"Copper!" Lottie snaps and the dog looks back at her, leaving me a brief window to make a run for the back table, past the fat pink-lipped lady with the bratty kid, and tuck into a folding chair next to Delaine and Evelyn. Copper follows me to sit before me, face again in my lap. Nervously I laugh and look around the table. Sympathy abounds on all three faces looking back, and I mentally curse the entire evening.

"Let's try getting started again," the party hostess announces in a loud voice. "I have a lot of things to show you tonight and I want to give you plenty of time to work on your pages, so we don't want any more interruptions." As if I plan to hold up the party. I refuse to buy anything from this party. The last thing I'll want is any memento from this night. I discreetly shove the dog away from my feet. My shoe slips off and he grabs it, running across the room—play time for Copper, not for me! Lottie turns around to give me a look which I ignore.

"Hello, everyone I'm Suzie Daniels, and I've been selling Happy Times scrapbook materials for two years now. I started scrapbooking five years ago when my daughter was born because I wanted to preserve every memory of her life and I didn't know what to do with all the photos I was taking. So, I started scrapbooking, and since I began, I've made twenty-eight scrapbooks, some of which you'll see tonight. I've learned that it doesn't matter how creative you are—good grief, I can't even cut a straight line—but with Happy Times I can make my memories into something beautiful and lasting." She treats us all to a huge, toothy smile and holds up what I presume is one of her twenty-eight scrapbooks. It's a pink, lace covered book with a photo in the center of the cover page of a phenomenally ugly baby with a few wisps of hair gathered on top of its head with a pink bow.

"Is that Pebbles Flinstone?" I lean over and whisper to Evelyn.

"Good Lord! Does she really think *that* will help her sell scrapbook supplies?" Evelyn whispers back.

"Why don't you open those catalogs to page twelve and I'll talk about our Happy Times binders—these are the best acid-free ones you can get for your money. You can go to a lot of stores and get your supplies for less money, but I guarantee you, in twenty years you'll see yellowing and fading. Happy Times has a lifetime guarantee on its product."

"Gotta love a lifetime guarantee from a company that's been around for less than five years," I mutter to Evelyn who snickers. I feel mean.

I thumb through the catalog and quickly learn that the Happy Times starter set only would cost me two hundred dollars. I choke as I read this and tune in once again to Suzie Daniels telling us, "You can give a scrapbook as a gift or keep it for yourself." Mentally I calculate the cost per page of this endeavor and determine that each page only should cost about three dollars, and assuming one can get between three and four photos per page, well… a photo album using Happy Times would only cost about sixty-five cents per snapshot. Holy shit! I will definitely *not* be purchasing anything at tonight's party.

"Ladies, if you'll take out the pictures you were supposed to bring along for tonight, we'll get started." She starts handing out pages of Happy Times binder fillers and envelopes full of stickers and colorful paper shapes. Evelyn and Delaine look at me and I shrug, reaching into my handbag for the photos I grabbed from my refrigerator door on my way out of my apartment this morning.

"I'm sure most of you have some sort of theme in mind like vacation, beach, birthday party, so you'll want to look at the exclusive Happy Times stickers for inspiration on those ideas." Suzie holds up the catalog once more, high above her head. "The stickers begin on page thirty-nine."

"Mom! Mom! I wanna glue pictures!" Tommy is back, knocking over scrapbook supplies with both elbows at his fat pink-lipped mother's table and I see one woman literally hunch protectively over her photographs.

"Okay sweetie, here you go. Momma will just watch you then." Pink lips smile indulgently at the little beast as he smears glue all over a page of paper.

"You don't need to use quite that much glue," Suzie says, and I have to look away. I look at Delaine and Evelyn's pictures; they both have vacation photos and I feel kind of stupid, as I only have school snapshots of Jane's kids and two pictures of Molly, Kara, Ben and me sitting at the Big Ten Pub before a Badger game last year. Not only do they not lend themselves to any sort of thematic display, I really don't want to permanently attach them to a scrapbook page when I have no intention of ever having a whole scrapbook to go along with it. I shuffle the sticker envelopes around in an attempt to look busy until I notice what Bernadette is doing.

Her page is covered in layers of patterned paper with the photos precisely and chronologically arranged. They are vacation photos of her family trip to Brazil last summer: her teenaged son and daughter, looking blonde and perfect against a backdrop of ancient ruins and her husband, laughing as he paddles a dugout canoe. "Wow, Bernadette, have you done this before?" I ask in admiration.

"Actually I have. I buy my products through Creative Treasures, though."

"You really have an eye for color."

"Thanks, I enjoy it. It's sort of a brainless hobby, just cutting and pasting, really. But it's a good stress reliever. I'm not as committed as some people are to doing it, but I've finished a few books."

"Will you be able to add these pages to the ones you have at home?" I ask.

"I'll just have to cut them down a bit, no big deal." At that very moment, Tommy and Lottie's son race through the card tables, upending the one closest to ours and sending scissors, photos, and paper flying.

Lottie rushes across the room and I see that Delaine has Lottie's son by his upper arm and he's squirming to be let loose.

"LET ME GO!" he shrieks in an ear-piercing howl.

"Not until you apologize," Delaine tells him through gritted teeth. I see how she raised four sons and never had any of them turn into juvenile delinquents.

"I DON'T WANNA! MOM! SHE'S HURTING ME!"

Lottie chooses to ignore her child while she kneels to pick up scattered scrapbook pages.

"*You will go over there and apologize and begin acting like a gentleman this instant or else you will learn a new definition of the word pain,*" Delaine whispers in his ear menacingly as her fingers turn white.

"Okay," he tells her sullenly.

"Do it *now*," Delaine commands and drops his arm. I actually feel a little sorry for him—until he sticks out his tongue and runs up the stairs, disappearing for the rest of the night.

"What an intolerable little brat!" Delaine shakes her head in disgust. "I've never seen such behavior! I'd slap my kids senseless if they behaved like that, in public or not!"

"I hear you," Evelyn agrees. "I'd swear the devil himself was mating with the women in this neighborhood if I didn't know any better."

Bernadette and I start to giggle and I furtively catch a glimpse of the fat lady, her bright pink lips pressed tight together. I also notice that Copper, the horny hairy beast, is chewing through the strap of my handbag. "Hey!" I yank it away from him. "Let go!"

The dog growls and bites down harder, forcing me to use both hands and pull. I'm gritting my teeth and holding back a flurry of curses. Its eyes narrow and its lips curl back to reveal nasty black gums and sharp-looking teeth.

"That's my favorite bag!" I tell it, as if I can convince the damn creature to let it go. Firmly, I plant my feet and lean back into the chair, straining against the weight of the dog and hearing the creak of the strap pulling loose from its stitches.

Evelyn leans forward and snaps, "Copper, drop it now!"

The dog's eyeballs roll up at her and, with a bark, the bag falls from its mouth and I fly backwards on my folding chair, legs straight up in the air, my skirt sliding down to my hips, showing the entire scrapbook party my underwear. Scrambling up from the floor, I see Delaine stifling laughter, and even though I know the moment is hilarious from her end, I'm too pissed to even smile. What the hell is wrong with Lottie to have two awful children and a gigantic dog carousing in the middle of a party? I tip the metal folding chair upright and snatch my handbag onto my lap, scooting as close to the table as possible.

"Are you okay, Sadie?" Bernadette asks. I nod, fearful that my voice will quaver into tears. Lottie appears at my side and asks about the state of my purse.

"It's fine," I tell her.

"Now that would have been something to preserve in the memory book!" Evelyn says and laughs, Delaine joins her heartily.

"I think the only thing worth preserving about this godforsaken night is my sanity. I should get going."

"Don't leave yet, I'll drive you home after this is all over," Evelyn pleads.

"No, I'd just as soon take the bus."

"Really?" Her eyes narrow as she searches my face. "No, you don't. Ride with me. I insist."

Before I can respond, Suzie Daniels is talking again about all the cute scrapbooking possibilities. "Look at what Evelyn did with her photos! She took baby pictures and surrounded them with the little foot and hand print stickers, backing the entire page with our yellow rattle print paper! And Dorothy included some of the tickets from her family's trip to the Milwaukee Zoo alongside the snapshots she took. She used the jungle print paper and our zoo animals stickers on her pages." Suzie holds these exemplary examples of scrapbooking creativity high above her head for the room to admire. "Does anyone else have a special page they'd like to share with the group?"

People exchange glances at their tables and Suzie waits with a hopeful expression for a minute before giving up. "I do hope you share your ideas at your tables. As I mentioned earlier, scrapbooking is a fun and rewarding hobby for even the least artistic among us. Now, I became a Happy Times representative to earn a discount while teaching people about a hobby I enjoy and selling a product I believe in. It takes very little time out of my schedule to be a Happy Times representative—I'm only gone one or two nights a week, which is a perfect schedule for a stay-at-home-mom, like myself. I earn extra income and have complete control over my schedule. If this sounds like a good deal to you, I invite you to turn to page sixty-seven in your catalog to learn more about becoming a Happy Times representative."

I tune out the rest of the rah-rah Happy Times speech and try to read Delaine's order form. She's getting the camping stickers, some paper, and tape. Bernadette has some stickers written down on her order sheet and Evelyn's is blank. "Are you going to get anything?" I ask.

"No, I think I'm going to stick with good old fashioned photo albums."

"But they're not acid-free, lignin-free, and buffered for the longevity of your photos!" Bernadette scolds her in mock despair.

"I'll take my chances," Evelyn replies dryly.

"Everyone, there is cake and punch and other good things to eat. Please come up and help yourselves!" Lottie announces, and I see her daughter standing behind the punch bowl, ladle armed and ready in her right hand.

"Her daughter seems well-behaved," I comment.

"One for three isn't bad," Delaine nods and stands. "I'm going for the free eats. Who's with me?"

We all stand to join her and I spend the rest of the hour safely standing between Evelyn and Bernadette, buffered from the evil forces of bratty boys and demon dogs.

"Thanks for the invitation, I'll see you tomorrow," Evelyn tells Lottie on our way out the door, an hour later. The neighbor ladies seem hunkered down for the night, and Bernadette and Delaine have already left.

"I'm sorry about your purse, Sadie."

"Don't worry about it." Evelyn and I furtively duck past Suzie Daniels who is camped out at the top of the basement stairs, ready to accost any and every potential customer before they leave.

"Are you ladies all set then? Did I get your orders?"

"We're just fine, thank you," Evelyn tells her and I nod while looking down the hallway for the girl who took my coat. Finally, she appears after an awkward silence passes between us and Suzie.

"Here's your coat."

I grab it from her, and Evelyn and I can't get out the front door fast enough. Evelyn raises her keys in the air and the headlights flash on as she unlocks the door from the driveway. Together we race across the street and jump into her car, screeching with laughter.

"Oh my goodness, that has to be the worst home party experience of my life!"

"I second that!" I agree.

"What a total rip-off that entire scrapbook scam is! You'd have to spend a mint just to complete one book!"

"*That's* what bothered you? I was far more offended by the dog in my crotch and the game of tag," I snort.

"And the dog attacking your purse like it's some sort of chew toy." Evelyn starts to laugh.

"And the punch bowl that had bits of cake floating in it."

"It did?" Evelyn looks at me. "I didn't notice! Is that why you didn't have any?"

"No, the fucking dog hair clumped in the center of the ice mold is what actually turned me off."

"Gross!"

"I think we learned a very important lesson tonight," Evelyn tells me as she turns onto the beltway.

"What's that?" I ask.

"Never go to the home party of a co-worker. You're just asking for trouble."

"You can't say that! You haven't had a party for me yet! You have to invite all the same people. They owe you, that's how it works. Reciprocity!"

"Bah! The cycle ends here, with me." She smiles. "Okay, one more party and then I swear we have to stop. It's just too much!"

"Agreed." I feel a twinge of guilt for not ordering anything at Lottie's party. The feeling passes, however, when I see the huge wet spot I've been sporting on the front of my skirt all night, kudos of Copper's wet face pressed into my crotch.

## Chapter Ten

**"Know your product line"**
*—Coddled Cuisine training manual*

Wednesday couldn't come soon enough. I had enough excited and nervous energy to clean off my desk at work, install new anti-virus protection on my computer, and finish unpacking my apartment. Feeling virtuous, I stuff the last of mismatched Tupperware and old Abercrombie sweaters into a bag headed for Goodwill and survey my apartment with satisfaction. I rolled over at two this morning wide-awake and wired. Consequently, my place looks immaculate. The coffee table gleams below a eucalyptus-scented jar candle and neat stacks of catalogs and magazines. A fuzzy afghan is invitingly draped over the edge of my armchair. Framed prints hang on the pale yellow walls, and on the deep window sill, lined up like so many uniformed schoolchildren, stand seven glass candleholders of various design. The room reeks of shabby-urban-chic.

Sydney suggested familiarizing myself with the Coddled Cuisine products by reading through the catalog several times; I diligently reviewed it three times a day since Saturday. This morning I memorized every word on pages twenty-three to thirty-two.

I bounce into the bathroom and study my reflection in the mirror. Despite my grey pallor, my eyes positively shine and my mouth can't stop twitching into a gleeful smile. Not a single spot of sophistication—I feel like I'm in seventh grade again, ripping open a love note found in my locker after lunch hour. The same giddiness flows through my veins now as when I discovered that Greg Carlson had a crush on me and wanted to "go out." I shake my head, still grinning foolishly.

Even Ron can't spoil my grand mood. I smile and agree with him when he snaps at me after the show.

"Might be a good idea to go over your show format with the show's host once in a while, don't you agree, Sadie?" Technically he doesn't say this *to* me, since he's walking away from me while he speaks.

Never mind that I had spent nearly two hours over my *lunch hour* doing exactly that. Never mind that a trained monkey could more competently conduct an interview than Dean, who managed to mispronounce our guest's name the entire hour. I just nod cheerfully and reply, "You know, I might try that sometime. Thanks for the suggestion, Ron."

He can take his crummy production job and shove it up his ass. I calm myself with visions of my new career with Coddled Cuisine taking off beyond my wildest dreams. Couple that with becoming the wife of a successful lawyer and remind me again why I need to take crap from an arrogant dwarf and his oversized lapdog?

My mood floats upward once again as I get a text from Ben:

> Hear you're starting a new career.
> Can't wait for Thursday's party.

I haven't even considered the potential of my relationship with Ben: he, the manager of two restaurants and me, a supplier of kitchens. I might get to leave the evil clutches of Ron and Dean sooner than I thought! Visions of cookware and credit cards dance in my head.

Pushing these thoughts to the back of my mind, I hunch over Dr. Leckwerth's folder, figuring a change in my body language might stave off intrusive daydreams. Dr. Leckwerth's a specialist in child behavior. These shows are always popular with our audience, but I absolutely hate them. Half of these kids' problems are the parents' issues, anyway. I mean, if you don't *like* how your ten year old dresses, then buy them different clothes! Meanwhile, "specialists" like Dr. Leckwerth make a hefty haul of cash by repeating the same message over and over: "You set the boundaries, you take control, you're the adult." DUH! I sigh and type up Dr. Leckwerth's credentials for Dean to read during the show's introduction tomorrow.

Back home, I bounce around my apartment, checking the window every two minutes. Finally I spot Sydney stepping up the curb under a load of two cardboard boxes, a shopping bag, and a purse. I rush out of my apartment to meet her downstairs.

"Great to see you, Sydney!" I call while I let her in the lobby.

"Hello, Sadie." She slides a bag from her shoulder into my eagerly waiting arms. I feel the heft of unknown kitchen implements in my arms—my future! I lead her up the stairs and into my apartment, where she begins emptying bags and boxes all over my living room.

"Holy crap! That's a lot of stuff!"

"It is, and I'll show you the most efficient way to pack and move it all so you don't spend half your life setting up for shows. Kimberly, the woman who taught me, she's a real pro. I have tons of great tips for you."

Sydney keeps opening boxes and sliding out plastic-wrapped items. Cushion by cushion, my couch disappears under the merchandise.

"I see you don't have much of a kitchen."

"Is that a problem?"

"Shouldn't be. You'll want to practice these recipes once or twice on your own here before you go out making them in public."

"I see." I grab a pen and notebook, feeling businesslike and serious.

"There's nothing worse than going to a show to make a recipe you've never prepared," she warns.

"Now then," she stands by the coffee table and picks up a fistful of spoons, "let's start with utensils and work our way from there. Everything in the Coddled Cuisine catalog has a point value, and when a hostess has a show, the point value of merchandise purchased makes up the free products she'll receive."

Half an hour later, my eyes start to glaze over while Sydney demonstrates the Glorious Grater. Has this been a huge mistake? According to Sydney I have to go out and purchase a fair amount of office supplies and storage containers for this gig. The start-up costs already double my original figure. As she turns around to pull up the food chopper, I take a deep breath and try to focus again.

"See how this just slides together? Again, this item is top-rack-dishwasher safe and has a one-year warrantee." She deftly demonstrates the chopper by banging it mercilessly against the cutting board on my coffee table. The entire stack of magazines and catalogs, carefully placed there at three this morning, shifts and slides to the floor as she pounds the chopper's top up and down.

"This is a great way to take out your aggressions!" she shouts, still chopping away.

"I see!" I yell back at her. Is this woman sane?

At last Sydney brings out a DVD and hands it to me.

"Watch this, it goes through all the steps of having a show and answers a number of questions you probably have. This," she scribbles a name and phone number on the front of the catalog, "is the name of our district director. She'll want to meet you and accompany you to your first show. Just to make sure you're doing things correctly. She's very helpful, actually."

"Should I call her?"

"I told her about you—she'll expect to hear from you before you book your first show."

"Anything else I should know?"

"Ummm…did I mention the monthly meetings?"

Monthly meetings? The horrible intuition that I have joined some sort of Amway cult makes my heart sink three inches. Gasping for air, I shake my head. "No."

"Oh," Sydney seems oblivious to my panic and shrugs. "We meet at Kimberly's house once a month, the second Wednesday, from seven to eight. She gives us product updates, that sort of thing."

One hour a month. That's not too bad. I watch Sydney brush off the front of her dress pants and stand.

"I'm off, then. Time to get home and pack lunches for tomorrow!"

I walk Sydney to the door and turn to survey the room. It's eight o'clock and Sydney has left me alone with a small mountain of plastic, metal, and paper. Poking at the pile, I debate in my head the merits of trying out a recipe or heading out to an office supply store. The recipe wins and I open the folder to choose one.

An appetizer I can bring to Kara's tomorrow night as a gift! Cream cheese, artificial crab, cheddar cheese, rosemary, mustard—I have no ingredients to make anything listed. Okay, add food to the start-up costs. So far, these Coddled Cuisine people have really pulled a fast one on this gal. But I recall Sydney mentioning something about food being tax deductible.

Sighing in defeat, I pull on sneakers and grab my purse. Groceries it is.

By ten I've successfully made cream puffs and mini egg rolls and dirtied every inch of my closet-sized kitchen. It takes an hour to clean up the mess, store the food and, as I run hot water into the sink for a third time, the memory of Uncle Bert hazily surfaces. Shit! I take on a burst of speed to finish cleaning up and scramble to find the flight information my mom gave me last week. Where did that go?

I thumb my way through a stack of papers on my kitchen counter and return to the living room. Okay, think. I take a deep breath and command my brain to calm down. Where was I when mom called? On the couch. I sift through papers and magazines on the coffee table, then scramble to my bedroom where I find it half sticking out beneath my lamp. I slide the receipt out and put it in my purse.

Too exhausted to deal with tomorrow's full plate, I scrub my face and teeth and drop onto my mattress, sleep overtaking my completely stressed out mind within milliseconds.

## Chapter Eleven

**"Gain self-confidence as a consultant"**
*—Coddled Cuisine recruitment brochure*

Thursday I plow through my work before leaving the office. There are only two hours before Uncle Bert's flight is expected to arrive. I have twenty minutes to spare by the time I leave the office, retrieve my car from the garage, and drive through downtown traffic cluttered with pedestrians, mopeds, and bicyclists to the south side of town where I waste another five minutes figuring out where to park.

For a brief moment, bigger isn't better as I glide through the narrow space between a Land Rover's front bumper and a Suburban's hulking mass. I'm rewarded with the blare of a horn and the muffled sound of a man's voice cursing at me. In my rear view mirror I see a finger raised and a shiny black Escalade glides past the spot. Sorry buddy, I have to pick up my uncle!

Inside the airport I study the arrivals posted. There it is, Midwest Express, flight 8769, gate eight! I look around for a sign to tell me how the hell to find gate eight and read that I'm headed in the right direction.

When I pass the obligatory newsstand and cheese shop, I spy the man from the parking lot, readily recognizable in his dark suit and red tie. I dart into the cheese shop and duck behind a display of Port Wine spreads. I can just see him over a box of crackers and he turns in my direction. Crash! Down go five tubs of Port Wine spread, knocked over by my purse swinging forward. I jump back and my butt knocks into a display of crackers—boxes slide and crash across the floor.

SUV guy glances up from the magazine he's studying and I turn to run out of the shop, the short elderly lady behind the counter half-rising to ask in a quavering voice, "Can I help you, dear?"

Shit. I don't have it in me to be rude to an old lady, especially one wearing a cow-print sweatshirt and cheese head earrings dangling heavily from each earlobe.

"Uh, no thanks. I'm just looking. I'm terribly sorry." I gather three tubs of Port Wine spread and set them back on the shelf.

"It's okay dear, happens all the time. I'll get it."

I feel grateful and then I notice the guy from the parking lot handing the cashier across the corridor money for the magazine. I bolt out of her shop, heading directly for gate eight without looking back. I don't even want to know if he's in my wake.

Breathlessly, I jostle past the crowd, no doubt fresh off the same plane Uncle Bert flew in on. I look around an embracing couple to see him standing perfectly still in the center of the emotional chaos that always ensues when planes, trains, and busses are involved. Waving my arms, I scoot aside to avoid a woman with a baby carrier and an exceedingly sticky-looking toddler.

Uncle Bert's face crinkles into a grin, the lines on his face deepening when he sees me. "My Sadie-gal!"

"Uncle Bert!"

We struggle toward each other through the crowd of people and finally stand eye-to-eye. He reaches into my hair and, with a flourish, pulls out a nickel. "Well, will you look at that?"

I laugh and throw my arms around his stocky shoulders. "Uncle Bert! It's so good to see you! How was your flight?"

"Not so bad. I sat behind the kid who kicks this time. Good for me, bad for the guy two rows ahead of me."

Shaking my head, I laugh again. This man is so funny and sweet. Tucking his arm beneath mine, I guide him out of the crowded terminal to the hallway. "Shall we go find your luggage?"

"This is it." He holds up a battered duffel bag and a briefcase and grins again. "I'm not trusting those airlines with my stuff again. Not after 1974."

"Okay then, let's go."

We move easily through the thinning crowd. I grab his duffel bag, which weighs more than I assumed from its size. "Mom tells me you're attending some magic convention this weekend?"

"Yes, very exciting stuff. I'm ready to take vanishing to the next level. Sadie-gal, is that a cheese shop ahead? I love cheese. Let's get some."

My cheeks blaze like embers while I follow him into the store, ducking my head in embarrassment as the old lady in the cow sweatshirt looks up at me with a grin. "Back for that Port Wine?"

# Chapter Twelve

**"A party can be a fun event with proper planning"**
*—Coddled Cuisine hostess brochure*

With Uncle Bert safely tucked away in a hotel room downtown and a promise to find him tomorrow for lunch, I return to my apartment to prepare for Kara's party—and my first official date with Adam. Ah, Adam. My cheeks flare crimson at the memory of Tuesday night.

A mere ten minutes until six remain and I perform a speedy makeover. Fresh swipes of deodorant under my pits, perfume applied to the places that matter, and a fresh coat of lipstick. Now to the closet to select an outfit that's stunning yet subtle.

Jeans? No, too casual. Khakis? Not sexy enough. I opt for a red chiffon dress with black heels. I hear a knock on my door while fumbling with the clasp of my necklace. I look one last time in the mirror. Hot. My hair curls softly and my legs look longer in my heels. Okay, Adam, I clench the necklace in my fingers. Here I come.

His expression registers immediate approval and I greet him in my most casual tone.

"Hi, Adam, I'm just about ready. Could you help me with this necklace?" I hold the necklace out to him and add, "I just can't seem to get the clasp to work." I drop the necklace in his right hand and turn around. I can feel the heat from his body as he steps behind me and lowers the necklace in front of my face, then my neck. His fingers brush the back of my hair as he connects the ends of the chain and then he runs both hands down my arms. I feel his breath as he kisses the nape of my neck and tells me, "You look gorgeous."

It takes every molecule of self-control for me to choose the cream puffs and the mini egg rolls over other delectable appetizers within my reach at the moment. I've never felt such a sexual vibe around a man before; he oozes seduction.

The ride to Kara's is quite sumptuous in the leather bucket seats of Adam's sports car. I'm gliding across the surface of the same streets with the potholes that rattle my teeth and make it impossible to drink a cup of coffee when driving my own car.

"This is a nice ride."

"Thanks, I've been very pleased with it. Lexus makes a good vehicle. Have you ever looked at them? The bumper to bumper warrantee is outstanding."

I look down at the platter in my lap.

"What?" He reaches over and rests his hand on my thigh—heat radiates from his hand.

"Nothing. It's just that a car like this one is out of my league as long as I command my public radio salary."

"I'm sorry. That was terribly insensitive of me. I should have realized." He does look apologetic as he softly massages my knee.

"No, it's okay. Besides, if we didn't have public radio, who would drive the hybrids and the rust buckets?" I point to the sign ahead of us on the road. "There's where Kara lives."

Adam whistles as he turns into the drive and stops before the imposing wrought iron gates. "Is there a buzzer or an intercom?" He pulls his hand away to steer and I feel my body relax.

"A buzzer. Drive forward a little further."

Adam easily stretches his long arm out to press the button that nine visits out of ten I have to leave my car to reach. Kara's voice sparkles through the speaker. "Helloooo?"

I lean forward, achingly close to Adam's broad chest and call back, "It's me. Sadie and escort."

"Splendid! Come right in!"

The gates open smoothly before us and Adam steers us forward.

"Drive to the next building, then take the first parking spot you can find."

"So this is how the other half lives," he comments while we glide past the groundskeeper's building.

"More precisely, the other two percent."

He slides into a spot next to Ben's SUV and walks around to help me out.

"Thank you."

Appetizers in hand, I lead the way up the steps, past the topiaries, to the grand oak door where Kara greets me before I have a chance to knock. Her mouth curves into a knowing grin and she steps back and looks Adam up and down, lingering for a moment for him to become uncomfortable before holding out her hand in a manner reminiscent of the queen of England. She declares approvingly, "You must be Adam. What a *pleasure* it is to finally meet you!"

Glancing at me, he steps forward to take Kara's hand and shake it gamely. "And you must be Kara. Sadie has told me all about you."

"Has she?" Kara raises her flawlessly waxed eyebrows into her platinum hairline. "I can only imagine. Sadie, you look fabulous. Love the dress. *Tres fantastique.* Everyone is in the gathering room, follow me."

We bustle in behind Kara, in her pencil skirt and ruffle blouse, and I catch the scent of something garlicky and spicy in the air. I can only imagine what she has concocted, considering nearly a fourth of the guests are strict vegetarians. I pray hard for meat to appear in at least a side dish.

Kara interrupts me as she calls back over her shoulder, "Sadie, you can bring the appetizers right with us."

In the gathering room Ben sits on the white leather sofa, his arm slung casually around a tall brunette with amazingly long legs and enormous breasts. Elizabeth is pouring a glass of wine off a cart for a very tall man with sideburns and hipster glasses, the bait for Molly, I presume. Kara's married friends, Kevin and Stacy Lookham, round out the party. Molly's nowhere in sight. Is she going to show?

"Sadie, this is Irving Glaston, my new accountant and business manager. Irving, Sadie and Adam. Sadie, you remember the Lookhams." Nods all around as Kara continues, "and of course, Ben and Rhonda."

"Very nice to meet you," I say and I notice out of the corner of my eye Adam struggling to tear his gaze away from Rhonda's thighs, which are topped by a thin strip of a black leather miniskirt.

Ben catches my eye and winks. Peeling his arm away from Rhonda's shoulders, he stands and walks over to us.

"Ben Armstrong," he announces, holding his hand out to Adam. I watch Adam take his hand and they shake vigorously. I cannot shake the image of two male wolves circling one another ready to attack and defend their position as the alpha.

"Adam Martinson."

"So how did you meet our Sadie?" Ben asks, flashing his dimples dangerously.

"At Kabul. We, er, ran into each other there, you might say. We live in the same building, though."

Nodding, Ben looks at me, a daring glint in his eye. "Pleasure to meet you. If there's ever anything you need to know about Sadie, feel free to ask."

Adam looks disconcerted by this comment and silently nods in response. I relax slightly; no one's pissing in the corners of Kara's gathering room tonight.

"Sadie, what have we here?" Ben lifts the cellophane off the platter of egg rolls and cream puffs. "Appetizers? Outstanding." He stuffs a cream puff into his mouth. Grunting and nodding, he reaches for an egg roll. "Delicious. Didn't know you could cook."

"You know I can't. This is compliments of Coddled Cuisine. You know that new line of kitchenware I told you about?"

"Yeah?"

"That's how I made these. They have the utensils to make any recipe within reach of a novice, such as myself."

Rhonda rises from the couch, giving everyone the full view of her bare legs, and leans over to set her glass of wine on the table in front of her. Even I cannot drag my gaze from her cleavage, nearly a canyon barely concealed by a tight pink cardigan, unbuttoned four inches lower than necessary, or prudent. Simpering next to Ben, she hooks her arm through his and flutters her lashes. "Benny? Is this the Sadie you told me about?"

Inwardly I groan, another of Ben's bevy of bimbos who seem capable of only asking questions, their voice rising at the end of even the most declarative of statements. I can picture her trapped in a burning building, asking, "Help?" I reach my hand forward and grasp the limpest excuse of a clammy handshake. "You must be Rhonda."

"Yes?"

"Pleased to meet you."

"Uh-huh?"

Kara swoops between us at that moment. "Sadie! Come and see my new sculpture. I have discovered the most amazing artist from Crandon, of all places. He uses all recycled materials in his art."

Obediently I follow, leaving Adam alone to discuss Badger football with Ben and Rhonda. Kara grabs my arm as we turn the corner and yanks me into the kitchen.

"It's in your kitchen?" I glance around her provincial French décor looking for wire clothes hangers and discarded beer bottles twisted together.

"Can you believe this one?" Kara hisses at me. "Where the hell does he find these women?"

I shrug. Guess there is no sculpture.

"I swear, Ben hasn't got a shred of integrity," Kara continues.

"She is rather obvious," I agree.

"Inflated and injected!"

"What does it matter anyway?" I ask her, confused by her sudden indignation about Ben's dating habits, which have not evolved as long as we've known him.

"It matters," she narrows her green eyes even further, "because this is exactly the sort of woman Scott dumped Molly for, and when Molly catches scent of Ronelle—"

"Rhonda."

"Whatever. When Molly sees her, she's going to regress back into her pity party mode."

"Kara," I say reasonably, "Molly knows what to expect from Ben's dates. Don't worry about it. If I were you, I'd be more concerned about her reaction to Irving."

Kara rolls her eyes at me and turns to see Elizabeth standing in the doorway.

"I just let Molly through the gate."

"I'll meet her at the door." Kara gives my shoulders a squeeze and tells me, "By the way, very nice work on finding yourself an escort, girlfriend!"

"Thank you for noticing. I'd hate for Ben to get all the attention," I say and she swishes out of the kitchen, leaving me alone with Elizabeth.

"You think she'll be very angry?" Elizabeth leans against the doorway.

I'll say this for Elizabeth, she is the least threatening partner any of us have ever had. Never possessive, always interested in Kara's friends, but she doesn't necessarily want to get involved with us. Not that I would mind. I think she'd be a lot of fun to go out with, but her residency takes a lot out of her. That and the volunteer work she does for the battered women's shelter downtown on top of her coursework. Still, if she were a guy, I'd probably have a huge crush on her because she's so confident and interesting and gosh-darn *nice*. I totally get why Kara loves her so much.

"Yeah, she's gonna be really pissed."

Elizabeth laughs. "We don't want to miss the show." She steps back and I lead the way back to the gathering room where Ben and Rhonda have reclaimed the sofa.

Adam stands talking to Kevin and Stacy. "I don't know, analysts say a market rebound is likely—"

"But a *jobless* recovery? I mean *really*, what is that but a nice way of saying the rich will get richer and the rest be damned!" Stacy declares while Kevin nods vehemently beside her.

"Historically, economies rise and fall regularly. America will work out its kinks in due time," Adam tells them in a judicious tone.

"Tell that to the working class family struggling to feed itself on minimum wage."

I know I should rescue Adam from these two, but I can't. If I get involved I won't get to watch Molly. I quietly retreat two steps and, with a loud clatter, collide with the cocktail cart. I whirl around, catch a wine glass with the my elbow, and send it smashing into the slate hearthstones. Closing my eyes, I feel tiny shards of glass bite into my knees and I hear the silence swell around me. The nylon bursts on my right kneecap, sending the run racing up my thigh. Great.

"I'll go get a broom," Elizabeth disappears back to the kitchen.

"Are you okay?" Adam crunches across the crystal shards and stops in front of me. I'm thinking he's relieved to escape Kevin and Stacy.

"I'm fine," I force a smile to pull my lips taut across my teeth. "Really."

I hear Kara's heels clacking toward us and she trills, "Everyone? Molly's here!"

Past Adam's shoulder I see Kara, all white teeth shining. Molly is beside her, predictably clad in her dinner party outfit of woven skirt, peasant blouse, clunky shoes and hair artistically arranged in what looks like painted chopsticks. She waggles her fingers at me and then spies Adam. The fingers freeze midair and her green eyes narrow. Quickly, she darts a suspicious glance around the room and deducts Kara's conspiracy.

It doesn't take a rocket scientist or even a Ph.D. in social behavior to predict her snarl and scowl when introduced to Irving.

"Yah." She defiantly looks him up and down and then turns on her heel towards the cocktail cart. "I need a beer."

I pity Irving. He stands awkwardly holding out a hand to shake with the now-vanished Molly. He looks from me to Adam and Adam gives him a sympathetic smile. "You're an accountant," he begins and I again congratulate myself on not only having found a date who is attractive, but willing to put others at ease as well.

Kara hisses as she strides past me to presumably give Molly a piece of her mind, "Go talk to him!"

I shrug at Adam and join Irving, trying to put my best face forward and smile engagingly. "So Irving, what is it like working for Kara? I always imagined it to be completely dreadful."

My kindness is rewarded with a feeble smile. Really he isn't bad-looking, he's just in the wrong place with the wrong people.

Finally Elizabeth summons us to the dinner table, decked out with crystal, china, and orchids. For all her ineptitude in matchmaking, Kara more than compensates in setting a festive table. A swale of candles curves through the center of the place settings, creating a dramatic flickering against the ruby tablecloth. I end up seated between Adam and Irving, across from Elizabeth.

As Kara and Elizabeth bring out course after course, I rescue Irving again and again from Molly's venomous tongue.

"I hear you work at the University. It must be fascinating to be on the cutting edge of research. I always hear that they make the latest discoveries over there." Irving thinks he's safe enough in this remark, but Molly shoots him down like a frostbitten fly.

"Cutting edge, that's what they'll have you think. If they let the experts actually *do* the research rather than force us to sit in our offices writing grants to fund our projects, we could probably get a lot more accomplished—" her tirade on ivory tower politics is interrupted by salads passed around the table.

Midway through the greens, Irving attempts again. "I just finished reading David L. Astrum's analysis of the Iraq war. Have you heard of it? Absolutely enlightening. I hear he's on the short list for a Pulitzer."

"David L. Astrum is a pompous post-colonialist lap dog for a blatantly conservative agenda," Molly says.

Irving falls silent until the pork tenderloin lands on his plate. "Wow, Kara, this looks fabulous."

"Pork is the lowest of all meat forms," Molly announces self-righteously while stabbing forcefully into a quivering square of tofu.

I sigh and look down the table at Kara, who is glaring at Molly. Poor Irving. I lean back a bit and attempt to redirect his efforts. "Irving, Adam practices law downtown."

Irving leans forward and eagerly dives into a long conversation with Adam on estate planning and recent legislation, which, before they lose me in technical talk, seems to have caused more problems than it purported to solve. I finish my meal ignored, listening to money talk on either side and catching wind of Kara and Molly verbally toying with Rhonda while Ben watches with amusement.

I want to kiss Elizabeth's feet when she stands to announce that dessert will be served back in the gathering room. I can't follow Elizabeth fast enough. I pause, however, at catching what sounds like the same sexy, husky voice Adam used last night on my couch.

When I turn around, I see his head turned toward Irving whose expression is placid enough. Must be a trick of my ears.

The evening winds down rapidly after that. Ben and Rhonda leave, groping and rubbing against each other on their way out. Molly follows them with the curt excuse of "an early faculty meeting tomorrow."

I don't even miss Adam since I enjoy Elizabeth and our married friends Kevin and Stacy so enormously. We've nearly rewritten a framework for public education when I realize he is nowhere in sight. I last saw him at the dining room table still engrossed in legal conversation with Irving, the rejected suitor.

"Uh, Kara?" I lean back to address my friend who is perched on the back of the couch, affectionately adoring every word from Elizabeth's mouth.

She raises her eyebrows at me while Stacy proposes sales tax as an exclusive form of funding public schools.

"Have you seen Adam?"

"I think he went to the kitchen." She sips her wine and looks up at Stacy, flushed with the heat of the conversation.

I cannot ignore the knot in the depths of my gut as I approach the kitchen. I hear murmurs and the quiet hum of the refrigerator. Turning the corner, my mouth freeze-dries at the sight of my date in a passionate kiss with another person. Horror pulls my body stiff while their heads turn slowly toward me. Irving.

The scream that passes through my lips pulls everyone else in from the gathering room and causes Adam to shove Irving aside and stride across the room toward me.

An hour later, Elizabeth gently convinces me to leave the bathroom where I've barricaded myself, perched on the edge of the swirling red-tiled bathtub, making liberal use of a box of tissues.

"They're gone. Can I come in?"

Sniffling, I stand and unlock the door. Elizabeth leans against the doorframe, her face all concerned. I can easily picture her as a doctor—she has the bedside manner of a saint.

"Do you want to sit in the sunroom? I've made you some tea."

Wiping the remains of my mascara away with a significant amount of moisture, I nod and follow her through the hallway and into the dimly lit sunroom where I collapse onto a wicker armchair.

Elizabeth hands me a mug of chamomile tea and frowns slightly. "Do you take milk or sugar? I forgot to get any."

"No, this is fine."

"Do you want to talk about it?"

"Not really. I just feel like such a total loser. First I get completely dumped by Henry, the bastard. This has been my first actual date in what seems like fucking decades, and here I am again, alone. What's wrong with me?" I know this was only a first date, but it seemed like this event defines so much in my life just now.

Elizabeth nods in response to my tirade and asks gently, "Did you really picture yourself with Adam? Did you really picture Molly with Irving?"

I shake my head. I guess I didn't really think he was the one. "I think I just wanted to get the transitional guy over with so I can get through Henry. I was looking to get through rebound territory, you know, so the *real* one can come along."

"You know, Sadie, it's not so bad being single."

"Easy to say when you're not," I mutter.

"My mother always told me that when you least expect something to happen, it will."

"I didn't exactly expect Adam."

She smiles. "Perhaps not."

We sit still for a moment, both the strains of a jazz CD playing on the stereo and the tea relaxing me. I'm really not sad. More shocked and embarrassed I guess, but who should be more embarrassed, anyway? I didn't do anything wrong. My self-esteem rises like a kite on a breezy day, easily catching any slight current of hope.

"Sadie?"

I look up from my tea and she continues.

"I hear you're going to start selling kitchen supplies. The Coddled Cuisine stuff? I'd love to make an order. I also know a few people at work who would probably be willing to have a party for you."

She's only being nice, but what the heck. Her pity translates into my profit. I wipe my nose and shift to discussing the possibilities of a catalog party with Elizabeth.

# Chapter Thirteen

**"Hostesses get a complementary sieve"**
*–Coddled Cuisine winter catalog*

I drag myself off the couch at two o' clock Saturday afternoon when I remember with a certain lack of enthusiasm that Evelyn's nephew expects me at four-thirty. My whole body feels positively fusty—even my mouth has a film of coffee residue. I haven't even bothered to put in my contacts—I'm wearing my old glasses and a sweatshirt over my pajamas. However, the day has not been a complete waste. My Coddled Cuisine supplies are now neatly packed in clear plastic bins and I organized several folders for future party hostesses. The mountain of Coddled Cuisine forms are filed in a bright orange accordion file folder. Flicking off the television, I eject the Coddled Cuisine training DVD and sigh.

Okay, Todd MacGynn, allow me to dazzle you with my wit and baffle you with my bullshit. Or maybe I can introduce you to the man of your dreams as I was able to do for my last date.

I linger in the shower, savoring the aroma of tea rose bath gel. When the steam clears my head and my hair squeaks, I turn off the tap and return to my bedroom to pull together an outfit casual enough for a hockey game but alluring enough, just in case. With a blind date, you never can tell. I've never been on one before, but Molly's have been unsuccessful, Ben's have been terrific, and my good friend Bethany Stadler from the Peace Corps married hers. The odds look favorable under this non-random sampling.

I settle on my grey v-neck sweater and denim jeans with boots; I'll be warm without looking like an over-stuffed sofa. Not really sure why I'm making such an effort, I strategically spray perfume and apply eyeliner. My stomach flutters a little at the prospect of meeting Evelyn's nephew. I decide he's tall, with dark brown hair, and blue eyes. Thin, but athletically built and not pierced or tattooed.

With this image in my head, I stack my Coddled Cuisine folders neatly on the table and look at the clock. An hour left before I need to be at Todd's hotel, so I pick up the phone and dial Kara.

"How are you, sweetie?" she asks when she picks up.

"I'm okay. Hey listen, you know how you said you would have a party for me?"

"Yes."

"I'm just getting everything organized and I thought I'd give you the first chance to book one."

"Okay—" I hear her open a drawer.

"When looks good for you?"

"How about two weeks from next Thursday, the fourth?"

"Super." I write this down on my calendar. "I'll drop off invitations and catalogs and a hostess folder to you right now, if that works out for you."

"Sure. What are you doing tonight?"

I hate to tell her this. It makes me feel like a pathetic loser, but hey, we've all been there at some point, right? "I have a blind date, sort of."

"You do?" She doesn't even attempt to keep the shock out of her voice.

"Evelyn's nephew is in town and I'm taking him to the hockey game tonight, then probably out for a bite to eat."

"You go, girl!"

"Whatever. So you'll be around for a while?"

"Yes. We're going out for dinner at seven, a little Pasta Per Tutti tonight."

"Sounds nice. Okay, I have to pick Todd up in about an hour, so I'll stop by your place on my way."

"See you then." Kara hangs up and I do a little dance by the table while I pull out a folder, four catalogs, and a stack of Coddled Cuisine invitation postcards. My first party. I'm officially on my way!


Forty minutes later I knock on a door in the downtown Best Western, very conscious of the fact that Todd will see me through the peephole before I'll see him, and this makes me nervous. Wiping my hands off on my jeans, I knock again, trying to sound confident. I mean, who cares if this is a bust? It's one night out of my entire life, no big deal.

Moments later, the door opens and I get my first glimpse: short and stocky. Todd has red hair, a neatly groomed goatee, and a healthy dose of freckles crossing the bridge of his nose. "Sadie?" He asks this in a low, raspy voice.

I hold out my hand. "You must be Todd. Nice to meet you."

"Wow. Aunt Evelyn said you were cute, but gosh."

I blush at his compliment; it's so earnest. His blue eyes crease when he smiles. I like him right away.

"Let me get my jacket, just a moment. You can come in if you'd like."

Inside the room I see two beds, one made and the other rumpled. A large bag of potato chips and a can of soda are on the table across from the television set, where I see Todd's been watching college basketball. He reappears around a corner, shrugging on a leather jacket and he gestures me out the door and into the hallway.

"Just another minute," he tells me and disappears. I hear the game abruptly stop as he turns off the television and meets me once again outside the door. "Okey dokey, we can go now."

As we amble toward the elevator I ask him, "What kind of conference brings you to Madison?"

"Magic. Actually we call them conventions, you know, a take on the old word coven, which meant a meeting of magicians. I'm a hack magician myself—it's a hobby."

"No kidding? My uncle is in town for the same thing! Bert Davis. Do you know him?"

Todd scrunches up his face in concentration, "No the name doesn't ring a bell. Do you know his stage name? I might know him by that."

"The Great Bertolini. He's out of Massachusetts."

"Ah yes, he specializes in vanishment. I met him yesterday."

"So, what do you do when you're not making doves appear out of a black top hat?"

Todd chuckles at this and replies, "I'm a veterinarian. But don't get too excited, it's not the glamorous job everyone thinks it is—all the spaying and neutering and birthing and such."

Laughing, I shake my head. "No I wouldn't expect it to be all fun and games."

"I specialize in farm animals, livestock, that sort of thing."

That explains the bulky shoulders and calloused hands. "When do you work the magic into your life?"

"Let's see, Janie Flannigan enjoyed several of my card tricks when I took care of her pony last Tuesday. I pop over once a month or so and do a regular gig at the Glenview Nursing Home, the occasional story hour at the public library, that sort of thing."

"That's where the glamour comes in, huh?"

"Oh yeah, forty or so old-timers in wheelchairs, walkers, and me. It's just a step away from the big time."

I smile and silently exhale. This could end up being a fun night out after all.

After dinner, where Todd made the salt, pepper, silverware, and the waitress's order pad disappear (much to the delight of the family in the booth across from us), we arrive at the hockey game just before the National Anthem.

"I love this game. In college they really let 'em play it the way it's meant to be played," Todd shouts to me above the din of the Badger band and thousands of screaming fans.

I eyeball the rink where the players race across the ice and ram themselves into one another ruthlessly. Not having a huge repertoire of hockey jargon, I nod along in agreement.

Two minutes into the game, the Badgers score and I have enough sense to stand up and cheer. Around me the fans begin to shout, "Sieve! Sieve! Sieve!" I watch Todd join in the cheer, heartily pumping his fist in the air.

"This is gonna be a great game!" he begins to tell me. "Alaska's ranked third this year and the Badgers are in second." He's interrupted by another goal, siren blaring, and lights bouncing off the ice and Plexiglas. Immediately we're on our feet again. At this rate, I'll be hoarse before the second period.

After the game ends Todd ushers me out of the arena, his fingertips on my lower back gently guiding me through the crowd of people whooping it up. When five college boys, shirtless and painted in red and black stripes, shove by us and yell in our faces, "Go Big Red!" I notice his good-natured grin and the way he shouts it back to them. He's not obnoxious, just personable.

When we reach the parking lot I realize in terror that I have no recollection of where I've parked. A black swamp of shame fills my stomach and the quesadillas I ate at dinner seem perilously close to reaching the back of my throat. I glance around the full parking lot, dimly lit under a black April sky.

"Ummm…Todd? Uhhh, I hate to tell you this, but I don't exactly remember where we parked." I want to close my eyes to block out the look of pity he'll give me for being so stupid. Or the look of irritation.

I open one eye and see a huge smile break across his face, revealing very even teeth. "I thought I was the only one who did stuff like that! Only one thing to do then, you know?"

"Start looking for it?" I am relieved at his nonchalance.

"Heck no! Call a cab! I'm not wandering around a parking lot all night!"

I look at him in astonishment. I can't leave my car here all night! What is this guy thinking? Will he pay the cab fare for my trip out here tomorrow to pick it up?

Todd starts to laugh, "Oh wow, you should see your face! You totally thought I was serious! Of course we'll go look for it. I was only kidding."

A laugh bubbles up from my throat and the quesadilla sinks back down. We step off the curb together and begin a long stroll through the rows of cars, vans, and trucks in search of my Honda. It doesn't take as long to find it as I feared. I quickly unlock the doors and jump in. Todd buckles himself in on the passenger side and looks over at me.

"Now what?"

"Your call. Your aunt suggested I take you down to State Street. We could stop for a drink somewhere.

Otherwise if there was something else you wanted to do…?"

"Nope, that sounds great. Let's go to State Street."

Magically, I find parking and we hike up the street toward the Capitol building. Todd seems to lean back as he walks, taking it all in with great delight.

"Don't you just love this old architecture? They usually just tear down old buildings rather than deal with their quirks and character. Wow! A kosher deli! I haven't seen one of those North of Chicago! Did you see that guy's mohawk? He must use a can of paste to make it stay!"

Normally someone so talkative would have gotten on my nerves by now, but not Todd. His curiosity is refreshing.

Finally we reach University Plaza and cut through to get out of the wind. Halfway, he spies the arcade. "Let's go in!"

I peer at the flashing lights, all the screens nearly hidden behind the hunched over bodies of teenaged boys and the occasional cluster of geeky college boys.

"Really?"

"Oh yeah, it'll be a blast!"

He purchases five dollars' worth of tokens and I follow him through the metallic beeping and electronic laser blasting to the rear of the arcade where a particularly creepy group of boys with green hair are clustered around a game called *Slaughter Field*.

"Look! *Ms. Pac-Man*!" He drags me over to it and drops tokens in the machine. "We have to play this. I can't believe they even have this old relic!"

"Seriously?" But he's already pushing the joystick around, directing his pink-bowed yellow dot through the maze. He maneuvers it through some blinking cherries and I watch the score crawls upward to one-hundred. Finally, two mazes later, I actually feel disappointed when it crashes into a ghost and melts away.

"Your turn!"

I grab the warm joystick and lean forward. It takes me a minute to get the hang of how fast it moves, and I'm sailing down a long row of dots when Todd's voice makes me jump. "Look out for the ghost! Turn left! Turn left!"

I yank the joystick to the left and grin when I evade the ghost and find my way up to a blinking cherry. The five dollars of tokens fall into the machine too quickly and, before I know it, we finish our last game.

"Nice. You got pretty good at that!" Todd holds up his hand.

"Thanks, you're pretty good yourself." I slap his hand, pleased with myself.

"I have Richard Fisher to thank for that—he's the one who trapped me in his basement for all those years through middle school to play this darn game! Good ol' *Ms. Pac-Man*." He pats the side of the machine affectionately. "She kept me out of trouble in my childhood. Let's go get a beer."

We weave back through the huddled masses of teenagers and college kids, and I look at them differently this time as I pass them. No, maybe they're not as hostile and angry as I thought. Maybe they're just in the best place to stay out of trouble.

Back on State Street I feel the wind pick up, whipping my hair and forcing a chill through my jacket and sweater. Folding my arms to block out the cold, I hurry and turn the corner to see Hawk's doesn't have a line out the door. I suggest it to Todd, who shrugs. We push through the heavy oak door to the raucous warmth inside.

"I'll grab a table over there if you'll order the beers," I volunteer.

"Sure. What kind?"

"Whatever's on tap is fine."

I bump past two gigantic college boys wearing matching red overalls and Bucky Badger earrings and catch somebody's elbow right in the center of my chest, causing me to gasp for air. I'm sure I'll find a bruise there tomorrow morning. I wiggle through a group of girls in tight jeans discussing someone named Chris who apparently had it coming. Just as I pass, I see one of them out of the corner of my eye giving me the glaring once-over women save for situations when they feel threatened. I can't believe it! I'm practically twice this girl's age and she thinks I am someone to watch out for? Her unintended flattery sends me floating to the table. I must still look good—not totally washed up.

Moments later Todd joins me, sloshing two pints of Killian's Red onto the table. "Whew, I forget how crowded the college bar scene gets."

"Not your usual hang out then?"

"Hardly. More the VFW Friday night fish fry and then over to the corner tavern for taps of beer with the gentlemen farmers."

Todd is very different from most of the men I've met in Madison so far. Even Ben, who I adore, is a real snob about where he goes for happy hour.

Too soon I hear the bartender shouting "Last call!" and the lights dim even more. Two o'clock already?

Todd repeats my thoughts as he looks at the thinning crowd. "I guess they'll kick us out if we don't get out."

"I suppose so." We leave our table and step over puddles of spilled beer. The jukebox is playing some Irish drinking song. It echoes in my head as I lead Todd back to where I've parked the car four blocks away.

The wind feels fiercer than before. "Spring takes forever to come in this state," I groan. "They aren't kidding when they say winter lasts six months out of the year."

"You think it's bad here, you should be up north. It's generally ten degrees colder." His nose glows a bright red under the streetlights but he doesn't seem to mind the icy blast hitting his face.

Opening the car doors, I begin to think ahead of the moment I'm in for the first time all night. What if he asks me in? How far would I like to see this go? Todd's definitely attractive in a boy-next-door kind of way, but his personality and humor put his average looks over the top.

I look over at him to see he is looking peacefully out the window, watching the city whiz past. "Do you have a lot going on tomorrow?"

"Sort of. I have three seminars I want to attend, the guest speaker for lunch is supposed to be pretty good, and then Aunt Evelyn and Uncle Dan are taking me to their place for dinner. I head back home on Monday."

I feel a twinge of sadness, like when I see the last leaves of autumn clinging to their branches when the snow starts to fly. I pull up to the doors and decide to take some initiative. "Would you like me to walk you up?"

"No, that's okay. I've kept you out late enough as it is. Thanks for a great time, Sadie. I hope to meet up with you again sometime."

Before I can open my mouth to reply, he leans across the seat and brushes his lips across my right cheek. I close my eyes and turn my face more fully toward him when I hear the car door open. I yank my eyelids open to watch him get out of the seat. He leans over to tell me good night before disappearing with a wave through the sliding doors leading to the lobby. I reach up to touch the warmth on my cheek where he kissed me. What just happened?

# Chapter Fourteen

**"Coffee pots & tea pots"**
*—Coddled Cuisine winter catalog*

Monday I track down Evelyn as soon as I arrive to work. She's pouring herself a cup of coffee and drowning it in cream and sugar when the sound of my voice makes her jump and spin around to glare at me. Fishing the sugar packet out of her cup with her fingertips she scolds, "You startled me! What's going on?"

I pull my mouth shut. I'm not sure how to proceed at this point. Do I risk looking like a sixth grader and ask her what Todd told her about me? Do I tell her that we had a nice time? I guess I figured she'd bring up the subject since she set us up. Finally I plunge ahead by gulping, "So, your nephew." Yes, very smooth introduction.

"Yes, Todd. How did that go? I hope you didn't mind giving up part of your weekend." She looks back at me with the benign and bland expression of a sphinx.

"Fine, I think. I had a nice time."

"Good. That's sweet of you to say so. He's a fine boy. I've always thought him very likeable. We enjoyed having him over for dinner Sunday. He's always such good conversation! Such an interesting life he leads."

He had a horrible time! He must not have liked me at all and this is Evelyn's kind way of letting me down. I can just picture him telling her, "Thanks for the blind date, but Aunt Evelyn, next time let me pick my own escort." I nod and muster a stoic grin. "Yes, he's a great guy."

Evelyn pauses, studying me suspiciously for a moment and then shrugs her shoulders, "I must be off, I have to catch Larry. He's putting in an appearance at a walleye festival this weekend and I've got to give him the details. Shall we do lunch?"

My frustration boils over. He must have liked me. For God's sake, how many eligible women can he meet up there in the boondocks anyway? "Did he like me?" I repress the urge to smack myself on the forehead.

Evelyn's face creases into a teasing grin. "You *did* like him! I knew you'd get along! I knew it!" Her coffee sloshes over the side of her mug while she dances a jig.

"What?"

"I was waiting to see what you thought of Todd before I said anything. I didn't want him to come off as desperate, you see, but now I know." She cocks her right eyebrow.

"I just asked what he thought of me," I say lamely.

"That's all you needed to say. Frankly Sadie, I hoped you'd come waltzing in with flushed cheeks and a gleam in your eye, but this is good enough for me. My favorite co-worker and my favorite nephew, a match made with my own two hands!"

"What did he say?"

"Oh, just that you are a really great girl, intelligent, passionate, attractive, and nice. The usual things you hear from a young man who is smitten."

"He told you all that?" My blushing starts at the base of my neck and crawls to my hairline.

Evelyn winks at me. "You'll be hearing from him soon, dear. I gave him your phone number when he asked me for it last night. Now I really must go." She hurries out the door as I slide into one of the blue plastic break room chairs. My heart feels weak and my breath comes in short little pants. He likes me! He's going to call me! I practically float to the studio to meet Dean. It doesn't matter that he keeps mispronouncing "judiciary" and "appellate." It doesn't even faze me when he expresses surprise to learn that state Supreme Court judges are elected and not appointed by the federal Supreme Court. Todd likes me!

I get a text from Kara before I can tell her the good news. She's full of apologies for the dinner party and begging to take me out for drinks tonight. I cave to her offer:

### Meet you @ Brothers @ 5:30?

Should we include Molly in this happy hour? No. She's too morose for my mood today. I hit send and dig into my Monday morning pile of confirmations and interview questions. I nearly have Wednesday's bio on a guest author complete when Evelyn raps on my door.

"Ready?"

We don't even discuss our destination—the Sunroom Café is a favorite lunchtime spot of ours. Settled next to a window, I open the menu while Evelyn studies the specials on the chalkboard behind the register.

"That spinach quiche sounds good."

"I'm in a B.L.T. mood today," I snap the menu shut and set it back in front of me on the table. "Tell me about Todd. What's the family like?"

She pauses, smiling at me. "He's the youngest of three boys, always was the one getting in the most trouble."

This intrigues me, but before I can find out more, the waitress comes to take our order. Did you want the fries or the salad with that?" The waitress glances up from her notepad, frowning behind her black-rimmed glasses to comprehend our order and using the toe of her left ballet flat to scratch the back of her right leg.

"I'll take the salad, house dressing."

"Okay. I'll be right back with the salad and your tea."

"Trouble?" I prompt Evelyn.

"Yes. Not bad or malicious trouble. More of the unfortunate, bad luck kind of trouble. Like when he crashed his go-cart into a city dump truck. It wasn't *all* his fault, but it was a terrible mess."

I nod to encourage her reminiscence. This is the sort of familial anecdote that really tells you something about a person. "Was he aiming for the truck?"

"Goodness no!" Evelyn laughs. "He was testing it out. He had just built this go-cart with his brother, Bill, and he won the coin toss to drive it for the first time. Well, they lived near the top of a steep hill and the brakes on this contraption probably weren't in complete working order. Anyway, as he's racing down the street, this city dump truck starts crossing the intersection. Todd tried to stop, then tried steering out of the way of the truck, and ended up crashing right into the rear tire. He spent a week in the hospital after that fiasco."

"Oh my gosh!"

"But he's a scrappy thing. I can't imagine there's a bone in his body he hasn't broken in one way or another. And the animals! He used to drive my sister nuts with his animals!"

"Animals?"

"Oh, he would adopt every stray creature he came across. It's bad enough to bring home puppies and kittens, but then a chicken, a snake, and a goat, too. He practically took over the shed in their backyard and made it into an animal shelter."

"So he's been in the animal business most of his life."

"He's always known what he's wanted to do. That's one thing about Todd: he doesn't mess around—he either loves something or he hates it. He's never luke-warm."

"Here." The waitress drops a basket of teabags on the table and unloads a tray of mugs, hot water and my salad with all the enthusiasm of a dead fish before shuffling away.

I shake my head and smile. "They sure don't train them here, do they?"

"Nope, the service is scattershot, but at least the food is good." Evelyn selects a bag of peppermint tea leaves and un-wraps it thoughtfully.

I paw through the herbal options and finally spy the lavender wrapping of an Earl Grey teabag and lift it out. "All set for that walleye festival?"

"It seems like springtime brings so many of these event appearances. It's good for the station, but dreadful for me."

Evelyn books all the "celebrity appearances" for the station, which range from book signings to odd village festivals. Normally this isn't too much trouble, but occasionally a diva like Dean or Maria Santolacca will make completely obnoxious demands and require all of Evelyn's abilities in diplomacy and damage control.

"Does Dean have anything coming up?"

"Sadly, yes. He's scheduled to speak at a number of high school graduation ceremonies and has been tapped to show up at a statewide broadcaster's conference later this month. I can just imagine him yelling at some poor high school principal for bottles of Evian and a better sound system."

I cringe at this and laugh. "I don't envy you."

Evelyn sips her tea and sighs. "At least I can say this: men's behavior is always predictable."

She's right on that point.

# Chapter Fifteen

**"Most marvelous margarita glasses"**
*—Coddled Cuisine recruitment summer catalog*

I enter Brothers and look around the bar for Kara. The wood-paneled booths are empty and the only other customers are a group of college guys shooting darts. Hefting myself up onto a barstool, I look around for the bartender while grimly noting the proximity of the entrance for the women's bathroom to the dartboard.

Moments later, Kara pushes through the heavy glass door and waves to me. "Sorry I'm so late!" She rushes toward me at the bar.

"I just got here."

"Let's take a booth. Margaritas?"

I shrug. "Sure."

I slide into a booth and Kara prances over to the dart players. Her voice carries over the hum of the coolers and the rattle of the radio. "Who's responsible for pouring drinks here?"

A scrawny young man in a Badger sweatshirt lazily stands up from his barstool and slowly walks behind the bar. "Me. What'll it be?"

Kara looks him up and down disparagingly. "A pitcher of margaritas, salt, not sugar on the rim, and we're right at that booth." She points to me and strides over.

"Unbelievable how bad service is with these college kids."

Smiling, I slip out of my coat. "Wasn't that long ago for us either."

"We had more brains and gumption." Kara jerks her thumb toward the bartender who is pulling down a pitcher at the same speed grass grows in August.

"Kids these days." I settle back into my seat.

"Honey, I am so, so, so, so sorry about the other night." Kara reaches over and grabs my hands in her warm, perfumed grasp. "I feel just *awful*."

"It's okay. Really." I look down at her fresh manicure— she's got tiny daisies detailing her fingertips today. Very spring-y. I look up again and meet her eyes while I smile bravely. "I guess it just wasn't meant to be."

"I mean, I have had scenes at my parties before, but never, never something quite like that! This is worse than catching Ben on top of our coats last Christmas with the caterer's daughter."

I release a genuine smile at that memory. Kara had not caught them. Ben's date, a vague blonde with enormous teeth, had walked in on them while looking for the bathroom. She shrieked so hysterically that everyone came running down the hall to her, dropping drinks and plates of food on the way, certain the house was on fire or something equally dreadful. We found Ben sheepishly tucking in his shirt and the caterer's daughter flushed and disheveled and pulling her dress down over her thighs. There was no mistaking what caused all the hysteria, and Kara had sternly escorted Ben and his date to the front door, returned to the gathering room and collapsed on the couch in a burst of laughter.

"There's something to be said for the shocking nature of sexual lust."

She nods grimly and whispers, "I had no idea he was bi. I usually can pick out a gay man within seconds. To think I had two within my radar and didn't peg either of them!"

So this is the cause of Kara's despair—she's losing her touch. Her despair has little or nothing to do with my feelings about the night. I can't even be mad though, since I've moved on to straighter pastures. "Hard to believe," is all I can say.

"And I promise you I gave Irving a talking to when he stopped by this morning, all full of apologies and flowers." She adds, "He won't be showing up at any more of my dinner parties, that's for certain!"

"He wasn't too keen on showing up at this last one, Kara."

She waves away my hint of criticism by looking around for the bartender who now has prepared our drinks and is placing them on a tray in slow motion. "Can you believe this guy? Typical college slacker. The motivation of a rock, and he'll expect fifty grand a year when he graduates with some lame-ass degree in Communications."

I let her rant in a different direction. I'd rather not relive the horror of discovering my date had thrown me aside for the guy she had claimed for Molly, but all the same, I'm keeping the news about Todd to myself for the time being.

We both watch the bartender shuffle past the empty tables and stop to watch an ESPN score update on the TV mounted above the bar. He finally makes it to our booth, sliding the tray onto the table as if it takes all his strength and effort to bring it to us. Silently, he lifts two salt-rimmed glasses and plunks them in front of us, then sets the pitcher of margaritas between us. As an afterthought, he drops a fistful of napkins on the table and actually grunts as he turns to leave.

"Thank you!" Kara gushes. "What's your name again?"

He pauses and half turns toward her to mumble, "Kyle."

"Kyle. Thanks and I'll be sure to let Chad know just how fine a staff he has working for him!" Kara chirps.

The kid turns and comes back to the table. "You want any chips with that?"

Suddenly I get the feeling he cares. "No, no thank you. This will be all."

"Just holler if you need anything. I'll be right over there." Kyle gestures to the bar, all nervous respect.

Kara nods, eyes slit like those of a cat comfortably sunning itself in a window, content with the brutal knowledge that she has made Kyle suffer. We watch him scurry away and huddle with his friends by the dartboard. Their faces turn to look at us and I finally speak. "I assume Chad's the owner."

"That would be correct."

"And you know him how?"

"Barely. I was introduced to him at one of those Chamber of Commerce events where the downtown business owners get together to schmooze and talk trash to one another. I've never met him since. That, my good woman, was merely a demonstration of the power of name-dropping."

I nod in approval. "Very nice. Quite effective."

"Isn't it though?" Kara pours our drinks and raises her glass. "To better love. And better service."

I clink my glass heavily against hers. "Cheers." The sweet-sour cold of the margarita rushes past my teeth and I let the saltiness rest on my tongue for a moment. Perhaps the guilt hasn't quite left Kara's heart. I dive in on the off chance she still pities me. "So Kara, what are you doing for dinner tonight?"

Bless her heart, she springs for Chinese food, too.

## Chapter Sixteen

**"Your district manager will contact you"**
*—Coddled Cuisine training manual*

The week flies by in a bustle of walking Dean through two shows on foreign policy (India and North Korea) and soothing Evelyn's ruffled feathers while Ron continues to wreak havoc on her Capitol news crew. I wake up at the ungodly hour of nine o' clock Saturday morning and get ready to shadow the Coddled Cuisine district manager at a show. This is the last step before my Wednesday night debut presentation of the products.

I rush to get ready, choosing khakis and a v-neck sweater. Casual, yet professional. I double-check to make sure I have the address and leave totally preoccupied with the morning ahead when I pause to check my mailbox. And who should I see but Adam, standing beautifully tall in a sweat suit, his face damp with sweat from a morning jog, checking his own mailbox. *I have nothing to be ashamed of. I have nothing to be ashamed of.* He looks up and sees me.

"Good morning, Adam. Have a nice jog?" I smile brightly at him while feeling my stomach lurch like a three-wheeled grocery cart.

He drops his keys and jumps back, "Hello Sadie, how are you?" He shifts from his left foot to his right, avoiding eye contact with me.

"In a bit of a hurry. Bye." I slip out the door, glad to have that first encounter out of the way. The door slams shut behind me and my face flushes at the memory of letting him kiss me hours before catching him with Irving. As the wind whips my hair into my eyes, I close them and concentrate my thoughts briefly on Todd. Ahhh. All better now. My frame of mind back in order, I retrieve my car from the underground lot down the street and curse the Wisconsin spring, which teases you one day with balmy weather and then punishes you the next with a storm of sleet and lashing winds.

I easily find the party house, two blocks off Mendota Avenue in an older neighborhood. Ringing the doorbell of the two-story stucco house, I begin to feel nervous about meeting Kimberly, the woman who will technically be my new boss. The door opens and I see a pleasant looking middle-aged woman in black corduroys with short burgundy hair. "Hi!"

"Are you Kimberly?" I hope so—she looks like the motherly type.

"No, I'm Carol, the hostess. Kimberly is setting up in the kitchen. Follow me."

Past a living room enshrouded in plastic slipcovers, I follow Carol down a long hallway and into a bright orange kitchen. I see a tall woman with long blonde hair busily pulling boxes out of wooden crates. She stands and extends her hand to me. "Hi, you must be Sadie. I'm Kimberly."

Her voice is low and smooth, like Bernadette Hill's radio voice. Kimberly looks barely older than me and exudes class from her expertly highlighted hair to her pointed leather heels. I shake her hand and catch a faint whiff of expensive perfume. Tanned, slender, and clad in black dress pants and a crisp white shirt, she could have stepped out of a magazine advertisement for Ralph Lauren. I can hardly picture this woman in a blue apron doing home parties, yet I'm about to.

"I like to arrive at least an hour before the party," she looks pointedly at the clock above the stove. "I expected you earlier, but I've gone ahead and carried in all the boxes from my car by myself. I'll use the kitchen counter back here as my display area and use the other countertop for my demonstration area. Put these folders and pens on each chair while I get the display area organized." She gestures to another crate where I find folders and pens to set on the ten chairs lining the back walls of the kitchen. I drop a couple more in the center of the kitchen table for good measure and peek inside one of them. There's a letter to the guests explaining the hostess benefits and the month's sale items, two catalogs, and an order form. I replace it and turn to watch Kimberly drape her wooden crates artistically with bright red fabric and use the different levels to set up the dishes and cookware.

Walking across the kitchen, I watch more closely while she effortlessly balances bamboo spoons and plastic spatulas among bowls and pans. "That should do it. Now, Carol," she calls down the hall where Carol has disappeared. "Everything I need is in your fridge, right?"

I hear Carol's voice call back, "Yes, it is. I'll be right back down."

Kimberly turns to me and explains, "She's doing the Bountiful Brunches party. We'll be preparing an egg casserole, triple-berry muffins, and Sunshine Punch. Most hostesses work off of a theme and select three or four recipes for the demonstration. My only criterion is that the recipes somehow include the food chopper, the stoneware, the cookware, and the Ultimate Mixing Bowl. These are our best sellers and practically every recipe uses them, so it's usually not a problem. If it is, I suggest an additional recipe. Let's pre-measure all of the ingredients and cook the meat for the egg bake."

I stand awkwardly with nothing to do but watch while she starts pulling stuff out of the refrigerator and piling it on the counter. "You can brown the sausages—you know how to do that, right?" She looks for my nod before continuing. "I like having plenty of time before the guests arrive to set up. The guests will want to look at the display before they even see the demonstration, so it's very important to get that ready. You also want the food ready to go, on the chance that the hostess forgot to buy an ingredient or runs short of something we need." I peel the plastic wrap off the sausage patties and watch her pour sugar, salt, flour, and milk into various measuring cups. "You can start the sausage—use that pan I set on the stove."

I'm browning the sausage when Carol returns to ask if she should make a second pot of coffee.

Kimberly clearly takes charge of every detail the moment she enters the kitchen. "Use the carafe by the sink for your first pot. You can put that out on your table with the number of coffee cups you think you'll need. Sadie, let me fix this for you." Kimberly chops the sausage into finer pieces using the edge of a fork.

In a flurry of activity Kimberly, Carol, and I have the food prepped as the guests begin to arrive. "Sit back there and watch," Kimberly points to the kitchen table. "I'll answer any of your questions afterwards."

Smoothing her apron, Kimberly takes center stage with a small cough and pause. "Welcome everyone to Carol's party. I'm Kimberly Carlyle and I have been with Coddled Cuisine for three years now…" She's a thousand times more polished than Sydney and she breezily works through the recipes, talking about the various products as she goes. It doesn't even seem scripted, although it must be if she has done this as often as I suspect. I watch in awe as the room, full of middle-aged women, whom must have well-stocked kitchens at this stage of their lives, fill in the blanks on their order forms at such a brisk pace I'm sure Carol's party will break a thousand dollars in sales.

Finally, Kimberly pulls the egg bake from the oven with a flourish. "Ladies, help yourselves to more Sunshine Punch and try this egg bake. I'll be in the living room to take any orders and answer any questions." She beckons to me and I follow her to the plastic-coated sofa where she plops down her briefcase and extracts a calculator, two pens, and extra catalogs. "Do you have any questions? They'll be a few minutes as they help themselves to the eggs. I normally would stay in there with them to answer questions, but I've seen a number of these women at previous shows, so I don't imagine they have a lot to ask."

"How do you do it? I mean, how do you talk about the products while you cook? I can barely follow a recipe and answer the phone at the same time!" I can't help gushing at her obvious grace in this area.

She shrugs. "I could make any of these recipes in my sleep. Any idiot can follow a recipe. As far as talking about the product, it's only describing what I'm doing as I'm doing it. It has nothing at all to do with the recipe. It's just about the tools that make the steps happen, that's all. The big key is preparation. Know your recipe, know your product line, have everything you need laid out ahead of time, and you're pretty much there."

"I'm impressed," I repeat in a small voice.

"It isn't that complicated. I love to cook and I enjoy people—I assume that's why you're here today."

That couldn't be further from the truth, but I want to impress her so I nod, feigning agreement.

"Why don't you take some of the orders today as practice so you'll have some practical experience under your belt before your first show?"

"Okay."

She hands me a calculator and set of pens and catalogs and directs me to the chairs across the room. "Call me over if you have any questions."

A minute later, I'm going over my first order form, filling in prices and adding in tax, shipping, and handling. I write in the proffered credit card numbers, double-checking the math along the way. I fill out two more order forms and anxiously show them to Kimberly as she thanks her last customer. "Okay," she frowns. "You need to write really hard so they are still legible by the third carbon copy. I'll just redo these." She pulls the orders from my hands.

"Sorry," I mumble.

"I should have just done them myself. Now, we have to pull Carol and talk her through her hostess benefits. Why don't you go get her while I finish the final tally?" She begins copying my orders on the final page of the first carbon order form.

Obediently, I head back to the kitchen, stomach growling for a plateful of muffins and eggs. I delicately extract Carol from her guests. "Kimberly wants to talk to you for just a quick minute," I tell her.

She stands, face beaming, and follows me. Kimberly announces to her, in a very pleased voice, "Carol, I have your final numbers." I get a flash of Regis Philbin on *Who Wants to Be a Millionaire* and I stifle a giggle.

Carol perches on the edge of the couch, hands wrapped together in anticipation.

"You earned 1300 points today. That's two free items and unlimited half-price items from the spring catalog!"

"That's fabulous!" Carol whispers.

"And that's not all," Kimberly pauses dramatically before continuing. "You have booked one party off of yours, earning five hundred additional points! Naturally, this does not include my own special hostess gift to you."

"Wow!" Carol clasps her hands beneath her chin.

"Now, you don't have to close your party yet. If you think you might have some catalog orders in the next few days, I'm willing to leave your party open until…" Kimberly opens her day planner and studies it for a moment, "shall we say Wednesday?"

"Sure. How do I close then?"

"You call me sometime Wednesday morning and place any additional orders with me and then we'll go through your order as well. Does that sound good to you?"

"Yes."

"Then you'll make out one check to me for the cost of anything not billed to a credit card at that point and, when I receive your check, I'll place your party orders and the products will be mailed directly to you within five to seven days."

Carol nods compliantly at this instruction and I note that at no point is Kimberly responsible for any payment of the orders until she has the money in her hand. "You go back and enjoy your guests. Sadie and I will clean up your kitchen and be on our way."

"Are you sure I can't do anything to help?"

"Absolutely not! You enjoy your time with your friends and family out there," Kimberly tells her in a tone of finality.

As Carol heads back to the kitchen, Kimberly quickly slides everything back into her briefcase and latches it shut. "Let's go do dish duty."

A minute later, I'm up to my elbow in sudsy water while Kimberly dries and repacks her stock. Every last spatula, pan, and platter back in its assigned space, she stacks her crates, folds the red fabric, and hands me a load to take to her car. I'm watching a pro. Kimberly slides each crate into the back of her Lexus, everything clean and ready for the next party.

"How many parties do you do a week?" I ask as we head back to her car with the second load.

"Three or four, it depends. My husband travels a lot with his work and I like to go with him sometimes, so I book my parties around him."

"I see." And here I'm thinking I'll book my parties whenever the heck anyone will have them. I'm gaining confidence that this stuff may actually sell itself and I won't have to grovel long before I'm profitable.

It's just past noon when I'm thanking Kimberly and promising to get in touch after my third show. "Don't forget our meeting on the third," she calls to me as she backs out of the driveway. "The summer catalogs are coming that night and you'll want to go through them with me!"

Intimidating? Absolutely. But she's a far cry better than Ron any day.

## Chapter Seventeen

**"The Chocolate Extravaganza party"**
*—Coddled Cuisine hostess brochure*

Wednesday I'm tight with nervous energy, tapping my pen, checking and re-checking my e-mail, sucking down a dangerous four cups of coffee. At four o'clock I speed out of the office and race over to Molly's.

Her kitchen is truly ideal for this sort of party, long and narrow. She has counters along three walls and an island in the center, smack in front of her dining table. She greets me with unusual enthusiasm as I haul in my first load of plastic tubs.

"I'm actually kind of excited about tonight." She grabs a plastic tub from my arms and leads me into her kitchen.

"Good, so am I. But probably for very different reasons."

She helps me haul in the last of my wares and perches on a stool to watch me unpack. What the hell did

Kimberly do with all of this stuff? I rack my brain to recall how she had her stuff packed. Did she have it in the original packaging? I'm about to hit the panic button when Molly interrupts my frantic inner voice with, "I have a date tomorrow night."

I nearly drop a serving platter at this newsflash. "A date? With who? How? When? Where?"

"His name is Francis. He just started managing the new coffee shop down the street. I met him when I went in there for coffee. We're going to the Elvehjem to hear the Eroica Trio perform and go out for a drink afterward."

"Great! I'm so happy for you! Tell me all about him." I preoccupy my mind with the details of Molly's new love interest while collapsing the cardboard boxes and vowing to pack my Coddled Cuisine wares in dishtowels in the future.

"He's from Washington originally, and he's into rock climbing and kayaking. He has a degree from Stanford, and when he's not running the shop, he's working with the Green Party on publicity and event organizing."

"Did you get this information off of eHarmony?"

Molly actually laughs at my joke and shakes her head, beaded earrings slapping against her cheeks. "No, it's just that you're the fourth person I've told about him and it's starting to come off a little canned."

"Does Kara know?"

"Are you kidding? She's the first person I told just so she'd quit trying to find me a date!"

I crack a smile and begin draping Molly's countertop with folds of a yellow and blue checked fabric I found on sale yesterday during my lunch break. The frayed edges of the cloth keep sticking out in pointy angles, and I can't get it to stay on top of the countertop. How did Kimberly make this look so easy? I grit my teeth and try refolding the cloth. I consider using masking tape to stick it down just as Molly comes over and begins tucking the ends in here and there, propping a platter and a few mixing bowls on top.

"There, that should keep it in place." She smoothes the front of a display of hostess serving dishes and turns to me. "I should have minored in interior design."

I thank her with relief—I can manage this display from here. Now to actually prepare the food and peddle the goods, the part of the party that really matters.

I start unwrapping measuring cups and spoons from their plastic bags and unfold the blue apron to pull over my head. "Hey Molly, where are your baking supplies?"

"Same cupboard as before. The only thing that isn't in there are the chocolate chunks—they're on the counter by the stove in the shopping bag. Is there anything I can do to help?"

I shake my head. The Chocolate Extravaganza party is pretty easy: a hot chocolate mix, double chocolate chip skillet cookie, and a s'more dip. Two of the recipes have fewer than five ingredients; I'll measure out as I go and I'll be fine. "No, as long as we lay everything out, I'll be okay. Maybe we'll just measure out the baking soda, salt, and flour. That should do."

After lining all my ingredients and essential utensils, I find my business folder, an accordion file folder I stuffed full of order forms, catalogs, and other Coddled Cuisine information. I slide out fifteen blue folders and snag a handful of pens from the bottom of the last plastic bin. Armed and ready, I place folders and pens on chairs as the doorbell rings, and I hear Molly greet someone at the door. I have no idea what to expect, probably a mix of co-workers, political activist friends, and Kara. Sure enough, Molly comes back to the kitchen with a tall woman sporting a crew cut and army-issue pants. I vaguely recognize her from Molly's office. Next to her stands a small woman in a tie-dyed peasant dress, one of Molly's research partners and a doctoral candidate.

"Sadie, you remember Kathy from my office, and Brenda, she's working on her dissertation in geothermal range measurements."

"Right. Hello, ladies." I plaster on my most competent and perky smile. "Make yourselves comfortable. We'll get started as soon as everyone is here. Feel free to look at the display items over there." I gesture grandly to my wares, not as many of them as Kimberly, but I'm just starting out, of course.

"Thanks," Brenda tells me, and Kathy brushes past me to sit down by the window. I see it all over her body language: she's like me at these parties. Absolutely no interest, here due to someone's coercion, and maybe good for about a thirty dollar sale, which she'll purchase just to be polite. Brenda sits next to Kathy while Molly escapes to answer the door once again. Fortunately, I'm not alone in the kitchen with these two for long. Within ten minutes Molly has the chairs filled up and wine and tea poured all around.

"Good evening, everyone. I'm so glad you could all come tonight and be part of the Coddled Cuisine experience." I watch Kara close her eyes and shake her head slowly in disgust at this. Ignoring her sarcastic facial expressions, I introduce myself and ask for introductions. I smile encouragingly as we get to Kathy, who nearly grunts her name.

"Kathy. I work with Molly. First party."

No other information forthcoming, I move along in what I pray is a smooth manner. "Okay then. Thanks for coming, Kathy. And Brenda?"

"I'm Brenda, I work with Molly and this is also my first party."

"Love all these first timers!" What the hell is my problem? I sound like some Vegas comedy show opener. I've become the really unfunny paunchy guy wearing a vest over a T-shirt, sent out before the real comedian to warm-up the crowd. "That's everyone, then. Raise your hand if you love chocolate!"

Three hands go up and the rest of the women shift in their seats, looking at one another uncomfortably. Kathy sighs and turns her head to look out the window. Great start, just fantastic.

"Chocolate is my favorite food group, so I was really glad when Molly told me she wanted to have a Chocolate Extravaganza party. You're going to love these recipes. They're easy and quick to make. But even more important, chocolate boosts the serotonin levels, gives you a natural high, and is delicious. Let's start with the Double Chocolate Chunk Skillet Cookie."

I talk through the recipe and products while I measure out butter, flour, and sugar. Then I get to baking soda and salt. In front of me are two identical white cups holding what looks to me like two identical white granular substances. Baking soda is more powdery, so I take my chances and dole out two teaspoonfuls of the smaller-grained powder and a half teaspoonful of the remaining cup. Okay then. I look up and smile, and my vision completely blurs so I only see dots of color.

"We mix this using the Super Whisk." I demonstrate by whipping the dough around in the bowl; the dough coagulates in one thick mess between the wires of the whisk. I try banging the whisk on the side of the bowl to loosen it off so I can finish mixing the ingredients but it sticks there, pasted between the wires. Finally I grab a spoon and smear the dough out of the whisk's metal grip and back into the bowl. The room is still dead quiet.

"The great thing about the cookware I'm about to demonstrate is that it can go in the oven or on the stove." I look up again and still find myself unable to focus on a single face in the crowd. My pulse has picked up and I feel a trickle of sweat start its journey down my hairline. Absolutely awful.

I grab a Sensational Spatula and finally ease the dough into the skillet. There are chunks of brown sugar and non-melted butter in the dough, but I figure it will melt itself into the mixture in the oven. "Now we cover the dough with another cup of chocolate chunks. Doesn't this sound decadent?"

No response. I wonder if a single one of these women has ever attended a home party. They don't even make the slightest sounds of feigned enthusiasm or polite interest you normally hear. I sprinkle the chips on top of the cookie and hold up the skillet. "Now we put this in our preheated oven. We're baking it at three-fifty." I turn to slide the skillet into the oven and, instead of a blast of heat meeting my face when I open the oven door, I'm greeted with the cool and dark cavern that clearly has not been preheated. Okay, this is embarrassing, but will it really affect the recipe if the oven isn't preheated? I put it in and discreetly turn the knob on the stovetop to three-fifty and spin around to face a room full of completely slack faces.

"While that's baking, we'll prepare the Scrumptious S'more Dip next."

The s'more dip assembles without a hitch and I slide the dish into the oven next to the skillet. I realize with relief that I'm now two for three and nearly done with this first party, which I know will result in a big, fat zero for sales. And even worse, no hostess benefits for Molly. I blink quickly to keep the tears back and my voice quavers when I turn to face the group of women once more. A few of them are talking to each other, their attention completely lost to my presentation and me. "So now we'll move on to our next recipe, the HaChaCha Hot Chocolate Mix." I demonstrate the quick measurements made with the Wet/Dry Plunger Cup and mix the cocoa, sugar, salt, and dry milk. I spill in the Coddled Cuisine flavor package and pour the boiling water out from the kettle Molly has prepared. The mugs soon swirl with the muddy mixture. I deftly top each mug off with a dollop of whipped cream and continue my spiel. "And *voila!* Let's see how things are doing in the oven."

The s'more dip looks presentable and I set it on the counter with a plate of graham crackers; I dive back for the Skillet Cookie, now a melted chocolate puddle in the middle of the pan. I shake the panhandle and the dough sloshes greasily in the pan and settles grumpily back into the center. It hasn't risen or baked through at all. Shit! I struggle valiantly to keep the panic from my voice and address the crowd, who has finally perked up slightly at the prospect of hot cocoa. "Well, our cookie isn't done yet. It looks like it might need a little more time in the oven. Meanwhile, help yourself to the hot chocolate and s'more dip. I'll be right over here to answer questions and take any orders."

Standing by the stove, I watch the women rush forward to grab their mugs and dip into the chocolate-marshmallow mixture. This is the most enthusiasm I've seen out of them all night. I lean over the oven, trying to figure out what went wrong with the cookie. I head over to the recipe card on the counter to double check the baking time when I hear the sounds of spitting and gagging all around me.

"Ugh!"

"What the hell?"

"Oh my goodness!"

Three mugs return to the tray and I see Kara frowning as she studies her own mug, now sniffing it as she holds it closer to her nose. "Ummm, Sadie? What did you put in this?"

"Why? What's wrong?" My face is growing redder by the instant. Something has gone seriously wrong. I screwed up worse on the goddamn hot chocolate than the liquid mess in the oven.

"This tastes, well, it tastes like complete shit. *What is that?*" She takes another tentative sip and scrunches up her nose. "It tastes like spaghetti sauce and chocolate mixed together. Disgusting!"

My hands shaking, I race back to the counter and look over the scattered ingredients and utensils—cocoa, sugar, I dip a finger into the cup I had taken for salt and lick it. Baking soda! "Molly? Can you get your baking soda?"

She obligingly heads to her pantry and pulls out the box I had absently shaken from and I look inside. Yes, the texture of table salt. I read the box. "Organic baking soda? Really?"

Scowling, Molly shoots back, "Why didn't you just use the original containers? You wouldn't have screwed up the recipe then by putting in the wrong ingredients."

Kara interrupts, "That still doesn't explain why it tastes like spaghetti sauce."

I pick up the empty packet of what I swear was Baker's Delight and read, in tiny letters beneath the Coddled Cuisine trademark, Italian Delight. "SHIT!"

Now I have everybody's attention. "Oh shit! I put in the wrong flavoring. Oh, I am so sorry." My hands are trembling so badly that I drop the empty packet on the floor. I turn around and look at Molly's friends and co-workers, who are either now looking at me bemusedly or in complete contempt at my stupidity. That's right, my first party and I hack it up in front of a bunch of college professors.

"It's okay." I hear Molly's voice in the distance, muffled beneath the rushing sound that has now invaded my head. "Do you have a packet of that other stuff? We'll just make the hot chocolate over again."

Kara is bent over, rummaging through my crates and she holds up a small brown packet victoriously. "Here we go—Baker's Delight. Dump your drinks girls, we're taking a mulligan on this recipe!"

Together, Kara and Molly commandeer the mixing of ingredients while I stand across the kitchen shaking my head and apologizing over and over to anyone listening. "I am so sorry, I had no idea. I am so sorry."

"Hey, Molly, this is a nice spoon." Kara holds up her bamboo mixing spoon and looks at it closely. "I could really use one of these."

"I don't know about you, but I'm digging the measuring spoon here, love the adjustable top on it." Molly and Kara sound like a couple of morning radio announcers bantering about the Packers. But I have no call to complain. I have royally fucked up this demo, and at least they're still game to try to save it. I poke my nose in once again to look at the skillet cookie, only to be rewarded with the exact same sloppy puddle as before. Probably the baking soda and salt was what I screwed up. Then I reach up to turn off the oven. I look closer at the knob. I swear I turned it to three-fifty but the dial is pointing clearly at "Warm." I'm not even cooking the damn thing! I whirl the dial around and reset the timer once more on the oven. Perhaps all is not lost.

"Well, Kara, what do you think?" Molly presents Kara with a mug, steaming and fragrant, topped with whipped cream.

Kara takes a slow sip and smiles in satisfaction, looking, I imagine, like she has just reached a point of ecstasy. "This is sensational," she pronounces and looks at the women who return her look with more interest than I have seen all evening. "What are you waiting for?" she asks them. "Belly up!"

In moments, hot chocolate is served around again. This time heads nod appreciatively and conversation begins at a murmur, slowly building. I feel my ribcage collapse in a sigh, releasing what apparently was a lungful of tension. Even Kathy appears to enjoy the hot chocolate. She licks her lips and nods thoughtfully. Molly busily pours seconds for a few women and the s'more dip gets scraped up onto a few more plates. Molly's friend, Starlight, pokes me on the shoulder, holding the food chopper in one hand. "Can you use this on herbs and nuts?" she asks, her ringed eyebrows wrinkled intently.

"Absolutely. You can chop anything at all: meat, nuts, any type of vegetable or fruit."

"I would never chop meat!" She interrupts, clearly appalled at the suggestion of making a meal out of a living creature.

"Oh." Uncomfortably, I shift against the counter. Silence and a forbidding glare from Starlight makes me want to sink through Molly's shining pine floor.

"I'll take the chopper. I'd also like a set of those bamboo spoons and the Measure All Cup."

"Let me get an order form for you and we can write this up," I volunteer, glad for the chance to no longer offend. I forget how careful you have to be around some of Molly's friends. I scramble to find a pen, my calculator, and an order form while another woman starts firing questions about the cookware. The line begins to grow in front of me and I hunker down on the wood floor and begin taking orders, answering questions, and tallying totals. The oven timer goes off at some point and I glance up to watch Molly pull the cookie out of the oven and begin to serve. It must have turned out okay or she wouldn't be putting it on plates, I figure, and focus on getting the order forms filled out correctly. By the time I come up for air, I see the skillet's empty save a few crumbs and the kitchen is nearly cleared out.

"How are you doing?" Kara booms across the room to me, up to her elbows in soapy dishwater.

"Hey! I'm supposed to be doing that!"

Kara shrugs and vigorously swipes at another measuring cup. "So?"

"No, the hostess and the party guests are supposed to enjoy their time together. My job is to clean up the kitchen and pack up my stuff. Come on, Kara, this is supposed to be training for me."

"Sadie, Sadie, Sadie." Kara shakes her head in exasperation. "What are friends for? Besides, do you really think I want to talk about boycotting leather and fur with Molly's PETA pals?" she asks. I get her point. Except for Molly and me, this isn't really Kara's crowd. Even as a lesbian, she isn't quite in the same liberal territory as the rest of them.

"I guess not," I tell her. "Thanks."

I heave myself off the floor and discover the lower part of my spine is completely numb from resting so long. Stretching out my back, I lean over to grab the order forms to tally up Molly's hostess benefits. I hear her in the living room, talking to the remaining guests.

"Hey, Kara."

"Yes?"

"How did that cookie turn out?"

"Pretty good. A little salty. I think you made the same mistake there, but there was so much chocolate in it that the unrefined palate probably didn't notice it too much."

"Good." I start adding up the totals. Molly has earned herself a nice amount of points to use. And I earned one-hundred and fifty dollars. The first thing I'll do is take Molly and Kara out for dinner, my treat. It's the least I can do after they totally saved my ass at this party.

I don't want to bother Molly in the living room, so I start packing my bins. I should bring Kara to every party. At the rate she's going, I'll be out of here in two hours! Seventy-five dollars an hour—not bad.

Finding it easier to pack my bins without all the packaging, I go to help Kara dry dishes and she starts giggling.

"What's so funny?"

She grips both sides of the sink and leans forward, catching her breath. Her chest is heaving and her cheeks are bright red.

"What?"

"It's just…" She takes a shuddering breath. "The expression on their faces when they tasted that first batch of cocoa!" She explodes into guffaws. "It was just so damn funny! And then you are all 'Well, I can't tell organic baking soda from salt!' I swear, I thought you were going to rip Molly's head off in front of everybody."

I feel my face crack into a grin. "It was pretty bad, wasn't it?"

"Bad? You probably set a new standard for Coddled Cuisine tonight. How anyone could even swallow that swill and still want to try another batch of it! And then you just stand there." Kara catches her breath and shakes her head. "You just stand there looking so pathetic in the middle of it all."

"I'm glad we can look back on this night and start laughing already."

"Don't be so sensitive! It's better to work out all your mistakes in the company of friends. I should probably only invite close friends to my party, just in case you have a few more things to screw up before you take this on the road."

"Very funny."

"How's it going?" Molly pokes her head around the corner and looks at me, almost afraid to see if I've lost it now that the party is over.

"Fine. Do you have a minute?"

"Sure."

I grab the stack of order forms and show her the show total so far. "This page outlines your hostess benefits. You might as well sit down with your catalog tonight and start making out your shopping list—you have a lot of points to use."

"That's great. Wow! We did pretty well, didn't we?" Molly looks elated.

"We did. All I need you to do is hold on to these forms until you close your party on Friday. Then you can give me your order and any other orders that come in at that time. And I'll help you figure out how to get the most of your half-price items and all."

"Super. Do you need me to do anything?" Molly looks around her kitchen. Even she could not find a stray crumb or spot as I admire the sparkling countertops.

"Nope. Kara's been awesome. I'm going to load up my gear and be on my way."

"You can stay if you want," she offers generously.

Kara interrupts her. "Absolutely not. Mustn't mix business with pleasure, right Sadie?"

Molly cocks her eyebrow at Kara. "Is that what you told your accountant when you invited him to your dinner party last weekend?"

"That was different!" Kara retorts indignantly. "That was pure pleasure, no business involved at all."

"Right." Molly nods wisely at me. "I'll call you later. Thanks so much, Sadie."

"Thank you! I don't know what I would've done if it weren't for you two tonight. Probably sat in the corner and wept while everyone scraped their tongues and left the party without placing a single order."

Kara pats my shoulder and resumes replacing gold bangle bracelets on her wrists. "You just need a little practice, that's all. You did fine, really."

"Besides, my friends aren't the best crowd for this sort of thing." Molly adds.

An understatement, but I dare not say so out loud. Instead, I nod gratefully.

"All right, back to the stem cell debate going on in my living room. See you both later!"

"See you!" Kara and I call back. I start stacking bins to carry out to my car. Kara follows me outside with her arms loaded up as well.

"I'm almost thinking I should get a free spatula or something for my extra work tonight," she teases me.

"Oh hell, I'll throw in a Measure All Cup, too."

My trunk is loaded in two trips and I wave to Kara as she heads down the street to her BMW. What would I do without my friends? I hop in my car, cringing when the freezing vinyl seat meets the backs of my thighs, and turn the key. At least my car starts up immediately. My next party will be better. I learned a lot tonight—leaving the ingredients out and measuring while I bake. With a little creativity, maybe some help from Jane, I can figure out an icebreaker for an opener. I just need to flesh out my routine. I don't need to copy Kimberly. I need to figure out my own spin on this Coddled Cuisine gig. Then I'll be on my way. I look down affectionately at the blue apron peeking out below my jacket—I'm practically official!

# Chapter Eighteen

**"Booking parties is easy!"**
*—Coddled Cuisine training manual*

I feel bleary at work. I remind myself to concentrate as Dean rambles on about the importance of physical fitness before introducing Curt Bellachi, personal trainer and fitness expert from Milwaukee. Clearly we hit on a topic dear to Dean's heart, as he repeats for the fiftieth time, "If your body is in shape, you feel better about yourself, and that reflects in your performance in the rest of the areas of your life." Yawn.

Curt finally gets air time, and it takes all my mental strength to keep from calculating my income from last night's party and reviewing what needs improvement (pretty much everything). I lean forward on my elbows in a physical effort to stay attentive to Curt's description of a client who lost fifty pounds after joining his gym and sticking to a diet regimen. I want to bang my head on the desk just out of sheer boredom and frustration.

Pure fluff, but occasionally we stray to heady foreign policy issues and environmental debates for the sake of balance. Fidgeting with my pen, I comfort myself with the knowledge that the rest of the week will deal with Indian cuisine, the politics of working motherhood, and pre-election analysis from a political science professor.

Fortunately, phone calls flood the lines. Evidently, personal trainers are a hot topic and the rest of the show goes quickly and smoothly. Dean actually looks a little disappointed when it's over.

"Great show today. Why don't we do topics like that more often? Seems like people really want to know how to get in better shape." Dean eyes my hips and thighs with a critical expression. "It only takes a small sacrifice each day to improve how you look and how you feel." He proves his point by patting his stomach, flat under his crisp blue-striped shirt. Honestly, you'd think he worked at *Cosmo* or *GQ* instead of Wisconsin Public Radio!

Dean inhales loudly, stretching his arms wide to further prove his state of physical well-being and then heads for the door, calling back over his shoulder, "We'll go over notes at three."

Naturally, he doesn't ask if that is a convenient time for me. What really matters is that his job doesn't interrupt his workout at the gym or lunch plans.

"We'll go over notes at two-thirty. I'm busy with an appointment after three," I correct him.

Dean shrugs and the door closes behind him. Shaking my head, I gather my coffee, notebook, and pen and walk back to my office to put the finishing touches on the week ahead. There's a mountain of reading to prepare for next week's guests, and I have nothing booked for much of April. Despite this, I pull out my Coddled Cuisine folder and start double-checking my math on the order forms. I text Molly to see what she thought of the party. I don't want to work today, I want to do another party and not screw it up. I need a confidence booster. I need to talk to Jane.

After checking the hallway for signs of Ron, I dial her number. In the next two weeks I have parties planned for Kara, Jane, and Evelyn. After that, I'm completely at the mercy of party guests booking off of those parties. One woman last night said she'd be interested, but I'll call her in a day or two so she doesn't feel too pressured.

"Hey! How did it go last night at Molly's?" Jane asks me.

I tell her the ghastly details, including the sloppy skillet cookie, and she laughs. "You have to start somewhere, right? There's nowhere to go after a party like that than up. What did Molly think?"

"I think she was pleased, overall. I don't know what I'd do without her and Kara, though. I can't have them at every party I do! I hope this is just a beginner's thing and I haven't made a huge mistake by getting involved in this whole home party business."

"Sadie, you'll do fine. You're good with people, and while I can't say much for your cooking, all you really have to have is enthusiasm for the product—that's the one thing you can't fake. People get into this sort of thing all the time and become very successful. It maybe doesn't happen overnight, but it happens eventually with hard work and patience. Give it time."

"You're probably right." No quick fix offered from Jane.

"Besides, think of all the free and discounted Coddled Cuisine things you can buy for your favorite sister, say, for her birthday or Christmas!"

"I guess, you mean, you really don't want that Magic Bullet I ordered off TV last night?"

"I only want it if you got me the Bullet Boost, too."

"I should get back to work. Dean LaRoche and the *Idea Exchange* waits for no man, or woman, in this case."

"Give my best to Dean."

"Yeah, right? Hugs all around at your end."

I felt encouraged after hanging up with Jane. She puts things in perspective; to expect instant success at my first booking was unrealistic. I need to lower the bar and focus on one party at a time. I pull out the notebook from my top desk drawer and open to the page where I wrote down my candle order, designating my gifting for next year. I turn to a clean page and begin writing:

> Coddled Cuisine Goals—
> Flawless product presentation by July.
> Clear $500 monthly profit by October.
> Party organization (packing, unpacking, processing orders, etc.) perfected by May.

I gnaw on the end of my pen as I read over my deadlines. This seems reasonable, doable, achievable. Besides, I can always bag it and move on to selling Avon if this doesn't work out. And I'll have a great new collection of kitchen supplies to show for my efforts.

But Coddled Cuisine isn't paying my bills yet, so I turn my attention back to the stack of papers piled precariously on the edge of my desk. I slide them toward me while glancing at the clock—plenty of time to tackle part of the pile by lunch. By the time hunger clenches my gut and makes me lightheaded, I have most of the pile sorted and discarded. Leaving my papers behind, I scout the hall for Evelyn, who's nowhere to be found. I'm left to eat a bag of chips and leftover pizza in the break room alone. It's hardly sufficient to bolster me for a meeting with Dean, but I have no alternative if I want to eat before explaining how Indian food varies by region (grits versus clam chowder) and by social class (Dom Perignon versus Bud Light) in terms he can comprehend.

# Chapter Nineteen

**"Icebreakers get your party started"**
*—Coddled Cuisine training manual*

I'm brushing my teeth before heading to bed when the phone rings, and I vault over a pile of laundry in the hallway and crash into a box of Coddled Cuisine cookware to grab it before the call goes to voice mail. "Hello," I answer, choking back a glob of minty foam.

"Is this Sadie Davis?"

"Yes…" The voice on the other end is smooth and female, not Todd's.

"This is Kimberly Carlyle, we met the other day?"

"Right. Hi."

"How did your first party go?"

Oh man, of all the people I don't want to rehash this with, Kimberly tops the list. Right next to my mother, of course. "Pretty well."

"Any questions? Areas you feel need improvement? Our novice consultants usually run into minor problems at first." Does she want me to fail at this? I hear the presumption that I will do poorly.

"I don't think so—"

"And your hostess?"

This must be her sneaky way of finding out how much I sold. I don't know how much of this is passed along to her from Coddled Cuisine corporate headquarters, so I tell her, "She ended up with seven-hundred and forty hostess points and one free product." This is about half of what Kimberly's last party earned. "But the party hasn't closed yet. We're waiting on a potential booking and there might be some catalog orders." Well, actually only one possible catalog order.

"Hmmm." The displeasure at this flows into my right ear and slams into my fragile ego like a truckload of concrete. "Not exactly record-breaking, but it's a start."

What does she expect me to say to that? Yes, I hope all of my parties combined earn less than a single one of yours? Yes, I'm an enormous loser, pathetically incapable of presenting the Coddled Cuisine products in the same perfect way you do? She breaks the silence with, "Before your next party, what is one area you think you might improve?"

I remind myself that she's trying to be helpful, like I wouldn't reflect on the party on my own. "I need more practice so I can move between products and recipes seamlessly." There. That seemed like a general enough improvement to make. Let's see what she has to say about that!

"Your practice should not only come at parties, in front of the public, you know. You should work on the

recipes and product presentation on your own, at home."
I bet she was the kind of girl who did all the extra credit
on every assignment in school. I bet this bitch never got
a zit, a parking ticket, or an overdraft notice from the
bank. I hate her.

"You're right," I concede, hoping to cut the
conversation short. "I'll do that."

"Fabulous. When is your next party? Next week?"

What is she, some kind of cookware secret police for
crying out loud? "Yes."

"Good luck with that. I'll be in touch soon. Feel free
to call me anytime with questions, concerns…"

"Thanks, I will." I clip each word, matching her
professional demeanor on the phone, even straightening
my posture and crossing my ratty Tweety Bird slippers
demurely under my seat.

"I'll talk with you after that. Good night."

I listen to the dial tone as I hang up. Is it my fate to
always work under unbearable personalities? She's harder
to take than Dean, probably because she's a woman, and
I pride myself on being fairly tolerant of others. Sheesh.

Returning to my bathroom to floss, I puzzle out my
introduction problem. How do I break the ice at these
parties? What would be a unique and engaging way to
draw in the party guest who doesn't enjoy home parties?
I'm still rejecting idea after idea when I flick off the TV
and head to bed. How do I make this home party crap
fun for a person like me?

On Friday, I bring my problem up to Ben, Molly, and
Kara while we sit, huddled around our table in the middle
of happy hour at the Big Ten Pub. Ben, bored by our

conversation, keeps glancing over at a table of college girls, obviously primed for a night out on the town. They keep giggling and flipping their hair, fully aware of their effect on the opposite sex.

"Maybe try an approach that sort of makes fun of the home party scene, you know, like ask them to relate their worst home party experience or ask them to tell why they're there for real," Molly suggests.

"Hey, why not learn a few magic tricks, like make a spatula disappear right away and have it turn up later when you need it during the show?" Kara dramatically attempts a demonstration of this idea using a chicken wing and a napkin.

"Right," Ben snorts. "I bet women everywhere want to buy a spatula that disappears."

I have to seriously consider even the most obnoxious suggestion. There might be a grain of good idea in one of them if I tweaked it enough. I think about what Molly said.

"So, can I tell you about Francis now?" Molly blurts out, and even Ben returns his concentration to our table, ignoring the preening coeds for Molly's huge news.

"Yes," I concede, glad for my friend and returning to the true spirit of happy hour, which is to *not* obsess with work. I take another sip of my margarita and lean forward to listen.

It hits me when I crawl into bed Saturday night after coming home from dinner and a movie with Kara, Elizabeth, and Molly. Bingo! Literally, Bingo, the game! I'll have the guests make up cards with cheesy phrases and/or occurrences that come up consistently at home parties. It'll be their chance to rip on the whole concept and to win prizes! I close my eyes and picture the squares on a Bingo card filled in with things like, "Introduce yourself and tell us how you know our hostess," and "Pitch for joining the company and becoming a sales consultant," and "Hostess Benefits." Not exactly the sort of thing Kimberly might approve of, but it'll keep their attention throughout the party while they fill in their squares. Even if someone loves home parties, they'll do well at the game—it calls on their knowledge of how they all work.

I throw back my sheets and roll out of bed, itchy with excitement. Before I flip on the living room light, I notice the answering machine light blinking. I hit 'play' and Todd's voice fills my ears, sending a tingle down my legs to my bare feet.

"Hi, this is Todd MacGynn, Evelyn's nephew, calling. Ummm." He pauses and I hear dogs barking in the background and what sounds like a radio. "You can call me back at 715-555-8160 if you want. Thanks." He sounds awkward and rough on the phone and I close my eyes, leaning against the doorframe, thinking of his calloused hands against my back, his raspy voice in my ear, his stocky muscular body pressed against me. I replay the message four times before going back to bed with my notebook and pen. At midnight it's too late to call anyone back, but first thing in the morning I'm dialing his number!

# Chapter Twenty

**"Cold calls can lead to new opportunities"**
*—Coddled Cuisine training manual*

I wake up Sunday before it's fully light. The dim grey March morning would normally have me rolling over and slamming my eyes shut, but even though my sheets feel soft and warm against my toes, the excitement of returning Todd's call has me too jittery to stay in bed any longer. I stretch and check my alarm clock—good grief! It's only seven!

Picking up my notebook, where I've begun a list of common home party phrases, I head to my kitchen to make coffee and plan my day. I have Kara's party Thursday night. Fortunately she isn't doing chocolate, but appetizers, which I've successfully prepared once. I double-check my list of ingredients (she's supposed to have them ready for me, but I'll have to remind her that day or she'll forget something) and using an envelope as a straight edge, create a Bingo template on a fresh sheet of paper. In neat letters, I print on the top of the page "Home Party Bingo" and pour a cup of coffee, mentally thanking Molly for getting me started on home brewing.

By eight, I'm crawling on the walls. My laundry is sorted, my kitchen is clean (even the pizza pan I burned cheese onto four nights ago), and my Coddled Cuisine stuff is so organized, I'm afraid to go near it again. Glancing outside I feel lured by the brightness of the morning. The early mist of the day has burned off already and I put on sneakers and sweats. Might as well power walk, get my nerves calmed before I call Todd.

Key in pocket, I feel virtuous starting down the sidewalk at a brisk pace. The cool quiet of this early hour is so peaceful; I hear birds chirping over the occasional passing car. I turn down Orchard and begin my trek past the row of fraternity and sorority houses, front yards littered with beer cans and hamburger wrappers. It's easy to imagine the occupants sleeping off the night before, in various stages of undress, all of them smelling like cigarettes and beer. One large college student is sprawled across the front porch of the Delta Kappa house. By the lakeshore, my breath comes in sharp pants and I wipe my forehead as I lean on my knees. What have I walked? Two miles, maybe? I better head for home if I plan on making it without involving the paramedics.

On the way home, I feel the jolt of a side stitch rip through the right side of my ribcage. I'm not even jogging, for God's sake! I feel like a seventy year old woman plugging up the hill toward my apartment. The shiny newness of the day has definitely worn off by the

Melissa Westemeier

time I step through a small, fresh pile of dog poop. The canine stench follows me home, reminding me of why I never want to own a pet of any kind. I try scraping my sneaker through the edge of a dew-drenched lawn and succeed in merely smearing it further across the bottom of the sole. Gross.

On the porch, I gingerly slip off my shoe before going in. I'll disinfect it in the tub with bleach. This is why people join gyms. This is why animals and humans should not coexist.

Dropping the stinky shoe in the tub, I slide off my other sneaker and find bleach under the kitchen sink. Perfect! I'll have my shoe cleaner than when I began this journey. I check the time—five minutes to nine. I can politely call Todd now.

He answers on the third ring.

"Todd? This is Sadie, returning your call."

"Hey—hi! Thanks for calling me back. I don't know what made me think I'd reach you at home on a Saturday night—"

"I was out to dinner and a movie with my friend Molly, Kara, and her girlfriend," I say, anxious to reassure him that I wasn't out with another guy.

"Ah…" I think I hear relief in his voice. "I was late at the clinic last night, just killing time. We had a Yellow Lab brought in, just about fourteen weeks old. Anyway, some asshole decided to toss it out of a car window, and some kids picked her up and brought her in. She's in pretty rough shape and I wanted to make sure she was okay before leaving her in a strange kennel all night."

"Oh my gosh!" My hatred for the canine species evaporates at his story. "What did you have to do? To treat her, I mean."

"She has a broken leg, which I cast, and a couple of cracked ribs, which I can't do anything about, unfortunately. I cleaned her up, treated her for shock, and put some ointment on her side where she had probably slid on the road. She's looking much better today. Ate like a cow this morning when I fed her."

Could this guy be any sweeter? "Wow. How're you doing?"

"Me? Fine. Just fine."

"Are you coming back to Madison anytime soon?"

"I don't know. My schedule looks pretty tight for the rest of the month. I lost my assistant to a better job, so I can't leave the clinic for any amount of time until I find someone to replace her."

Her? "What kind of a better job?"

"She was an intern and found a job at a clinic over in Rochester, Minnesota. Now I have to either wait until one of the colleges sends me another intern or go looking for someone I can train. It's a crappy job, actually. Involves a lot of shit, literally."

I laugh at his joke. "Well, if you make it this way, look me up."

"I will."

I don't know what to say next, and after a pause he says, "If you ever make it up to Neillsville, you can look me up."

"I'll do that," I promise, wondering what sort of excuse would make me travel that far north.

"I hate to cut this short, Sadie, but I really have to go in and feed some creatures and hose out some kennels. Talk to you soon."

"Okay, bye."

He hangs up and I feel down in the dumps. Why wasn't I home last night when he called? Why did I have to go out with Molly, Kara, and Elizabeth? Because if I stayed home every night, I would become a lonely recluse. I would be the kind of single woman who rushes home to watch *Wheel of Fortune* while wolfing down a pint of ice cream every night. The kind of woman who ends up living with eighteen cats and pursing her lips at any hint of fun or craziness. I hope next time he calls I'm around to pick up the phone.

The rest of the day looms ahead of me, so I call Molly to see if she's up for lunch or coffee—anything to get me out of this apartment.

No answer. I dial one more number and my brother-in-law, Erich, picks up.

"Erich, it's Sadie. Are you guys going to be around today?"

"Sure. We've got a few projects going on, but nothing major."

"Mind if I come out?"

"Not at all. I'll tell Jane. What time?"

"I'll be there about noon."

"The kids'll be thrilled! See you then, Sadie."

My mood again matches the clear sky outside as I practically skip to the shower.

Later that night, as I head back to Madison, I flip on my car radio and start scanning through the stations to find something to help pass the time for the next hour of driving. Country—ick. Top Forty—is it a sign of my age or do all of the songs start to sound alike after a while? Oldies—not in the mood to sing along. I tune in my own station, but realize with horror the instant I hear a few bars that it is the folk music segment of the weekend. As if I really want to hear a bunch of old hippies singing protest songs about war, unions, and Tom Joad. Finally I find a jazz station, crackly as it's coming from someplace in Milwaukee. But the wail of the saxophone and easy beat help me relax in my seat and settle into the drive.

My stomach is comfortably full after a free-range turkey dinner, complete with all the traditional fixings including an apple pie, brimming with cinnamon and allspice. We played a rousing game of Scrabble and I left feeling glad I had made the trip. Olivia gave me a sheaf of pictures she had drawn for me. Davis and Samantha packed my front seat with a care package from Jane: leftovers from dinner, a fresh loaf of bread, and a tin of lemon bars.

With the lazy day behind me and food to tide me over into the middle of the week, I feel more than ready to take on the week ahead. Even the parts involving Dean, who informed me helpfully on Friday that, starting Monday, he'd like to try a new format where we open with listeners calling in to comment on the previous day's show before introducing our new guest and topic. Translated, he wants more ego stroking during his broadcast, and this is a way to do it while simultaneously eliminating between five and ten minutes of actually having to discuss a topic with a new guest. Ron knows nothing about this yet, so I have to decide whether to ruffle Dean's feathers by insisting on his approval or going ahead with it and hopefully laying Dean out to take the heat when Ron hears it live for the first time. Or the other option, which crept through my mind as I had sat at dinner next to Samantha, who begged me to stay the night so I could join them on a field trip to Walden West: call in sick. Call in sick—three simple words loaded with all the promise of Christmas morning. Terribly irresistible. Tapping my hands to the easy rhythm of "Jelly Roll Stomp," I reconcile myself to the sad truth that I will end up at the station tomorrow morning and do the right thing by talking to Ron first.

# Chapter Twenty-One

**"The modern woman enjoys shopping"**
*—Coddled Cuisine training manual*

Bracing myself for the noxious fumes of Ron's morning breath, I inhale deeply and knock on his office door with my clenched fist.

"Come in."

"Ron, do you have a minute before Dean goes on air?" What the hell died in his office this morning? His room reeks like a cross between gasoline and old Limburger cheese.

"What is it, Sadie?" He peers up at me from behind his desk, motioning with his left hand to take a seat, but I won't. I don't want to stay and I don't want to play power games with him, either.

"Dean has an idea for his show that he'd like to implement today, but I thought it would be best to run by you first." I rush ahead, wanting to keep this as brief as Ben's last romance. "He wants to open his shows with listener comments on the previous day's show. This is a major format change and it's something that—"

Ron interrupts me by standing to his full and unimposing height of five feet two inches, slapping both hands on his desk. "That's fantastic."

I can't tell from his remark whether he is pleased or being sarcastic, so I stay silent, breathing through my mouth.

He walks around his desk and opens his office door, offering me a gust of what I will accept as fresh air, even though it has been recycled through filters and air conditioners. "I can't wait to hear this."

I start back down the hall toward the studio. "Okay." I say hesitantly. "Does that mean let him do it?"

"Oh yes, absolutely." He pauses and looks closely at me for the first time ever. "Let him do it."

That figures Ron is all in favor of Dean the Drama Queen getting a few more strokes. All I want is to go stomping down the hall, past the studio and to my office, grab my bag and leave. But I don't. I pull my chin up and enter the studio, slide into my seat, get the guest on the line and nod silently to Dean, who grunts as he enters the room.

"Did you talk to Ron?"

"Yes."

"And?"

"He said to go ahead and do it."

I swear the bastard smirks as he leans back in his chair and waits for the signal to start the show. A minute later, our listening audience is treated to his self-promoting format change.

"We care about our listeners and what they think of our show. In order to let you have more input on *Idea Exchange*, we will begin a new format starting today to allow you to share your thoughts and comments on the previous day's show. So, we'd like to open today by inviting you to call in with your comments on last Friday's guest, Srikahn Singh. The topic was Indian cuisine. Our lines are open now for your calls…"

I can't help but feel sympathy for today's guest, whom has been pushed back five minutes. Closing my eyes, I pray no one responds. I can almost hear Ron's wheezy panting as he stands outside the studio door listening to this fiasco unfold. Five seconds pass and Dean is talking to Sharon from Prairie du Chien. "Loved your show Friday! I've never tried Indian food before, quite afraid of the spice factor, you know, what with bad heartburn and all. But I tried the curry stir-fry recipe and I can't wait to experiment more! Thank you Dean, for opening up a whole new world of cooking for me."

Ugh. I can't escape quickly enough to my office where I shut the door behind me and sit down, slowly thumping my forehead against the desk. I hate him; I hate him. Ihatehim, Ihatehim, Ihatehim.

Quiet knocking interrupts my mental chant and I sit up straight, sighing deeply as I get to face Ron or, worse yet, Dean again this morning.

Evelyn slips in, edging the door shut behind her and bursts into hysterical giggling. Is she nuts? But then I join her, tears streaming down my cheeks as I laugh, gasping for breath when she pretends to talk into the pen in her hand as a microphone in her deep Dean voice. "Good morning. Before we begin today's show, I would like everyone to tell me how great I am and how much they love my show. Call in now."

"He's a piece of work."

"A piece of pretentious dog shit is more like it."

"Thanks, I feel much better now that you've shown me the humor, albeit dark, in this whole situation."

"A station with integrity, we're not." Evelyn says dryly. "Let's commiserate over lunch today. My treat. Keep your chin up."

Gritting my teeth, I e-mail the guests lined up for the rest of the week, informing them of the format change and advising them that I will call them five minutes later than originally agreed. I hope an e-mail is somewhat binding.

# Chapter Twenty-Two

**"Amazing appetizers"**
*—Coddled Cuisine hostess brochure*

Duct tape bouncing and sliding on my wrist, I arrange the cookware on the gingham fabric that I've taped to the countertop in Kara's kitchen. The ingredients are set out, ready to chop, dice, shred, and stir. Folders are on each chair, pens clipped to the front cover alongside the computer labels I generated at work yesterday afternoon which read

### *Coddled Cuisine*
### *Sadie Davis, Sales Consultant*

My recipes are in the order by which I shall prepare them, next to the utensils I plan to demonstrate. I put the finishing touches on my display like a worried mother fussing and picking, and grab my Home Party Bingo cards while Kara starts greeting guests. Within a half hour, the room smells like a department store perfume counter with Kate Spade and Coach handbags lining the floor.

I survey the room, filled with Kara's bevy of gallery regulars, mostly aged thirty- to forty-something. Wives of Madison's power brokers make up the bulk of the guest list. A few friends from college and one of the owners of L'Etoile, a very chi-chi downtown restaurant, round out the table. Clearing my throat, I take a breath and dive into my spiel.

"Hello all, and welcome to Kara's Coddled Cuisine party! As a twist on introductions tonight, I'd like you to pick up the Home Party Bingo card I've placed in front of you and spend a few minutes filling it in with common phrases, words, and concepts you've heard at previous home parties. If this is your first home party, you can write down what you fear will happen. Or copy your neighbor's ideas."

I'm rewarded with genuine laughter and my shoulders drop a full three inches in relief. Approving nods and commentary follow, and I feel myself slip into a comfortable groove. "You'll use the Bingo card all night. Mark off any square you see or hear during this evening's party, and remember, bingo counts as five across, down, or diagonally. I have prizes for all winners!"

Conversation builds quickly while cashmere and silk-clad women fill up their squares. They're hooting, giggling, talking, and having a grand time while I wander around the table, checking to make sure they're all on the right track.

Finally, I pull their attention back for some quick introductions and I plow into the pitch with the first recipe: Cheesy Crab Canapés. I stuff the Better Baking Tube, slide it into the preheated oven (triple-checked for temperature setting), and set the timer. Before I know it, the egg rolls and canapés are finished, the almond cookies are perfectly browned along the edges, and the Super Slush Fruit Punch is sparkling and fizzing in Kara's cut-crystal punch bowl. With all the grace and finesse of my wildest Coddled Cuisine fantasies, I arrange the appetizers on the Perfect Party serving pieces in elegant fan patterns and set them on the table.

"Feel free to help yourselves and ask any questions! I have many of the products over here for you to look at more closely. I'll be in the gathering room to take your orders."

The clutch of nerves in my throat obstructs any swallowing as I watch the women serve themselves. I hold my breath and study their expressions to see if I succeeded this time. Murmurs of pleasure and delight fill the room as they chew, swallow, even take second and third bites. Thank God!

I linger a moment longer in my glory, answering a few questions about products and recipes before heading out to the gathering room, where I've stashed a bag of tissue-wrapped boxes of Godiva truffle samplers I picked up at the mall the night before. I'll have to check the tax-exemption status of prizes, but I'm pretty sure this prize will be a hit with Kara's crowd. I can slum it with future party prizes, but tonight I wanted to go all out to make sure absolutely everything in my power was completed to perfection.

Eventually the guests trickle out to me placing orders, and a couple even booked parties. Never mind that I won't get home until nearly eleven, Kara's friends more than compensate for my shopping therapy.

"I just *love* this product," says a very tan woman with a black bob, "it's much better than the Cephalon cookware at Marshall Field's."

Nodding in response, a blonde in the very same Ann Taylor outfit I admired in a display window last night chimes in. "And you simply *cannot* consider your kitchen well-stocked without their utensil collection."

The owner of L'Etoile looks up from her catalog quizzically. "Which utensils?"

"Oh, *all* of them, darling. Aren't you one of the girls from that bistro on Pinckney Street?" The blonde looks at her more closely. "I've seen your picture in the paper, I think."

She sighs and nods. I can practically read her mind from here. She extends her hand graciously.

The blonde grasps it. "You must meet so many interesting people in your line of work!"

The L'Etoile owner replies dryly, "You can meet interesting people anywhere."

I jump in after quickly folding up the last order packet. "Who's next?"

Blondie hands me her order form, every line filled in. "Wow. I thought you had a lot of these products," I tell her as I look over her list.

"I do, these are for gifts."

"Ah." I'd love to have a friend like her. Or boss. Or whatever.

"You must know Kimberly Carlyle," she continues conversationally.

"I just met her two weeks ago, in fact."

"Isn't Kimberly *divine*? I don't know about you, but if my husband were CEO of a paper company, I wouldn't waste my spare time peddling kitchen supplies. But that's Kimberly for you. She's so down to earth and *real*."

Right, she's so real. "That's exactly what I thought when I first met her!" I agree, battling to keep the sarcasm out of my voice. I start punching in numbers on the calculator and send Blondie on her way back to the party while L'Etoile watches and grins at me.

"Don't you just find the new Lear jet *divine*? So much better than their old one!" She impeccably imitates Kara's friend. "Where the hell does she find these women?" L'Etoile plops down on the couch and crosses her clogs delicately. "I love Kara and all, but she has got to learn to keep business separate from pleasure!"

"I'm assuming you fall into the pleasure category?"

"Speaking of that, why don't you come out Saturday night? We have a wine tasting scheduled. Straight up from Alsace. I think Kara and Elizabeth are coming."

Knowing my weekend prospects are empty, since Todd is stranded in Neillsville and, from the sound of it, not coming to town any time soon, I nod in agreement. What the hell, maybe Molly and her new guy will want to come down. Besides, when you're lonely, bored, and single, few places are more likely to cheer you up than a restaurant full of wine-swilling girlfriends. I've always found it comforting to go out to a bar where you don't want anyone trying to pick you up.

"Great! I'll look for you. Thanks." She puts the order form in her satchel and gets up from the couch.

Tallying up Kara's benefits, I take vicious pleasure in the fact that she has double the bonus points than Kimberly's had earned. I'll ask her about sharing a few with Molly, who got ripped off with hers being my first party and all. Besides, it's not like Kara needs the free products.

I start washing dishes and packing my gear while listening to Kara's gallery groupies discuss the better private academies and the preferable spring vacation destinations. Must be nice to have such choices. Shit, I can't even afford staying at a water park in Wisconsin Dells right now.

It's eleven-thirty when I break free from the party, waving enthusiastically to my future party hostesses who coo to Kara, "Wherever did you find her? She's such a doll!"

I'm a hit!

## Chapter Twenty-Three

**"Coddled Cuisine can even replace your existing job!"**
—*Coddled Cuisine recruitment brochure*

I'm positively head-achy and cranky when I drag myself out of bed Friday morning, for no plausible reason since last night went exceedingly well. I didn't even get a stain on my blue apron! I yank a black v-neck over my head and pull on fatigue-green cargo pants and sneakers. Feeling rebellious and moody, I wolf down some Wheaties and race to the office, sunglasses protecting the general populace from my angry glare while I push past the early morning rush of Madison citizens heading to school, work, or wherever.

In my office, I slam my door and try to meditate a moment before facing Dean and his stupid new show format. Why am I angry? I had a great party last night, I have at least four more booked in my immediate future, it's Friday.

Glancing at the calendar, I realize my mood is a combination of P.M.S. and irritation with Dean and Ron, so it's not likely to fade soon. I'll have to drown it tonight at happy hour. I grab the folder and pen and head down the hall to the studio to listen to everyone call in and tell Dean how great and wonderful he is before actually hearing him do any work.

"Wow, are you playing war games this weekend, Sadie? I didn't know you were in the Reserves." Dean comments. I glower at him, earning me more attention. "Or, perhaps this is the new fashion? It's quite…butch." He slowly eyes me up and down, and I want to scream at him but swallow some coffee instead, burning my throat.

"I'll—ACK! Just get our—ACK! Guest on the line." I barely choke this out between coughs. I want to leave.

I listen in literal and figurative pain as Dean mispronounces the name of every Chinese leader (they *are* spelled out phonetically on his notes) and comments to our guest, "I don't see why they can't just go in and take Tibet by force, I mean, what's the big deal anyway?"

Certain that the blood vessels around my brain could burst any moment, I ignore Ron in the hallway and stalk back to my office without so much as a nod. Why do I work so hard on getting these incredible guests? If I worked for *The Connection* with Dick Gordon or *On Point* with Tom Ashcroft, my talents would be appreciated. Here with Dean, they're not only wasted, but insulted!

I stand inside the doorway of my office and look at my desk. What do I really need to accomplish before Monday? Nothing. I don't even turn on my computer. I repack my bag and make my retreat. Passing Lottie at the front desk, I mutter, "I'm going to be out the rest of the day."

She's signing for an enormous box with a picture of a car seat along the side. "Okay," she mumbles as I push through the doors into the bright sunshine.

Friday morning and I'm sick of the whole world. What am I going to do? I walk towards home, not really wanting to go there either, when I suddenly get a crazy idea. I'll go to Neillsville. Why not? I've never been there before, and I have every reason to believe Todd would be happy to see me. I have no idea where he lives or where his clinic is, but how big can that podunk town be, right? My fog lifts and a helium-like bubble expands in my stomach. I'll pack a bag, get some cash, fill up my car with gas, and head north to Neillsville.

An hour later I'm on the road, the Indigo Girls condoning my decision on the radio. I keep glancing at the map, the millimeters slowly creeping between my car and Madison, the gap closing between my destination and me.

I've never driven through this part of the state before, so I pay close attention. Farms, hills, and a state forest that creeps me out when I don't spot a single trace of human life for a half hour of driving. Lots of Amish farms, and I pass several horse-drawn buggies, fluorescent orange triangles nailed to their backs as a nod to the modern world they travel through. When I near the outskirts of a tiny township, it occurs to me that I should show up with some sort of gift in hand. I execute a U-turn into the gravel parking lot of a cheese factory. Inside, I fill a shopping basket with cheese, a bottle of wine, three cow pies (chocolate covered caramels cleverly marketed to look like cow shit), and a jar of "Betty's Homemade Jelly—Raspberry." It's not grand as far as gifts go, but it's something.

Finally, I see a green highway sign; it's the first indication that I'm nearing my destination:

## Neillsville—58 miles

My stomach is totally fluttery now. I feel sweat start on my forehead and I nervously tap the steering wheel, involuntarily changing the radio stations as I drive closer and closer.

Should I check into a hotel and then go look for him? If I show up with no place to stay, would that seem a bit forward? Maybe I should turn around and head back, make some cheese sandwiches and drink wine in the safety of my apartment. I can feel my nerves jangling all the way from my fingertips to my armpits as I pass the next highway sign:

## Neillsville—27 miles

What is Evelyn going to say? What if Todd already has plans and is busy all weekend? Then what?

My heart races with panic by the time I reach the city limits and pass the Neillsville Country Club on my right, and a convenience store on my left. I look along the road for signs of a veterinary clinic, but see nothing. I decide to drive around and get my bearings, then look for a place to stay before I find Todd.

Neillsville has one hotel, the Sandman Motel. Pulling into a parking spot in front of the office, I see no other cars. All the rooms are curtained shut, but the vacancy sign, lit in red neon, blinks steadily. Pushing open the orange door, I walk into the smoky front office, concentrating to keep the theme music from *Psycho* out of my mind. On the counter a note card, grimy with age, instructs:

**Ring bell for service.**

I tap the bell and hold my breath. What will come out of that back room? Faintly, I hear a thump over the hum of the heater and what sounds like a television game show in the background.

Moments later, the door opens slightly and a stooped old woman with the thickest coke-bottle glasses I've ever seen peers over the counter at me. "Hello?"

"Hi. Ummm, I'm here to see about getting a room for a night or two?"

Slowly she shuffles forward, grabbing the counter for support, and fumbles with a huge guest registry that she drops on the counter. She turns page after page and finally reaches a blank space and pushes the book toward me. I notice as I'm filling in my name and address that the last guest was Herman Melville, back in July 1997. I'm not sure which is more odd: the name or the date.

Scratching away at an ancient pad of carbon paper, the woman calculates the cost of the room. I try not to stare at the skin under her neck; it wobbles to the rhythm of her writing. I'm face-to-face with the original Mother Bates.

"Two nights?"

"Yes, please."

She scribbles some more, then rips the page from the pad and hands it to me. "That'll be forty-seven dollars and eighty-seven cents."

I dig out my wallet as she selects a key from the rack, filled with identical bright orange plastic key chains numbered one to twelve. She seems to waffle between five and six, touching each key twice before choosing room five and handing it over to me. "Motel policy states no pets, no illegal substances, and no unpaid guests on the premises."

"Right."

"There's coffee in the lobby starting at seven each morning and you can ring the office from your room by dialing zero if you need anything." She looks at me doubtfully. I'm sure she's wondering what she might possibly do for me.

I nod again and hand her two twenties and a ten. Shakily she takes it and tells me in a weary voice, "I have to go back here to make your change. Wait."

I take a closer look around the lobby while she's gone. Two vinyl orange chairs, an oak coffee table covered with fishing magazines and tabloids, the most recent edition from 1992. Sheesh. A time capsule. The lamp next to the chairs is coated with cobwebs; just looking at it makes my nose itch to sneeze.

By the entrance is a display rack of brochures for area attractions, some are as far away as the Wisconsin Dells, which is a good two-hour drive from here. I take a brochure about the largest block of cheddar cheese, kept in a giant semi-trailer just on the outskirts of town, and another brochure for some renovated one-room schoolhouse. A semi-trailer full of old cheddar sounds disgusting, but I never know when something might trigger a good idea for a show. There seems to be no other local attractions. I'm too early in the year for the tractor pull and the county fair, and a couple months too late for the ice fishing festival. Damn.

The old lady returns and drops my change on the counter for me. "You can let yourself in, if you don't mind."

"Thank you." I leave the stuffy office and take my car to the parking space directly in front of room five. Feeling ridiculous since I'm the only one there, I lock my car door after grabbing my bag and let myself in. It's freezing! I walk straight to the window unit, flip it on high, and immediately smell the familiar odor of burning dust particles. They fly up from the vent and float in the air. In the light sneaking between the plastic drapes, I see two queen sized beds, covered in bright yellow and orange bedspreads, a nightstand with the obligatory Gideon Bible, lamp, and phone book. A glance into the bathroom reveals a shower with mold crawling out of the caulking and a cracked and warped mirror above the sink. The toilet seat is wrapped in paper, stating it has been sanitized for my protection. I just pray the sheets are fairly clean. My brilliant, spontaneous idea doesn't seem glorious anymore.

I sit carefully on the edge of the bed. The mattress sinks six inches beneath me, and I have to position myself further in so I don't fall off while grabbing the phone book and looking up the vet clinic: Clark County Animal Clinic 6704 Larkspur Lane. This shouldn't be too tough—I just have to find the streets that have flower names. Or is a larkspur a bird? Whatever. I check my reflection, and when I lock the door behind me, I feel like I'm being watched.

I look all around the empty parking lot and then at the motel windows where the curtains hang as still as graves. No one in sight. I'm just out of my element, that has to be it. I get in my car again and my stomach unclenches. I probably felt tenser at my first Coddled Cuisine show; this is just silly nerves.

Driving through town, I find the post office, a downtown café that looks promising for breakfast tomorrow morning, three bars, the VFW, the Catholic and Lutheran churches, and a grocery store. I drive down High Street, Main Street, Seventh Street, and Fifth Street. No Larkspur Lane. I head into the residential part of town, passing the school. No Larkspur Lane. I drive into the country and cross train tracks. No sign of a lane by any name.

I turn around and head back into town, thinking this will be harder than I thought. Where would a logical location for a vet clinic be? I came in off the highway and didn't pass it there. Down Polk Avenue, I see a person walking a dog.

I pull up alongside the man and his Collie and roll down my window. "Hi there! I'm looking for the animal clinic and can't seem to find it. Can you give me directions?"

"Sure." He pauses and squints into the sun, as though asking the heavens to guide his advice. "Turn around and take the first left at the stop sign, drive until you reach, I think it's Livingston Avenue—anyway, it's something like that. Turn left there, go until you pass the Co-op on your left, and you'll see it on your right."

I repeat his directions and look at him for confirmation. "Yep," he nods and sneezes loudly into his sleeve.

"Bless you. Thank you."

Blowing his nose into a huge white flag of a handkerchief, he nods again and I drive off, the Collie barking ferociously at my departing tires. I come up to Limestone Street and consider it for a moment before turning onto it and, within two blocks, I see a large green-lettered sign for the Dodge County Animal Clinic. Outstanding! I pull in and study the building. It's square, nondescript and covered in grey aluminum siding. Looking into the windows, I see cupboards and cages, but no sign of Todd. I'll just head inside and announce myself.

The bells on the door jangle loudly and I look around an empty waiting room. The reception desk has a sign taped to it, and I cross the room to read the scrawling message:

**Will be back. Call 555-4542 if emergency.**

So far this plan is a total disaster, and the clutching in my gut intensifies again. I hear scratching and barking coming from the rear of the building, but content myself first by looking around for clues of Todd's life here. The magazines are about what I'd expect in any waiting area, except instead of *Highlights*, he has *Dog's World*. The office behind the reception desk is cluttered, but ordered. A few posters of magicians and an embroidered picture of a Dalmatian adorn the walls. The fridge is covered with pictures drawn by children— guess he gave a tour to a second grade class recently. The most intriguing object I find is on the desk next to the phone, a Post-it note with my name and phone number. I smile, encouraged by this discovery. Nothing in the script indicates his feelings about my phone number, no hearts doodled along the edges. But I also don't see any phone numbers on Post-it notes beside my own. All the other names and phone numbers are typed on a sheet next to the phone, numbers for other vet clinics, supply houses, the Department of Natural Resources, and poison control. Pretty run of the mill stuff.

Peering into the refrigerator on the back wall, I discover a dozen cans of orange soda, several bottles of medications which I hope are for the animals, the remains of a sub sandwich, and an economy-sized box of popsicles in the freezer, next to a cache of ice packs. Curious. A grubby looking quilt and a pillow in a flowered pillowcase are stacked on the sofa. He must spend the night here sometimes.

Finally, I gain courage and open the door to where the animals are kept, if the racket on the other side of the door is any indication. The barking, scratching, and growling cease momentarily as I enter the room and I feel twenty or so sets of eyes watch me, probably wondering if I'm here to feed them or take one of them home with me. I walk past the cages, taking a peek inside each one. Some of the puppies climb up the sides of their pens, tongues hanging out and paws reaching through the wire. The cats mostly sit towards the back of their cages, staring with golden eyes. I'm startled by the discovery of a huge brown-speckled snake in one of the cages, and on the floor next to a door leading outside, a pig asleep in a bed made out of an old towel. From the looks of it, Todd definitely has his hands full. I can barely keep a houseplant alive, and those only require weekly watering.

The sound of a car engine cuts my exploration of the animal kingdom short. Through the windows, I see a pick-up truck pull into the parking spot next to my car. I hurry to settle myself back in the waiting area on a chair with a magazine, spying over the top of *Good Housekeeping* to see a middle-aged man in a cap and blue flannel jacket tenderly remove a greying Black Labrador from the passenger side of the truck and carry it toward the door. I jump up and open it for him.

"Is Doc around?"

"Uh no, no he's not."

He walks over and reads Todd's note, then takes the dog over to a padded bench where he sets it down and sits next to it, patting its back.

"Belle got hit by a car," he tells me, interrupting the silence with his quiet voice.

"Is she going to be all right?" I lay the magazine on my lap and look at the dog, with her head resting on her owner's lap, eyes closed and back slowly expanding with each breath.

"I don't know. It caught her from the back, seemed to just nudge her off the road. But I'm sure a ton of steel and metal *nudging* you at seventy miles an hour feels pretty brutal. I can't tell if she can move her back legs or not."

"You saw it happen?"

"Yeah. Live just off of Cooper Road. Belle was by the mailbox when this sports car, think it was the Jensen kid, comes screaming down the road and swerves. Son of a bitch hit her on purpose." The man's face looks both tired and angry and I feel his rage lift in my own chest. What kind of a person would swerve to hit an animal?

"That's awful. I'm so sorry."

"Yeah, well they say it takes all kinds to make this world. Just wish that kind would make their home someplace else. I'm Tom, by the way, Tom Jacobson."

"I'm Sadie Davis."

"You new in town?"

"No, visiting."

He raises his bushy eyebrows but doesn't say anything, and then we turn our heads at the sound of gravel crunching under tires. A green pick-up pulls in next to Tom's. I recognize Todd's red hair and compact build when he hops down from the cab and grabs a bag out of the back end of the truck. I hold my breath, nervous as hell about what he'll say when he sees me. I hope he doesn't notice me until he has Belle patched up, or whatever he does with a dog that was hit by a car.

He strides through the front door and goes straight over to Tom and Belle. "Hey Tom, what's wrong with Belle?"

"Hit by a car. Caught her from behind on the side of the road."

Todd doesn't even notice me as he kneels in front of Tom and Belle, hands deftly moving across the dog's body, gingerly probing and poking along the length of her back. "Can she move her legs?"

"The front ones for sure, don't know about the back. I carried her in."

"Let's take her back to an examining table. I'll give her something right away for the shock and we'll take a closer look. Can you carry her okay on your own?"

"Yep."

Todd stands up and turns, and the moment he spots me, his entire face lights up. "Sadie! How are you? Listen, can you wait here a while? I—"

"Go take care of Belle. I'll be right here."

"Okay." He leads Tom and Belle down the hall, concern in his voice as he asks for more specifics on what happened.

I get comfortable again with the *Good Housekeeping* magazine, flipping past pages of recipes and diet plans. What will I say to Todd when he returns from taking care of this dog? *What brings you to town?* he'll ask, and I'll reply, *you* in a suggestive and meaningful way. Of course he won't ask me that exact question, and I'll sound like a pathetic stumbling idiot as I tell him I had absolutely nothing better to do and wanted to see him. Will he be flattered or will he be afraid?

I obsess my way through old issues of *People*, *Field and Stream*, and *Time*. I'm about to cross the waiting area for a new magazine when I hear voices down the hall.

"I'll stop by tomorrow morning and check on her, okay?" Todd says.

"Sure thing. We'll be there."

"Say hello to Darla for me. Tell her thanks for the pecan rolls!"

"Sure will. Thanks again." Tom tells Todd and nods to me as he leaves, dog wrapped in his arms, Todd helping him out the door and into his truck. They stand outside a moment longer before Todd returns, standing in front of me with a huge grin.

"So, what brings you to Neillsville, Sadie Davis?"

Panic chokes my resolve and I gulp. "Thought I'd take a little drive."

He cocks an eyebrow. "That's quite a drive."

I nod.

"Where are you staying?"

"The Sandman."

He laughs. "I can't believe the sight of that dump didn't scare you off. You sure you want to stay there?"

"No, not really," I tell him, uncertain of where he's headed.

"I have a spare room at my place. If you don't think I'm being too forward, would you feel comfortable staying with me instead?"

"Maybe I'll take a look and then consider my options."

He nods seriously at this. "Good idea. I won't have complimentary bars of soap, but the rates are pretty decent."

"They are?" Is he propositioning me? I can't really tell.

"Yep. For the pleasure of your company at dinner and helping me out with a few chores around here, I'll knock ten bucks off of whatever they're charging you over at the Sandman."

I stand and stick my hand out to shake on this arrangement. "Deal."

He eyeballs my hand and then tells me as he walks behind the reception desk, "I can't shake on this until I wash the blood off."

Dropping my hand to my side, I follow him back. "Nice place you run here."

"You think? You oughta see it when I have some help! It's already falling to pieces."

"Is that dog, Belle, going to be okay?"

"Hard to say." He turns off the water in the sink and shakes his hands before toweling them dry. "She's old, which doesn't help the healing process any. She might pull through and yet there remains a chance that she might need to be put down. The x-rays showed two broken ribs and a fractured hind leg. Other than that, I think she's okay, but the next twenty-four hours are going to be real critical."

"Why did you send her home?"

"Because Tom and Darla will keep her more comfortable there. She's been through enough without having to spend the night listening to puppies whine and cats scratch. I'll head out there in the morning and take another look."

"What's going to happen to the guy that hit her?"

"You ask a lot of questions."

"It's my job, remember? I'm the *Idea Exchange* girl."

Todd sighs and shakes his head, rubbing his palms across his hair. "Realistically, nothing. Geoff Jensen is the sheriff's son, and a spoiled shit of a human being, to boot."

233

"That's crazy! Tom saw him do it. He told me!"

"And Geoff will just as easily say he didn't swerve, and it's one man's word against another. Believe me Sadie, the politics don't stop at the Madison city limits. Things are unfair all over. Let's discuss something more pleasant, like helping me clean out kennels."

"Oh yeah, that sounds pleasant."

Todd wiggles his eyebrows and lets out an evil laugh. "Follow me, Miss Davis, and *I vill show you zee zecrets of zee inner circle of veterinary science.*"

# Chapter Twenty-Four

**"Make your party guests happy & comfortable"**
—*Coddled Cuisine training manual*

Two hours later, I sit down and slide off the large and slippery rubber boots Todd loaned me for mucking out the pens. I'm thoroughly convinced that I never want to own a pet. Even though they're cute and friendly and have big brown eyes, animals are disgusting. I know it's not their fault, but let's face it, they are. All that hair and fecal matter…

"Sadie, do you want to get your things and come to my place, or would you rather check it out first and then decide?"

"You know, I think I'm going to take you up on your offer sight unseen."

"Great, I'll drive. Your car will be fine where it's parked."

I tie my shoelaces and follow him out the door and wait as he locks it. He gallantly opens the truck door for me and I climb in. Country music blares through the stereo speakers the minute he starts the engine, and he reaches over to turn the volume down. "Drowns out my singing if I keep it turned up loud enough," he tells me.

Outside the Sandman Motel, Todd waits for me in the truck while I grab my duffel bag. Then he follows me into the office, where the old lady eyeballs me and says, "It'll be ten dollars extra for overnight guests."

"No, no I'm not staying. Neither is she. She's just here to return her key," Todd explains.

"I'm sorry?"

"Change of plans. Sadie's going to stay at my place. So, she won't need a room here. She's returning her key."

Her wrinkles deepen as she frowns at this news. "But she paid for two nights."

"Yes, and she changed her mind. She didn't use the room, and here's the key." Todd stares back at her and places the key in the center of the counter.

"I'm going to have to charge *something* for my trouble."

"Fine." Todd turns to me. "What did you pay for one night?"

"Twenty dollars," I mumble, wishing the old lady would just take the damn key and not look so offended that I won't stay in her creepy, dusty old motel.

Todd turns back to the old lady. "Why don't you refund her all but ten dollars? That should compensate you adequately for the—what was it? Five minutes it took you to check her in?"

"Hrumph." Breathing heavily, she takes the key and shuffles back to the room, behind the office. I glance sideways at Todd, studying a huge cobweb hanging above the sign that's telling us the Sandman is air conditioned *for your comfort*.

A moment later, she returns to sluggishly count out my change across the desk. Todd sweeps it over to me and sings out cheerfully, "Thank you very much. You have a great evening, then!"

"Hrumph."

I fold the bills back into my wallet and drop the wallet into my purse before I follow Todd through the door, conscious of the old lady's stare burning a hole through my retreating back. Any place has got to be better than this place. After that whole scene, I'm relieved not to have to stay at the Sandman—it freaked me out more than I'd realized.

"Well Sadie, since I managed to regain much of your money for lodging, I think it's only fair you offer to buy me a beer."

"And where might one do that on a Friday night in Neillsville?" He's going to tell me the VFW or the Elks' Lodge.

"It just so happens that I know the perfect place for drinking a beer in the spirit of gratitude."

"And that would be?"

He gives me a huge wink in response, so I lean back into the seat and enjoy the scenery from my perch in the truck's cab. Even in the muddy-grey, not-quite-green stage of late April, Neillsville is clearly a clean and well-kept town. Several houses have tulips and daffodils in bloom near the front doors, and only a few yards have any stray junk in them at all. The street gutters are lined with leaves and twigs, not the empty beer cans and fast food wrappers that are so common in Madison's streets.

We turn down a side street behind Hansen's IGA and pull into a parking lot behind what looks like a huge barn. I follow Todd's lead and get out of the truck, just missing a huge puddle of water with my right foot, and hop carefully across the gravel surface past the array of pick-up trucks and Cadillacs. "Where are we?"

"Only at my favorite watering hole of all time! The VFW."

I knew it.

Passing a row of dumpsters, we enter through a back door and head through a narrow hallway, paneled in dark wood. Ahead, past the mens' room, ladies' room, pay phone, and coat room, I see a huge banquet hall and, beyond that, a bar area. No one sitting in either section of the building appears to be under forty-five.

Todd waves to and greets several people as we pass tables, stopping at one to ask about a calf and assuring another couple that he'll be in first thing Monday morning. I feel the curious gazes and I look straight ahead, pretending I come here every Friday night with the town's beloved veterinarian. He's Neillsville's own James Herriot.

Todd puts his hand on the small of my back and guides me to a tall table flanked by five barstools off to the side of the pool table. "Here we are." He pulls out a stool for me and shrugs his flannel jacket from his broad shoulders.

"Sit," Todd tells me and, within moments, a woman

old enough to be my grandmother appears with a round cork-bottomed tray in hand.

"Hiya, Todd! I see you brought some company tonight. Who's your friend?" Her bright mauve lipstick stretches into a wide smile and she swipes at the table with a rag.

"Gladys, this is my friend Sadie, from Madison. Sadie, this is Gladys, Neillsville's finest Friday night fish fry waitress and probably the state's best knitter, too."

"Oh, Todd, you know that isn't true!" Gladys flutters her bright blue eyelids at us both. "I'm probably the best knitter in the Midwest!"

Todd guffaws and Gladys turns to me. "He just says that because I knitted him a scarf and mittens one year for taking care of my dog. Watch out for this one, he's a smooth talker!"

"Gladys! After all I've done for you?" Todd feigns wide-eyed innocence as his goatee stretches into a grin.

Snorting at him, she leans over to me. "What can I get you, dear?"

"We'll both have a couple of Old Fashioneds, whiskey-sweet. Mushrooms in both." Todd answers.

"Be right back. Keep those hands where I can see 'em." I watch Gladys return to the bar, skinny legs clad in dark tan pantyhose, rising like two twigs above clunky white orthopedic shoes.

"I hope you aren't jealous of Gladys and me; I haven't got the heart to break it off with her, you know," Todd tells me.

I ask, "Whiskey Old Fashioneds?"

"Yup, house specialty. They pickle their own mushrooms, too."

"I guess I always thought that was an old person's drink."

Todd considers this for a moment before looking around. "When in Rome…"

"So this is Friday night in Neillsville? For real?"

He bobs his head in the affirmative. "It probably seems lame compared to Madison, but these folks here are really nice. And to be honest, the younger crowd down the street at the Corner Bar aren't really my speed. Most of them are in their early 20s, went straight from high school graduation to the mill and want nothing more on the weekend than to get drunk and talk about how drunk they were the weekend before. I'd just as soon come here for a couple drinks, flirt with Gladys—who is married by the way—eat my perch dinner, and go home to catch a ball game on TV."

"Wow—almost as exciting as my life." It's a little scary how content he sounds. It's hardly about to change for him anytime soon, and he's young to be so settled down.

We're interrupted by Gladys, back already with two glasses sloshing an orange-tinted foam. She plops them down in front of us. "The usual?" Her pencil is poised in her claw-like fist and Todd nods.

"Miss Sadie?"

"What's the usual?"

"Perch fry with twice-baked potato, coleslaw, and bread."

"Sounds great. I'll have the same."

"Be right back with your fish." Gladys slips her order pad and pencil into her black jumper and descends on the next table to begin clearing dishes.

"Doesn't it seem cruel to make someone that old wait tables?"

Todd considers this and I study the way his lashes curl up at the edges of his eyes. He even has freckles on his eyelids.

"No, it gets her out of the house and in the middle of the fun on a Friday night, and she probably makes enough to cover the cost of her hobbies. Besides, she's young compared to some of the others here."

I take a look across the dining area and concede this point. One woman actually uses a cane as she pushes a cart piled with plates full of fried fish. I don't think I've ever been in the same building as so many old people in my entire life, except maybe when visiting a nursing home with my high school choir to sing Christmas carols. I sip my drink through the straw and like the bitter sweetness; I've never tasted one of these before. "These aren't bad." I take another sip through the skinny red straw.

"So, Sadie, why did you come to Neillsville today?"

I've been waiting for that to come up in conversation at some point, but the direct way in which he asks surprises me. "Ummm, I guess I just needed a mini-vacation. Had to get out of the city for the weekend."

He nods and, over the most delicious fried perch I've ever tasted, I tell him all about Dean, Ron, and Coddled Cuisine.

# Chapter Twenty-Five

**"Do you want to share your gifts with others?"**
*—Coddled Cuisine recruitment brochure*

I'm full and slightly fuzzy around the edges, thanks to three more drinks before returning to Todd's house. I follow him up the porch steps while he carries my bag for me and opens the front door. Stumbling across the threshold, my shoulder slams into the wall to my right and I rub it while Todd switches on lamps all over the living room.

The man has no style. This living room is direct from 1974, complete with an orange plastic chair in the corner and a heavy oak coffee table taking up the center of the room. Clearly he took hand-me-downs from somebody—it looks clean, but shabby.

"Welcome to my home sweet home." He sets my bag down next to the steps leading up stairs and crosses to turn on some music. "Would you like another drink, or do you want to see the guest bedroom first?"

Courage, girl. "I'll take the drink."

When Todd leaves the room, I walk around the living room, looking at framed photos on the wall. I recognize Evelyn and her husband in two of them. A snapshot of a very young Todd in a baseball uniform with longish bushy hair sticking out of the sides of his cap has me giggling when he returns, holding two bottles of beer.

"Cheers," I say, taking one. I settle into the center of the sofa and Todd looks at me uncertainly before sitting next to me. I take a long drink and place the bottle carefully on the table in front of me before leaning back against the cushion, sliding my hands down the fronts of my thighs to wipe the sweat off of them. There is *definitely* some tension in the air. The only question is how to cut it.

"So, do you follow basketball…?" I ask and turn my head to look him fully in the face, and he breaks off the question mid-air and gulps. Our faces are inches apart.

"Not really."

"Oh." His eyes are the bluest blue, his nose deliciously crooked toward the bridge and he has the nicest broad shoulders. He leans back into the sofa cushion, and I move my face toward his, aiming for his lips as he leaps off the couch, yelling, "Oh, shit!"

Oh shit? I snap back to sitting up straight on the couch and see that his lap is wet with spilled beer. Giggles well up inside my chest and tears stream down my cheeks as I howl. Drunk and laughing, I realize that the moment for romance has passed any tension I sensed has disappeared like water into a bucket of sand.

Todd wipes at his jeans and excuses himself while I try to stop laughing. Each time I try to compose myself, the giggles overcome my belly and then the hiccups hit.

I'm choking on a giggle-hiccup combo when Todd returns, dishtowel in hand. He wipes off the table and sits down again, smiling at me. "Pretty funny, huh?"

"I'm so sorry," I gasp. "I don't know why it's so funny that you spilled beer—"

I don't get to finish because Todd's hands are suddenly holding my shoulders in the most tender way and he is kissing me, startling the giggles and hiccups away, and sending my blood racing through my chest, thighs, and toes in frantic, hot longing. Melting between the effects of whiskey and his hungry lips, I stop giggling altogether.

# Chapter Twenty-Six

**"Do you enjoy new experiences?"**
*—Coddled Cuisine recruitment brochure*

Groaning, I roll onto my side to feel the residual effects of last night's whiskey pulse between my head and my gut. "Uuunnngh."

"Sadie? Are you awake?"

The rest of last night swims in a foggy haze that has overtaken my brain. I remember kissing Todd, kissing him quite passionately and for quite a while, then falling asleep. I wiggle my toes—my shoes are next to the couch. A quick and subtle exploratory search reveals that all my clothes are still buttoned. My entire body is covered in a patchwork quilt and my head is resting on a very flat pillow that smells slightly of mothballs. Based on the circumstantial evidence, I'd say Todd was a gentleman and didn't take advantage of the situation. Or me, for that matter.

"Yes, I'm up." I heave my body upright and the pain rushes straight to the back of my eyeballs.

Todd walks in from the kitchen and hands me a glass of orange juice. "Here. I hope you slept okay. I didn't carry you up to the spare room. You kind of fell asleep right here, and I didn't want to risk banging your head on the banister or something…" He trails off and rubs his bearded chin, looking away from me.

I take the orange juice gratefully and swallow it in two gulps. "Wow. I guess there's a reason I don't drink whiskey. Ever."

He chuckles and sits on a rocking chair on the other side of the coffee table. My bladder is throbbing and the pressure nearly makes my eyes water. "Where's your bathroom?"

"Up the stairs, second door to your left."

"Thanks." I feel him watch me climb the stairs. What's he thinking after last night? Either he thinks I'm a total slut who can't handle her liquor, or he thinks I got carried away and pities me. At the top of the stairs I pause, temporarily blinded by bright blue-flowered wallpaper, and I make out four paneled oak doors, two on each side. I pick the second and open it. The bathroom is straight out of 1957: black, white, and pink tiles with a toilet that has one of those old-fashioned tanks above the back. I settle myself on the seat and, a second later, feel a rush of relaxation surge through my entire body. Amazing how having to pee can be a total body experience; even my headache recedes as my bladder empties.

Poking through the stack of magazines next to the toilet, I'm gratified to see they're all on magic or animal care. No nudie magazines for this guy. Unless, of course, he keeps them in his bedroom. I stand up, flush, and walk to the sink to examine the damage. My hair sticks up oddly in the back and mascara is smudged beneath my eyes. Otherwise I don't look as hideous as I feel. I use a washcloth from the linen closet to wipe my face clean and brush my teeth with my finger and a dab of Todd's toothpaste. Much better.

Back downstairs, Todd's still in the rocking chair, sitting patiently.

"What time is it?"

"About eleven. You hungry?"

I remember the man and the dog from yesterday. "What about that dog that was hit by the car?" I struggle to remember anyone's name.

"Belle. She'll be okay. I stopped by this morning."

"You did?"

"Yup, on my way to the clinic. Animals can't get their own food and water—they're pretty bad about cleaning out their own cages, too. I just got back a while ago."

"Wow, I really slept in."

"You did?" He raises his eyebrows.

"Yeah. I'm not what you'd call a morning person, but I'm usually up and moving around before eleven."

Todd smiles suddenly and stands. "Would you prefer to eat out this morning or do you want me to make you something here?"

"Whichever."

"Let's eat out then. You want to shower before we go?" He looks doubtful—he must be starving. After all, he put in half a day's work already.

"No, I'm good for now."

"Okay, let's go."

As Todd drives us through town to the café on Main Street, I close my eyes in the bright sun beating down through the window on my arms and face. "This sounds terrible, but I could take a nap already."

He laughs. "Well, that's one way to spend the afternoon."

"Did you have something else in mind?"

"Actually, I did."

"What's that?"

"Let me surprise you."

Inside the café, I immediately sense that Todd is a regular here, too. "Hey Todd, how are you today?" the grizzled woman in a hairnet behind the counter asks, as we sit down in a booth. She stares at me curiously. Does Todd know anyone under the age of fifty-seven?

"Great. Hey Ethel, I'd like you to meet my friend, Sadie. Sadie, Ethel."

I nod and tell Ethel it's nice to meet her, and she juts her chin at me before leaning forward on her elbows to address Todd again. "So, the fish tank has been cleaned and I put a new thermometer in there, but I still found a floater this morning. What do you think?"

His eyebrows furrow as he thinks this through. A very pregnant woman about my age wearing a pink uniform comes over to drop menus on our table and slides a coffee pot and two mugs in front of me. She smiles at me, revealing the cutest dimples I've ever seen and winks before waddling back to a booth full of what look like fishermen, judging by their waders.

"Maybe the temperature in the room fluctuates too much. It's possible, you know. You keep the fish in that room above the garage, right?"

"Yeah."

"Remember, I can birth a cow and spay a cat, but fish are a whole different line of vet work. I'd say your next move should be a heater, but check with the store first. "

"Will do." She turns and heads into the kitchen behind the counter. I flip the plastic menu cover open. It's eggs or pancakes here, no bagels or quiche in Neillsville.

"Ethel recently began a new hobby. As you probably guessed, she's still working out the kinks of the aquarium."

"Gotcha."

The waitress comes back and again shows off her dimples and straight white teeth. "Hey, Todd. What'll you two have today?"

"Give me a bacon cheeseburger and fries. Coffee is fine."

"I'll have the short stack of the blueberry pancakes, please."

"Any meat with that?" She looks up from her order pad.

"No, thanks."

"Do you want anything else to drink?"

"Coffee's fine."

"So when's that baby coming, Amy?" Todd asks.

She giggles and pats her enormous stomach. "Any day now. We're due Tuesday, but the way I feel, I'd be happy to spit the kid out this afternoon!"

"I'll be anxious to hear how it goes for you."

"We'll keep you posted. Bret's so proud, he'll take out a front page ad in *The Herald* probably!" She taps the table and walks away.

Todd grins, leaning forward. "This is their first."

"I see."

"They're pretty excited, as you can tell."

I nod. My stomach is making a racket and I wish I'd ordered the tall stack, but in my experience, pancakes in restaurants are always the size of a dinner plate.

"So how's the future of your cooking business look?"

Cooking business? Oh. "You mean Coddled Cuisine. It looks okay. I told you that my show Thursday night went really well. I booked another one off it, and your Aunt Evelyn is hosting one for me this week. I'm hitting my goal anyway, which is one show a week."

"How does it compare to radio work?"

"Good question. I can't really compare it yet—I haven't done it long enough to know."

"Huh. I think it'd be tough to sell anything. I don't have it in me. It takes a certain kind of personality."

"You're right, it does. But this stuff seems to just sell itself. My hardest job is to show it in action, demonstrate it, and then people either think they need to buy it or not."

"And so far?"

"They seem to need it."

"That's good!"

Amy returns with our food and I look enviously at Todd's burger, oozing cheese, ketchup, and grease from the bun. My pancakes, as predicted, are the size of the plate and I just pray to God they aren't too rubbery.

After leaving a five dollar tip for Amy and promising to get a phone number of a fish expert from La Crosse, Todd pays our bill and I follow him out to his truck. "Let's go back to the house and you can shower, change, whatever else it is you women need to do, and then we're out of here."

"To where?" He didn't let anything slip at the diner.

Grinning at me he opens the truck door, which lets out a loud creak. "That's a surprise, I said."

"Well, what if I need to wear something or bring something wherever we're going?"

"Don't worry about it. Just come along for the ride. This is your adventure weekend, right?"

I nod, and settle back into the sun-warmed vinyl seat. "A shower is exactly what I need now. Between that, my full stomach, and the coffee, I feel much, much better."

At the house, he walks me upstairs and pulls towels from the linen closet for me.

"Sorry I haven't got much to offer you in the way of fancy shampoos or anything, just Ivory soap and some Head and Shoulders shampoo."

"I've packed my own." I hold up my duffel.

"I'll be waiting downstairs until you're ready."

"Can you at least tell me if this is an indoor or out-door thing we're doing?"

He just grins and shakes his head before retreating downstairs. I strip off my funky clothes and pull out clean jeans and underwear. Arranging my makeup bag on the back of the sink, I wonder if this bathroom has seen any women lately, or if I'm his first female houseguest outside of family. I'm betting on the latter.

Forty minutes later, I emerge from the bathroom in a swirling cloud of steam and hop down the stairs. "I'm ready!" I trill.

"Okay, let's head out."

I pull my purple scoopneck sweater over my head and follow Todd out to the truck, no clues yet as to where we're going.

He turns onto the road and begins driving through town, along a country road and then to a highway. His head nods slightly to the country music playing on the radio, and I lean against the headrest, my hair ruffling in the wind coming through the half-opened window. I turn to look at him. He's a good-looking man, once you accept the red hair and freckles.

"What?" He glances over at me and raises his eyebrows.

"Nothing."

"Then why are you staring at me?"

"Was I? I'm sorry. I was just sort of spacing out," I lie and look away. It's possible to imagine dating him, but I can't figure out how we would negotiate the distance between our lives. I have no desire to leave Madison and I don't get the sense that he's in any rush to leave Neillsville, either. I don't feel like a long-distance love affair. I could've had one of those before leaving the

Peace Corps and didn't do it then, why on earth would I pursue one now?

I mull over the people who have gone down that road—all unsuccessfully. Kara had a short-lived fling with a grad student who headed to France after they got started; the affair ended within two months. Molly had a boyfriend for years whom was stationed in Germany while in the Air Force; she was miserable the whole time. Jane had a boyfriend her sophomore year of college. She had met Steve over the summer, and in the fall they headed off to their respective campuses, only to break things off by Christmas break because, as Jane put it, what's the sense of staying in a committed relationship with someone you see only twice a month? She told me she felt more involved with the cashier at the grocery store she shopped at, since she saw him more regularly.

The more I think it over, the more I'm wondering why I made this trip to Neillsville.

The car slows down and I look through the windshield again. We pass a bar and a gas station and then Todd pulls into the parking lot outside of a roller skating rink with a huge yellow sign reading Skate City. The outside of the building is painted with silhouettes of people on skates, girls with ponytails, and boys wearing bell-bottom pants. He parks beside a minivan and takes the keys out of the ignition. "Here we are."

I look at him and smile uncertainly.

"Let's go!"

I feel like a sixth grader as I glide around the skating rink, holding hands with Todd under the circling disco light. The love ballad playing—something by Foreigner—pulls at a longing inside of me and I sneak a glance at Todd. He grins and squeezes my hand, sending a jolt up my arm and straight through my thighs. I find myself willing to happen tonight whatever didn't happen last night.

Is it the power of a love ballad? The dizzy feeling of motion that remains when I take off the roller skates two hours later and stand on firm ground in my tennis shoes?

"Come on! Let's give *Ms. Pac-Man* another go!" Todd pulls me over to a bank of video games and starts dropping quarters through the slot.

I stand very close to him, my breasts brushing against his upper arm every time he moves, my thigh resting alongside his leg. I'm coming on strong; if he doesn't read the signals, he's either totally uninterested or too slow for the speed I'm raring to go.

Leaning over after the screen flashes *Game Over* for the fifth time, I breathe in his fresh Ivory smell and go for it. "So, what do you have planned for us next?" I whisper in his ear.

I'm rewarded with a slow grin and a quick kiss on the lips. "Dinner. Let's go!"

Across our table at the River-Rail Supper Club, Todd glances at me over the top of his faux-leather menu. "What sounds good?"

I want to say *you*, but chicken out and answer, "I'm thinking about the tenderloin."

"You have to try the twice-baked potatoes here. They're out of this world."

We make small talk through our salads and, when the waitress arrives with our steaks, I decide to plunge in. What the hell, right? Either this trip is a dead end or I'm heading down this road again.

"So Todd, how do you feel about long-distance relationships?"

He chews his steak and swallows, then takes a drink of water. "Depends."

"On what?"

"On where the relationship is headed."

Okay buddy, you're not evading this. "Where do you see this headed?" I ask directly. "I mean, is this something you want to do again? Do you see any point in—I don't know—in trying this whole thing out?"

"Sadie, you're the most beautiful woman I've met since I've moved here. I admit it's a bitch that you live three hours away, but I'm glad you came up here."

"And?" I set down my fork and knife, my hands starting to tremble.

"And I hope you come up here again."

"And?"

"And I'll try to see you in Madison again?" he asks. "Look, what kind of answer do you want? I'm not involved with anyone right now and I definitely want to see more of you. Can I give you more of an answer a month or two from now? Probably. It's good that you came here, yes. But what more do you want me to say at this point?"

I blush, confused. "That you want to see me again."

"Didn't I just say that?"

After dinner we leave the restaurant and drive back to Todd's house in a sulky silence. This is stupid. I wasted the trip here, not even sure what I was looking for.

We reach the front porch and Todd turns to look at me. "You're staying tonight, right?"

"I don't really want to drive back to Madison at this hour."

"You're cute when you pout. Listen," he turns the key in the lock, "I'm glad you're here. I'm terrible at saying the right thing, probably why I never get a second, let alone a third, date with anyone. But yes, I want to see you again. Can that be enough right now?"

I nod and Todd grabs my arms and pulls me close, leaning down slightly to look me in the eye. "Let's watch some TV or something," he suggests and I follow him inside. Wordlessly, we head to the couch and he switches it on, grabs a quilt and pulls it across our knees. "You want something to drink?"

"No, thanks." I still feel sullen and rejected.

He rests his arm on the back of the couch and I feel the heat of his body next to mine—the surge of longing pulls through my core. He did say he wanted to see me again. I settle back into his arm more comfortably and he turns his head to look at me. Turning my head to return his gaze, I again notice how blue his eyes are. What would it be like to kiss, really kiss, a goateed man? My wish is granted when he leans forward.

His lips are warm and his beard scrapes my chin softly while I sink into his arms.

"Sadie?"

"Uh-huh," I moan when his lips pull away minutes later.

"Tell me when you want to stop."

"You're a true gentleman, Todd MacGynn." I grab the back of his hair and pull him closer, pressing my chest against him. His hands slide up my back, beneath my sweater—hot, but causing goosebumps. I'm not stopping him, not at all; not when he unbuttons my jeans, not when he kisses my knees, not when he slides my panties past my hips and down my thighs.

I don't stop him when he leans above me on his forearms and raises his eyebrows in question. "Come on. God, I want you."

Later, both of us satisfied, we snuggle naked beneath the quilt on his couch. All my uncertainty has ebbed out of me as he strokes my leg with his strong, calloused hand.

## Chapter Twenty-Seven

**"You'll be excited to share your new venture with your friends and family members"**
*—Coddled Cuisine training manual*

I leave Neillsville at five on Sunday, calling Jane before Todd's even out of sight. I turn onto the highway and accelerate to sixty. My foot bounces up and down, and I turn the dial on the radio, pausing each time I get reception, trying to find a song playing that fits my mood. After five rings, Jane answers.

"It's me. How are you?"

"Hey, Sadie. Fine, just cleaning out flower beds. What's up? You coming over?"

"I'm on my way home from Neillsville."

"Neillsville? What were you doing there?"

I rehash the reasons for my trip and then start sharing the good stuff; that is, what happened once I got to Neillsville. "Then he took me roller skating."

"Roller skating?"

"I know. How completely seventh grade, right? But cute. We get there and it turns out that he's good friends with the owner. The only other people there are a bunch of kids having a birthday party. We rent those disgusting beige skates with the red laces and start moving around the rink. They have the disco lights going and everything. The lights are low, and Brad, his friend, starts playing all these old slow songs, like REO Speedwagon, that kind of thing."

"You're kidding, right?"

"It gets better. So we're skating along together, holding hands, and it's so completely cheesy, I can't stand it. We eat popcorn and play video games. After we turn in our skates, we go out for dinner at this supper club where he doesn't know anyone, so we're able to talk uninterrupted the entire time. Then we head back to his house to watch a movie together, all snuggled up on the couch."

"And?"

"Quit yelling."

"I'm sorry, I can barely hear you. You're breaking…p"

The line is completely silent, and a moment later I hear the dial tone. Just when I'm getting to the good part! "Argh!" I look down at the phone—roaming. Figures.

I turn up the radio and fiddle with the dial for a few miles before I dial Jane again. This time she picks up on the first ring.

"And? Is my little sister coming home from Neillsville a woman?"

"Geez, Jane. I came home from my junior prom a woman."

"Ew! With Randy Bremski?"

"No, with Henry."

"Oh, Henry." She says this thoughtfully. "How is the old sleazebag these days?"

"I didn't call you to talk about him."

"Right. So you watch a movie all snuggled up on the couch and…?"

"And it was fabulous." I drive out of the city limits and accelerate to highway speed.

"*It* it? Or the movie *IT*?"

"*It* it."

"Really." She sighs.

"I'm coming home a much more satisfied woman than I did on prom night."

"Good for you. You deserve that."

"He was so thoughtful and slow, not all rushing it to make himself happy. He really took his time. I bet he doesn't tear wrapping paper off of presents. He's the kind of guy who sets the bow aside, unwraps the ribbon, then peels the tape off of the paper, sliding his hand up the back of the gift—"

"Whoa! Are we still talking about unwrapping presents?"

"Ummm, no. We're not."

"I gathered that. And this morning? Awkward? Weird? How was it?"

"Just as good as last night." I tell her, my toes warming at the memory of waking up to Todd burrowing his goateed chin in my shoulder.

"Not the sex, you idiot! The goodbye, the…whatever you want to call it! When you left, how did you leave it?"

"It was okay. I don't know when I'll see him again. We didn't talk about it. I guess it was just sort of understood that we'll be in touch. We kissed goodbye—he stood and waved until I disappeared."

"Huh."

"Sounds strange, but it was comfortable, like we've been together for ages and were just going to be apart for a little while. I don't know, we haven't really said anything about where this is at, what we're calling this whatever."

"You sound really happy," Jane says, and I can tell from her voice that she's smiling.

"I am. I really am."

The rest of the drive to Madison goes quickly as I replay the weekend in my mind over and over again. His arms around me while we played *Ms. Pac-Man* at Skate City, the warm pressure of his biceps against my arms. His face, all serious and concentrated as he leaned over to kiss me on my lips Saturday night, his breath warm on my face. The way he pulled my sweater up over my head while we sat on the couch. He stopped and looked at me in the most appreciative way, then reached over to kiss me again and run his hands over my shoulders. Amazing.

And even more amazing, rather than obsessing over what the future holds, trying to figure out where things are going, I'm just content with the right now. It feels so relaxed and natural to simply enjoy this man and not worry about when he'll call next. Then it occurs to me: is *this* normal?

## Chapter Twenty-Eight

**"Weekend parties are the most popular option"**
*—Coddled Cuisine hostess brochure*

I'm in the middle of writing Dean's questions for a program on creating a Constitutional amendment when Evelyn pokes her head into my office. "Good morning, Sadie. Good show today."

"It was, by Dean's standards."

Evelyn smiles, and I suddenly feel very uncomfortable around her. Why? She doesn't know about my trip. Why do I feel oddly guilty? Her expression is so guileless that I finally burst out with it. "I visited Todd this weekend."

"You did?" She looks pleasantly surprised at this news.

"You're okay with that, right?"

"Of course I am! If I weren't, why on earth would I have introduced the two of you?"

"I don't know. I guess I was just nervous about what you'd think."

"Did you have a good time? What did you do?"

I tell her about the fish fry and the movie we watched, the roller skating and helping him at the clinic. I leave out all the details she probably wouldn't want to know about her nephew's sex life.

"Sounds like a nice break from Madison. How do you like his house?"

"It's a little—"

"Old. It's okay, you can say it." She laughs. "Todd bought the place from my mother, his grandma. The last time I was there it hadn't been redecorated in quite some time. I'll assume the place still reeks of old lady taste?"

"It does," I giggle. "Hardly a man's domain. The crew from *Queer Eye* would have a field day in there!"

"I think it's laziness, or not caring, more than any actual affection for crocheted afghans, lace doilies, and rust-orange upholstery."

"I hope you're right. Otherwise there's a whole side to Todd that I'm not sure I want to know about."

I'm about to ask her if she thinks Todd plans to live in his grandma's house forever when Dean interrupts us to ask why he has to talk about tariffs in a show about free trade. "A tariff's a tax, right? So what's free about a tax?"

Evelyn crosses her eyes and waggles her fingers at me and leaves, unnoticed by Dean. I sigh and dig deep for patience.

## Chapter Twenty-Nine

**"Have a great time with your friends"**
*—Coddled Cuisine hostess brochure*

Tuesday night, Kara's heading towards me on State Street. She puts a jog into her step and grabs my arm when she reaches me. "We have to wait out here for Molly."

"Molly's coming, too?"

"Without Francis. A girl's night out. Love the scarf!" she adds, nodding at my neck.

"Thanks, got it at ReThreads."

"*Tres* stylish. Oh, here she comes!"

I turn and it takes me a moment to recognize Molly without her glasses and wearing, I have to squint to be sure, *lipstick*? "Molly?"

Kara smiles smugly at me. She knew of this transformation no doubt, and I shake my head in disbelief. "Molly Ryan wearing lipstick?"

The left side of her lips curls and Molly whispers, "Contacts, too."

"Holy shit!"

"Hush." she hisses. I gape while a flush creeps up her neck and her face turns blotchy shades of pink and red—Molly blushing is not a pretty sight. Yet, who would've guessed I'd see Molly blush one day, let alone wear make-up?

"After we sit and order, you have to tell me all the details."

"Right here?" Kara grabs a chair at the huge table in the center of the dining room.

"Looks perfect," Molly agrees and we drop our jackets and bags on the seats.

The two hostesses look at each other before the taller one comes over with menus. "How many will be dining this evening?"

"Just us." I smile.

"Three beers, right? What dark beer do you have?" Kara looks at the hostess.

"You have to place your order with the waitress. I'll get her."

Kara shakes her head. "The hostess takes the drink order and the waitress takes the food order." She explains in a singsong voice, like she's explaining to a two-year-old how to wash hands.

"I just started here."

"Don't you know what dark beers you serve?"

"Well, I just started." The girl tells her defensively. Kara goes into attack mode.

"Are you getting defiant with me? Do you have any idea who I am? We come here all the time and I think it's reasonable to expect our service to be consistent. I want to see your manager, right away. Go get Ben."

The girl's eyes narrow and her cheeks turn red, but I can see fear build in her eyes at the mention of Ben's name. "I'll go get a list of our beers from the bar."

"Get Ben for us right now." Kara stands and places both hands on the table. "I insist!"

The few other diners turn in their seats to watch the drama unfold, and we fight to keep straight and indignant expressions as the twenty year old tart flounces to the kitchen. She throws open the kitchen doors in a huff. Kara leans forward. "We do want to drink beer tonight, right?"

"I was thinking soda," I tell her.

"I kind of want an iced tea," Molly says.

Kara shrugs and laughs. "He's going to be so pissed when he sees us."

"Not half as pissed as that hostess will be!"

A moment later Ben follows the hostess out of the kitchen. His face is composed as he braces himself to deal with ornery customers. He's wiping his hands off on a white towel and looks elegantly rumpled in spotlessly tailored pants and sleeves rolled up to his elbows. Five steps into the dining room he stops mid-stride, and his face relaxes into a grin. He's chuckling by the time he reaches our table, and the hostess scowls at him.

"This is the table?" He looks at her, struggling to appear sober and serious for her benefit. He furrows his brow, but there's a wild twitch at the right side of his mouth.

"Yes, these ladies would like to speak with you," she snaps, jutting her chin at us.

"I'll take it from here, Keely. Go back to the hostess stand." Ben waits for her to walk out of earshot and then leans forward. "You nasty bitches!"

We can't hold the laughter in any longer and I feel sheepish when I see Keely angrily whispering to the other hostess. Ben slides a chair out and sits beside Molly. "You picked a great night to show up and be obnoxious. I'm training a new cook and this is Keely's second week on the job."

Kara shrugs and grabs a breadstick from the vase in the center of the table. "Ah well, I'm sure you'll live." She waggles the breadstick in front of her face like a cigar.

"But will they?" He jerks his head toward the hostess stand and pulls both hands down his face. "Tell you what, be nice and drinks are on the house."

"Ben, we didn't come here for a free night out," Molly protests and Ben looks at her with sudden interest.

"Holy—Molly! What happened to the angry, establishment-hating intellect I once hated? You look fantastic! Must be the effects of a man in your life. The rumors are true, then?"

She blushes. "Flattery will get you nowhere. And you don't have to buy our drinks."

"No," Kara argues. "We act nice and *dinner* is on the house!"

"You drive a hard bargain, Kara."

"Take it or leave it. But I guarantee Miss Keely will tattletale on us at least five more times before our night is over."

Ben exhales and stands, the wooden chair scraping the floor as he pushes it back. "Diane will be your server— she'll be right with you. Let me get this new kid trained and I'll join you for dessert in an hour."

"This is a *girl's* night out, Ben," I point out.

"Sometimes I feel like a woman." He sings a falsetto imitation of Shania Twain and saunters back to the kitchen.

Diane is one of the three or four waitresses Ben hasn't slept with. Grinning, she flips out her order pad as she strides toward us. "Giving Keely a hard time, eh? Be kind, she's only a child."

"We'll try." Molly promises.

Kara leans forward after Diane leaves us. "How long until Keely becomes another one of Ben's harem?"

"Oh Kara, come on! She's practically still a teenager. Ben's a pig, but he's got *some* standards."

"He's never gone for jailbait before." Molly says.

"Hey, I'm having a party for your friend, Lydia, next month." I change the subject.

"You are? Cool." Kara nods in approval. "I haven't gotten an invitation yet, but I'm sure I will."

"How's that whole thing going anyway, Sadie?" Molly asks.

"Pretty well. I have a party for Evelyn this week, Lydia's in three weeks, and I can call Jane when this streak dries up. I figure one a week is a fabulous start."

"I couldn't believe how quickly the stuff arrived at my house."

"It came already?" I ask.

"Yeah, plus the company sent me a gift, some dip spreader thing."

"I didn't know they did that. On a serious note, I want to thank you both for being so supportive."

"What are friends for? It's not like you've never helped us out," Molly insists.

"Molly's right. It's the least we can do," Kara agrees and grabs another breadstick.

"Still, friends or not, I appreciate it."

Molly and Kara shrug. "You're welcome," Molly finally says.

"Now I want to hear all about Francis. Enough about work—it sucks, it sucks, it sucks. Let's talk about something that doesn't."

Molly radiates happiness while she tells all the details about Francis. He holds doors for her, keeps napkins in the glove compartment of his car, is a card-carrying member of the Green Party, and smells like Ivory soap. It makes me so glad to see her like this. She's completely different now. When she was with Scott, she slumped through life, always insecure about where she stood with him. What would she think of Todd if I told her? I decide to keep Todd to myself for now, though. Molly never gets to shine; it's her turn tonight.

An hour later, we slowly push our plates away, the remnants of pasta sticking to the edges of the plates. "Ugh, I can't eat another bite," I complain.

"But you must! Dessert!" Kara urges.

"I know, but I feel so full. Thanksgiving full. I just want to take a long walk." I look longingly out the front windows of the restaurant and imagine the sun setting by Lake Mendota, the lights along the walking paths just starting to turn on while the shadows of the trees stretch across the pavement. I want it to be a hot summer night—the kind of night before mosquitoes begin breeding; when you can walk for hours and feel the fresh air in every pore of your body.

"Me too." Molly nods. "I know this is bad, but let's skip dessert for some nice coffees."

"I really wanted a bite of Ben's tiramisu." Kara looks mournful, but I know she's just as full.

Diane returns and begins clearing the plates. "Nothing to wrap up for home?"

"It was so good," I moan.

"I get that a lot," she cracks. "Any dessert?"

"No!" Molly and I chorus adamantly while Kara reluctantly shakes her head.

"But we'll have some coffees," Molly adds. "Tell Ben to get his ass out of the kitchen and join us."

"I make no promises. This new kid needs all kinds of training."

"What do you guys have going on this weekend?" Kara asks.

"If no one invites me to some stupid dinner party to get hooked up with an accountant, I'll be spending it with Francis." Molly shoots Kara a look.

"Doing what?"

"I'll leave you to figure that out," she smiles. "But there's a jazz combo playing at Mother Fools Saturday night. Anyone interested?"

"I would be." I should have *something* to look forward to since I'm not going to Neillsville. I was bold enough last weekend, but now it's time to let Todd make a move.

"I'm in, too," Kara says. "What time?"

"Seven. They'll play until ten or eleven."

Girls' night out comes to an unofficial close with the arrival of Ben and a tray of coffees.

# Chapter Thirty

**"Monthly meetings allow consultants to network
and learn about new product promotions"**
*—Coddled Cuisine training manual*

After work Wednesday, I head to the ladies' room to
brush my teeth and check my hair and make-up. My first
Coddled Cuisine district meeting is in half an hour and
I'm curious and nervous. Curious to see what will happen
and purely nosy about getting a look at Kimberly's house.
I bet her mansion looks like something out of *InStyle*,
complete with an in-ground swimming pool and a
painted portrait of her face above the fireplace. I'm as
nervous as a kid on the first day of school when I think
about meeting the other saleswomen and making a good
impression.

I retrieve my car from the lot down the street and
head over to Edgewood. It figures that Kimberly lives
in the quietly prestigious, but not ostentatious, part of
town. She reeks class and I envy her so much. I pass

through the wide boulevards and enormous brick houses. Gigantic maple and oak trees edge the street, and ahead, a cluster of cars are parked along the side of the road. That must be where I'm headed.

The address checks out when I read the brushed nickel house numbers hanging to the right of two heavy wood doors. I park and grab my notebook and purse, the whole time admiring the expensive topiaries in cement urns along the impeccable brick-paved walkway.

I pause to listen to the sounds of birds twittering in the trees and the quiet hum of traffic a few blocks away before ringing the doorbell. Twenty seconds later, Kimberly opens the door. "Sadie, you're the last one here. We're about to get started. Follow me."

I follow Kimberly through the airy space of the front hallway, taking in the chandelier, flower arrangements, and her skirt suit. Her suit is a shade of blue-grey that no one I know would buy, except maybe Kara. None of my friends wear clothes in such specific colors; it costs too much to accessorize.

In Kimberly's huge living room I see my Coddled Cuisine colleagues. Seven women of varying ages and sizes turn their heads to check me out. Sydney stands up and calls across the room. "Sadie! I'm glad you made it!" She motions to the empty spot on the couch beside her and I self-consciously cross the floor to take my spot.

"How's it going? Have you had any parties since we talked last?" she whispers to me while Kimberly settles herself into a leather Murphy chair and begins rustling papers.

"Great. I've had three parties and I have two more booked." I whisper back and I return the smile of a large woman in her fifties with a head full of thick, grey curls.

Looking over the group, I realize I'm the youngest person here by at least five years. Three women fall into the thirty-something mom category, one of them pregnant, and another wearing a purple long-sleeved shirt.

All chatter ceases when Kimberly takes center stage. "Welcome," she begins in her smooth voice. "I trust everyone has had a successful month since our last meeting. We have some exciting new things in store for our summer party line, and I also have some news regarding the consultant benefit awards. Let's get started."

Catalogs pass from hand to hand and I listen intently as Kimberly points out changes in product lines, new specials, and a few promotional items. She reminds us that to stay current, we need to book a minimum of one party per month.

"Now then, the consultant benefits. Starting June first, any consultant earning five thousand dollars in party sales is eligible to enter a drawing for a trip to Hawaii. The contest ends August thirty-first and for each five thousand dollars achieved, you get another chance to win."

Appreciative murmuring fills the air.

"The trip is for four people, with no blackout dates, seven days in an all-inclusive resort."

More appreciative murmuring.

Kimberly goes on to describe some other details about the trip and my mind wanders to Hawaii. I'm wearing a brightly colored sarong, walking along the beach, holding hands with a tanned (but not freckled) Todd. Just as the thumping sounds of a luau echo in the background, I realize everyone around me is standing up and moving around. What did I miss?

Sydney turns to me and reads the confusion on my face. "We're headed to the kitchen to sample the new summer recipes," she explains excitedly.

Leaving the sumptuous leather couch, I follow her into the most gleaming copper kitchen I have seen outside of a magazine. Bold yellow sunflowers on a cobalt blue background fill every inch of wall and ceiling space, and the appliances are top of the line. I would never go to anyone else's kitchen if I lived here.

Kimberly positions herself behind the island and gestures to the platters and bowls in front of her as she describes each one. "Take a sample and recipe card of each," she invites us. "I think you'll find the Fiji Fruit Parfait and the Sombrero Salad very refreshing and light for summer entertaining."

In turns we help ourselves, filling the square white plates (Coddled Cuisine Hostess Collection) and Kimberly hands out bottles of water while we taste. The mom crowd perches on chairs next to the island. I follow Sydney and the two older women to a table nestled in an alcove of windows looking over the back yard and patio.

I nod and mumble a "hello" to both around a mouthful of blueberries and vanilla yogurt.

"Nice to meet you Sadie. Good to have you on board," one says while the other nods and chews.

"A person could sell this stuff five days a week, twice a day, and still turn down parties." Sydney looks to the others for affirmation.

"Really?"

"Uh-huh."

"I guess I had no idea." I digest this and the Fiji Fruit Parfait while the rest discuss a grad class they're enrolled in at the University. Kimberly leaves the mommy club at the counter and comes over to our table, carrying a huge bowl of fruit salad.

"Sadie, I trust you've met everyone."

"Yes, thanks."

"When will I be able to see you in action at a party?" She asks this casually enough, but from the look on her face, I know I better have an answer this time.

"Well, I have one booked tomorrow night. I know that's short notice but—"

"I'll be there. What time? Where?"

I write down Evelyn's address and the time of the party for Kimberly, using the notepad and pen she hands me. The Fiji Fruit Parfait leaves a slightly sour taste in my mouth at the prospect of Kimberly watching me in action.

"I'm looking forward to tomorrow night, then. It will be good to see firsthand how you're really doing." She turns and walks away, busying herself with the rest of the food at the counter.

"I'm really nervous about doing a show in front of her. Can she fire me or something if I screw up?" I ask Sydney.

"Don't worry about it. She came to watch me once and it was no big deal. She had some suggestions for how I could improve, which she shared with me after the party was over, and that was that. I think it's required of her to watch all new salespeople, kind of a corporate Coddled Cuisine commandment or something."

"Okay." I feel less confident than I sound when I say this to Sydney. She pats my hand gently and then leans in closer to whisper in my ear.

"Bet you're wondering why Kimberly does this at all when you look at her digs, eh?"

"The question has occurred to me," I admit, hoping she'll tell me more.

"Have you seen her husband?" she asks conspiratorially.

"No." I look around the kitchen. Did he just walk in the room?

"Check out the photos on the fridge."

I squint and see the side of the cavernous refrigerator (stainless steel, sub-zero temperature controls) is plastered with snapshots. Among them are several of a tanned Kimberly wearing a bikini, looking glamorous, and leaning against a grey and wrinkled man, who looks about sixty years old. Her father? Not kissing like that, he isn't. I eyeball another snapshot of the couple on a boat. "Wow."

"Yup."

"But how does this explain—?"

"It doesn't, I just wanted to see your face when you realized that Kimberly Carlyle has a sugar daddy." Sydney giggles as she says this and I can't help feeling catty since the woman we're gossiping about is twenty feet away from us and we're in her kitchen.

"Any kids?"

"Nope, not yet, anyhow."

"Huh."

"What do you think of the Polynesian Salad?"

"Really good," I mumble around another mouthful, which suddenly doesn't taste so sour anymore but light, fluffy, and refreshing. After swallowing, I ask if all the monthly meetings are like this.

"Pretty much. We don't always have food, but they're fast and painless."

She's right. Forty minutes later I'm back in my car, leaving the lush Edgewood neighborhood and heading back into the constant stream of noise and smells that surround my downtown digs. No matter how many parties I work, I'll never be able to upgrade to that standard of living. But it sure is nice to dream about.

Before I know it, it's Thursday and I'm setting up for Evelyn's party. I feel like an old pro when the gingham fabric drops into neat pleats and stays there while I arrange my display on the crates. Briskly, I circle the table, slipping folders and catalogs out of the stack in my left arm and onto the folding chairs Evelyn set up in a semicircle around the kitchen table. I move through one more time with pens and double-check the ingredients against the recipes and set the oven temperature. Ready to roll. I glance at the clock one more time while the doorbell rings. I hear Kimberly's cool, murmuring voice respond to Evelyn's cheerful greeting.

She follows Evelyn into the kitchen and takes a quick look around. "Hello, Sadie."

"Hi, Kimberly. You've met Evelyn, I guess."

"Yes, I have." Kimberly looks impeccable in grey dress pants and a lavender cashmere sweater, topped with pearl earrings and necklace. "I'll sit over here so I don't get in anyone's way." She perches on a stool behind the counter where I'm planning to demonstrate the recipes.

I nod at this and gulp for air when the doorbell chimes again.

The friends and neighbors seem to arrive at once, and within minutes we're starting the party. Evelyn's friends are sweet, but what did I expect? I'm doubtful about middle-aged women needing kitchen supplies, but you never know, so I give it my best shot. This is my second time through the appetizer party and I'm more confident about knowing my stuff. I explain the food chopper and quickly disassemble it. "This is dishwasher safe, of course, top rack. Notice the cap for the blades, very handy if you are chopping small quantities of food. The cap measures a quarter cup exactly." I snap the entire ensemble back together with the efficiency of a seasoned mechanic and show everyone how quickly the chopper takes care of vegetables.

I make more eye contact with Evelyn's guests while chopping up the peppers, onions, and ham. I crack a few jokes. A few women cry "Bingo!" before I finish the punch, and I honestly believe that even if they don't buy much, they had a good time, which, while not doing much for my bottom line, can't hurt either. I pass out the Bingo prizes (not Godiva this time, but Lindt truffle bars). "Ladies, I'll be in the other room if you'd like to place any orders or ask any questions."

Leaving them to dig into their canapés and dips, I wander around Evelyn's living room while waiting for orders. There are family pictures on top of the entertainment center and I pull one down to study. There's Todd in the second row of what looks like a birthday party. About thirty people are lined up behind a white-haired woman in a wheelchair. Most of the people are wearing party hats, some little kids sit cross-legged in front of the wheelchair, clutching party horns and balloons.

Todd's wearing a party hat and standing next to a man with the same red hair and stocky build—must be his brother. The woman on the other side of him has her arm wrapped around his neck tightly, and she's leaning into his shoulder. A cousin? Sister? She's an attractive blonde with a huge smile. I'll have to ask Evelyn about her.

I don't see any other pictures that include Todd, so I make myself comfortable on the couch and begin sifting through papers as the first wave of women joins me. Kimberly sits across the room from me, seeming to be absorbed in looking over a catalog. I pen in the first few order forms. Nothing amazing, most of them ordering the obligatory thirty-dollar amount to be polite when Evelyn joins us.

"Sadie, my friend Candace," she indicates a tall woman with yellow-blonde hair clipped back with a pony tail and huge bangs, ratted five inches above her penciled eyebrows, "wants to hostess a party for her daughter. A bridal shower. You do those, don't you?"

Evelyn and her friend look at me expectantly. I read that you can do this kind of party, but I have no experience as a bride or otherwise in having one. Nonetheless, I nod enthusiastically. "Of course we can." I glance at Kimberly who nods imperceptibly. "Did you have a date in mind?"

"Nikki's wedding is in June, so I'd really like to have the shower in April. You know, April showers." Evelyn laughs at Candace's joke, so I chuckle along as well.

"Are you thinking during the day? Like on a Saturday for brunch? Or in the evening during the week?"

"Nikki works on the weekends and at night sometimes, so I think a week night would be best."

"How about a Wednesday, say five-thirty? That gives guests time to arrive after work, but it's still early enough to have any type of menu you might enjoy."

"Fabulous! What about two weeks from this Wednesday?"

I consult my calendar: the twenty-seventh of April. I never have plans on Wednesdays, anyway. "That'd be great. Where will we be having the party? At your home?"

"No, we'll do it at Nikki's apartment." Candace gives me directions and her phone number. Even though Evelyn's party won't break any sales records, at least I booked another party off of it.

"Her daughter's planning a fairly large reception," Evelyn tells me. "Tell me again Candace, something like four-hundred guests, right?"

"Three-hundred and ninety-three." Candace proclaims proudly. "The groom is originally from out of town, so that makes the guest list bigger."

"Wow." I act duly impressed.

"Her dress is covered in handmade lace from Spain. It costs four-thousand dollars," she continues. "And of course, the veil is another seven-hundred and fifty."

Holy shit. I could buy a new wardrobe for that price, but I smile and act interested. This is the paying public, after all.

After I know the color combinations (red and black), number of bridesmaids (seven) and flower selection (roses and lilies), Evelyn and Candace return to the kitchen. I tally up two more order forms before closing up shop in the living room. Kimberly finally sets the catalog on her lap, resting both hands on top of it lightly, giving me a clear view of two enormous diamond rings, one on each ring finger. "How did I do?" My insides flutter and my face heats up, but what's done is done and I can't go back and change anything. I would say things went well, but who knows what the ice princess saw?

"Not bad. You know your product line passably well and have a friendly approach to customers. I have questions about the Bingo game, but it seemed effective tonight."

I nod, immodest pride welling up in my chest.

"But it's obvious to anyone who cooks that you don't. Cook, that is. You don't know any of the hints and shortcuts that someone who spends a lot of time in a kitchen expects to hear."

"But I'm single, Kimberly. It's hard to cook for just one person!" I try to keep the whine from my voice.

"That doesn't matter. Practical expertise and experience are imperative in this business. Especially when selling to this sort of customer." She nods toward the kitchen.

"What am I supposed to do then?"

"Get serious about practicing more or quit if you can't commit." She stands and walks across the room toward me, and I think she's going to offer to help clean the mess in the kitchen. "I'm meeting my husband for dinner and he's waiting for me as we speak. I'll see you next month." She lets herself out through the front door. I feel like I've just been visited by a fairy godmother that found me too lacking to help. But she wasn't terribly harsh, I remind myself, and I return to Evelyn's kitchen to clear away my gear.

Up to my wrists in hot soapy water, I wash all of my kitchen supplies. When I turn off the water, I hear Candace again, center stage with details about her daughter's wedding. I feel a sharp pain in my chest while I dry the food chopper. I thought I'd have had a wedding by now. I hadn't gone so far as to fill in the details about flowers and stuff, but I'd dreamed about that future with Henry. Not that I miss him *that* much, but I feel kind of robbed of being the new bride—Mrs. Henry Kendall, owner of a pretty diamond ring and new dishes from a department store registry. Married women get a sort of dignity with their status. No one asks a married woman if she ever thought about *not* being married.

No one asks married women where they're headed in life, skeptical because they're missing a key accessory (strong, dependable male partner). I sigh heavily and the sound of my own breath brings me back to the reality of Evelyn's kitchen, resplendent in hand-stenciled pigs and roosters. There's enough time to be sad when I have to do this wedding shower. With any luck, most of the guests will be singletons like me and I'll feel right at home as a member of the majority.

Evelyn walks me out to my car, carrying a crate, despite my protests that she's supposed to enjoy her party guests. "I need a breath of fresh air. Candace really sucks it out of me."

"Really? I thought she was a good friend of yours."

"Neighbor. There is a huge difference between a neighbor and a friend. I've found it's safer to stay on good terms with neighbors, regardless of what you think of them personally. No matter, we got you another party booked and that's the main thing, right?"

"Well, yes."

Evelyn smiles brightly at me. "Don't worry, her daughter's even worse than she is!"

"Can I ever thank you enough?"

"Sure, you can tell me all the gory details about Nikki's shower after you work it," Evelyn cackles. "How did it go with your supervisor tonight?"

"Pretty well, she said I need to cook more. I guess it's pretty obvious that I'm a novice." I want desperately for Evelyn to deny this charge up and down, but she nods her head thoughtfully.

"I guess I can see that you don't cook. If you did, you'd probably have more to say besides 'the chopper can chop onions.'"

"So, you don't think I did well?"

"I didn't say that, I just observed that if you did cook, you'd have more to say. Like with anything else, it's all in the details that you share. For example," she pauses and frowns a little while she thinks of what to say next. "The spatulas you have are great, but you only talk about how they don't melt over a hot stove. You don't talk about how the rubber is slick enough to scrape the batter completely out of a pan and the handle is sturdy enough to pull through bread dough."

"I guess I don't know those things." I hate to concede that Kimberly may be right.

"It may not matter most of the time," she reassures me. "But it could be a selling point for some people. I guess it depends on how committed you want to get to this whole thing."

"I guess."

"My guests are probably wondering where I am, so I better head back. I'll see you at work tomorrow. Have a good night. And thanks for the party!"

I slam my trunk shut and turn to her. "You, too."

Evelyn's still standing outside her house when I drive down the street, barely visible in the dim glow of the streetlight. I feel a little wounded by her criticism, although I see the truth in it. Maybe I should make more of an effort to cook, to learn the subtleties of the kitchen. It's a thought, especially if I plan to cook for someone other than myself one day.

## Chapter Thirty-One

**"Book your parties at least two weeks in advance"**
*—Coddled Cuisine recruitment training manual*

"Jane," I whine into my phone. I'm feeling exceptionally needy and Jane's one of the few people I can act pathetic around.

"Yes, dear sister."

"You have to have a party for me. A *good* party with lots of *fun* people."

"A party for you or a party *for* you?"

"A Coddled Cuisine one." She's got to do this for me.

"Uh-huh. What makes you think I would hostess a party for the likes of *you*, dear sister?"

"The fact that you told me you would."

"Oh. Right. Okay. When do you want to do this?"

"You make me feel so special," I tease her.

"Oh, but you are. Truly. I suppose it had better be on a Saturday. Do you prefer brunch or an afternoon thing?"

"Hey, it's your party, Sis. Whenever you want to have it."

"All right, brunch then. How about three weeks from Saturday?"

I double-check my own calendar. "Hey, why not invite Mom?"

"We could do that. It would help expand the guest list if she'd bring a few friends."

"Why don't you call her and I'll get some recipes together?"

"Well done, Sadie. Well done. You not only made this party sound like my idea, but I'm responsible for Mom now, too."

"Is that what you think?" I raise my voice to its most innocent pitch. "Tell you what, if you're low on guests, I'll bring Kara and Molly, too."

"Plan on that. I have to go, we have clay in the oven and the timer's going off."

"Bye." I hang up and do some quick mental calculations. If I manage my current average, I can clear an extra thousand dollars in April. This means paying down my credit card by June, including my recent shopping spree, and then I can start saving for something like a vacation. The idea sends chills down my arms.

Dean's voice blaring down the hall sends a new wave of chills.

"Where are the transcripts from yesterday's show?"

What? When has he ever cared about a previous show? Much less shown any urge to read anything?

"Right here," I pull it off my desk and hand it to him. "Why do you want to look at it?"

"Apparently," he pauses dramatically and sniffs, "yesterday's guest died last night. Can you imagine? I thought we might do some sort of memorial on tomorrow's show."

What the hell? "Dean, a memorial? Really? For a one-time guest who was a not-terribly-notable author of a book about traveling in Peru? I mean, it would certainly be thoughtful to mention the guest's passing. I don't think this merits an entire hour! Besides, we have a guest booked for tomorrow's show. We can't just cancel them."

"You don't understand." He puffs his chest out and expounds somberly on his new concept. "We need to memorialize all of our guests who have died. The whole hour we'll remember those who have contributed to the *Idea Exchange* before their passing. You can research our list of guests and find out who else has died."

I struggle to keep a composed expression. "Dean, I doubt more than two guests have died on us in the past two years. I really don't think there's much of a show here."

"And once again, I have to disagree with you, Sadie. I think Ron will be very interested in this idea. No one has done it before."

No one has done this because the idea sucks, you idiot. "Okay, bounce it off Ron and let me know what he thinks."

"No, you need to come with me."

"I'm sort of busy here, Dean. Is there a reason why I need to join you?"

"To present a united front. With only two of us working on this show, we should always be involved on every aspect of it together."

Right. Unless, of course, that aspect involves actual work. Resentfully, I follow Dean out of my office and down the hall to Ron's. Evelyn catches my eye as I pass her and she raises her eyebrows. I shake my head and frown to indicate I'm on a mission against my own free will and better judgment. She mouths, "We'll talk later." I'm nodding back at her when I enter the stench of Ron's office, forgetting to get a last gasp of clean smelling air before entering. Damn.

"Ron, I have a proposal to pitch." Dean begins and Ron looks up from his desk.

"What is it, Dean?" He sounds exasperated.

"As you probably know, our guest from yesterday's show died last night. I think it would be appropriate to have a program in his memory. Also in memory of former guests who have passed on," Dean says while sitting in the one empty chair.

"Was this a regular guest?"

"Well, no. I believe he was just on this one time. Right, Sadie?"

I nod. I'm having as little to do with this as possible.

"And how many other guests would you be memorializing?"

Dean looks at me and I finally speak. "Ron, we don't really have that information." It's tough to keep contempt for this idea out of my voice.

"Um-hum." Ron frowns at Dean. "And is this your idea and Sadie's?"

"I came up with this idea by myself. Sadie accompanied me since she is the show's production manager."

Ron then focuses his frown on me and I shrug my right shoulder. Finally he looks at Dean again and grunts. "Lousiest idea I've ever heard. Leave the producing to Sadie, Dean." With that, he returns to the papers on his desk and we're dismissed.

I feel almost drunk with joy leaving his office. Did Ron and I just take the same side on something? Did I detect some impatience, annoyance even, in Dean's direction? This can't be, yet it sure seemed like Ron's star host fell a few cosmic feet.

"Some people just don't recognize genius when it's right in front of them." Dean blusters as we retreat down the hall. "It's a great idea. He's an idiot. I guess we'll just have to go with the planned format for tomorrow then."

I don't bother pointing out that any change would've just made more work for me, anyway. I'm still coming to terms with what just transpired in Ron's office. An actual decision made that I agree with—will wonders never cease?

Later that night, when I've just turned on the television and kicked my feet under an afghan, the phone rings. Grunting, I swing my legs off the couch again, reluctant to miss the opening scene of *CSI* and leave my couch. "Hello?"

"Hello? Sadie?"

It's Todd and suddenly I don't mind standing barefoot on the cold linoleum in my kitchen. "Hey, Todd. What's up?"

"Just thinking about you and thought I'd give you a quick call before turning in for the night. Any chance you'll be around weekend after next?"

"Sure. Why?" My cheeks flush and my chest tingles.

"I found somebody to watch the clinic for me that weekend—an old buddy from college who's actually between jobs. He doesn't start his new position for a couple of weeks and told me he'd help out so I can get out of here. Thought I'd pay you a visit if you're okay with that."

"I'd love for you to visit!"

"Super. I'll be in Madison Friday. I've got to be back Monday for regular clinic appointments."

"I'll see about taking Friday off."

"Great! I have to run. I've been swamped here lately, but I'm looking forward to seeing you."

"Me too."

"See you then."

I blow a kiss into the telephone, but an echo and the dial tone fills my ear. Todd's coming back to Madison! He's coming to see me! I snuggle back into my afghan on the couch and blissfully plan what we might do, where we might go, who we might see. I think I'm almost half of a couple again, and it's a really good thought.

# Chapter Thirty-Two

**"A Coddled Cuisine party
can be for special occasions"**
*—Coddled Cuisine hostess brochure*

After a few wrong turns, I finally locate the address of the bridal shower party and pull into a parking spot close to apartment seven. It's in a block of nice, cookie-cutter buildings, completely lacking character, but clean and well-kept. I pile two crates into my arms and slam the passenger door shut with my hip before heading up to nudge the doorbell with my knuckle. The sky is still bright. I wish I didn't have to work a party on such a fine spring evening.

Moments later I am face-to-face with a bleached blonde wearing enough make-up to clear out Tammy Faye Baker's cosmetic case.

"Hi, I'm Sadie, the Coddled Cuisine consultant. You must be…" I trail off, taking in her considerable tanned cleavage, dipping into a long "V" before disappearing into a bright pink tank top and a diamond ring conspicuously sparkling on her right ring finger that she pulls through her chemically treated locks.

"Nikki. Nikki Sandburg. Come in." I follow her into the apartment that smells faintly new, like paint and carpet. The room strikes me as somehow familiar. The furniture is new, black leather, and I can tell that Nikki enjoys shopping at Pier 1 Imports. Most of last fall's collection of wreaths and swags hang all over the walls.

"Hello, Candace!" I greet her mom. I'm taken aback by this pair of tanned, talon-nailed, bleached-out bimbos, but I'm not giving that off. I have to handle these people with integrity, and, with luck, I'll probably never see them after tonight.

"Hi, Sadie. How are you? You look a little pale, you need some color. I figured you'll want to get started setting up right away, so I'm almost done here."

I set my crates down on the linoleum floor and survey the dining room table, covered in doilies, umbrellas, and pastel colored Jordan Almonds. Someone's been reading *Bride Magazine*, circa 1985.

Nikki sits down on a stool at the counter and pulls out a nail file, working away at a hot pink claw while I slide the punch bowl and platter of deviled eggs aside. "I'm going to need most of the counter space, I'm really sorry. Do you have a card table I could use for these things?"

"We're using the card table for gifts," Candace tells me doubtfully. I meet her stare defiantly. "All right, we'll put the gifts on the entertainment center."

"Thank you," I tell her sweetly and begin unpacking. Silence floods the air and I arrange my utensils, pulling out the pieces I'll need for the canapés and wraps. "I'll be right back," I announce after emptying the first two crates. "I have to get a few more things out of my car."

Candace and Nikki ignore me as I walk out, a little annoyed that they don't even offer to help. When I head back into the apartment, I again study the living room to figure out why the place feels so familiar. I stare at the entertainment center, the black screen of the television catching my eye. It's not the television. Not the furniture. But there is something unsettling about how it feels like I've been here before.

I heft the crates up a little higher on my hip and walk to the kitchen, where Candace is pinning a corsage to Nikki's tank top. "Okay, I should have this all set up in about twenty minutes. Are the ingredients in the fridge?"

"Yes," Candace mumbles around a stick pin clenched between her teeth. "Or in that bag by the stove."

"Great." I start putting the countertops in order. I look up at Nikki who is, again, sawing away at a fingernail. "So, a June bride, right? You must be pretty excited."

"Uh-huh."

"Is everything going as planned so far?" I'd like to strike up some kind of rapport before the guests arrive, but she's not making it easy.

"Pretty much. I just have to finish the centerpieces for the tables. We're doing flowerpots filled with tulle and baby's breath. Kind of a garden theme."

"Neat!" I tell her, more enthusiastically than I feel. "Hopefully tonight will fill your kitchen for a great start to married life. Do you have your wish list filled out?"

"Yeah. But we've been living together for almost a year, so I don't need a lot of stuff."

"You should add to your list anything you want to replace, too."

"Huh. I guess I might want to do that." Her nasally voice grates on my ears and I force a wider smile at her. The doorbell rings and she looks at Candace, who straightens up from the party favors she's arranging all over the table.

"I'll get it." Candace says.

Nikki returns her attention to her nails once more and I hustle to get the folders placed on everyone's seats. Candace greets the first guests and I turn to see two tall and tanned women with big brown hair (what Kara sneeringly refers to as "mall bangs") ratted high above their heavily-lined eyes. "STACY!" Nikki shrieks, dropping her nail file right in the middle of my mixing bowl with a clatter. She races over, emitting ear-piercing squeals while hugging her friends. I gather both of them are named Stacy. I close my eyes to pray for a boatload of patience to pull me through this evening.

By the time I finish setting out, measuring my ingredients, and tying my blue apron around my waist and neck, the room is full of Nikki's and Candace's friends; the only difference between the generations is the number of wrinkles acquired by years of year-round tanning. Nikki sits at the head of the table, a veil anchored in her bleached hair and a corsage bouncing atop her right breast each time she moves. The seven bridesmaids sit on either side and various aunts, cousins, friends, and co-workers are across the room. I ask Candace if I can use the bathroom before we get started.

"Second door down the hall, to the left. Did you see the dresses she picked out? Fabulous. The matchbooks have their names and the wedding date embossed in gold."

Candace's voice follows me into the bathroom where I shut and lock the door and lean against the sink, taking three deep breaths before opening my eyes to focus on my reflection in the mirror. Just as I hear Candace's next words, I see a photograph taped to the edge of the bathroom mirror.

"My Nikki will be Mrs. Henry Kendall!" There, in the photograph on the mirror, are two smiling people with their arms wrapped around one another's necks, Nikki and my ex-boyfriend, Henry. My heart beats into overdrive as my chest fills up with an icy feeling. Numbness freezes my hands and fingers motionless on the grey-swirled countertop. Henry. I'm in his new apartment. That's why it feels so familiar. Staring at the picture, I take in his thick eyebrows, dark hair curling slightly above his forehead, and straight white teeth. I scrunch my eyes shut again and attempt three more deep breaths. Weakly, I suck air into my lungs and wonder if I can leave the party right now. I can't though, I'm already started. Everything is set up and besides, this is for Evelyn's neighbor. I'll just go really fast and pray that he won't show up until I'm long gone.

I pee and wash my hands, the whole time fixated on the photo taped to the mirror. I try to discern between still having feelings and simply lacking closure, but I can't tell the difference.

I leave the bathroom and force my lips into a smile that probably looks more like a grimace. "Good evening ladies, and welcome to Nikki's bridal shower! You'll find folders and pens on your seats. I hope you've had a chance to look through the catalog! Nikki's wish list is being passed around right now and, of course, you can place orders for yourselves, as well. Before we get started, let's break the ice with a game called Home Party Bingo."

I distribute the Bingo sheets and race through introductions, noting that a cluster of Nikki's friends keep referring to themselves as numbers. "Hey Two, did you see she wants a new pizza slicer?"

"Yeah, imagine needing that with Henry!"

I try not to wince and concentrate on figuring out why they refer to each other by number rather than by name.

"Okay then, our first recipe tonight is Cheesy Crab Canapés—they're easy to make and very impressive to bring to a party. I'll start by showing you the food chopper, which is the primary utensil used in assembling this recipe." I slam the chopper's blades down again and again, yelling over the banging, "As you can see, the chopper is an excellent tool for taking out aggression, too!" Candace raises her eyebrows at a coppery red-haired woman her own age. Who cares what they think of me? It's all I can do to keep from bursting into tears right now.

I slide the tray of canapés into the oven and whip through the next two recipes in record time—only forty minutes having passed between Bingo sheets and finish. The food isn't even done in the oven by the time I ask if there are any questions before placing orders. The guests don't seem to notice that I've dragged them through a cooking demonstration at warp speed, if the empty boxes of white zinfandel by the recycling bin are any indication. The bridesmaids are all flushed and tipsy. Nikki's veil droops over her left eye.

"Okay, I'll be in the living room to take any orders."

First in line are the aunts and cousins; I'm guessing they want to get out of here before the core group gets any drunker. I process orders, mostly gifts for Nikki, and then have to wait for the rest of them to get on with it. Finally I go over to Candace, who's standing by the stove with a friend, glancing constantly at Nikki who has spilled wine across the paper tablecloth and is trying to mop it up using two fistfuls of napkins. Candace's eyebrows and lips are equally pinched together.

"Candace, um, do you think anyone else will want to be placing an order here tonight? Otherwise I think I'll start packing."

"Oh no, not yet. Has everyone ordered?"

"No—"

Like a foghorn, she cuts the din of laughter and chattering. "If you haven't placed your order with Sadie, you need to now!" She turns to me. "Are you in a hurry to leave?"

"I think you'd like to enjoy the shower without me since I'm nearly done." That's an understatement.

"Okay," she frowns at me again and turns to her friend. "Excuse us just a moment."

Candace follows me to the couch and sits down. "Where are we at for free stuff?"

"Right now you've earned two free and three half-price items. If you give me Nikki's wish list, I'll figure out the best deals. Does that sound all right to you?"

"Is that what most people do?"

"Usually. I know the catalog like the back of my hand and I know the specials, so it takes me less time to figure out the best way to place your order."

"Okay. I'll round up any remaining orders. Stay here."

I obey less than willingly and glance at my watch—seven-forty. If I can get out of here by eight, I'm convinced I'll miss running into Henry.

Candace returns with three tipsy bridesmaids in tow. "Ladies, go ahead and place those orders and then you can go back to the party."

I race through the forms, rewriting two of them because they're illegible with scribbles and crossed out math mistakes. I hurry back to the kitchen while the last bridesmaid is still putting away her credit card. Maybe I won't wash the dishes here, just haul them up to my apartment and do them there.

Just when I put the first platter into the bottom of a crate, the front door opens and, for the second time this evening, I freeze in my tracks. Henry walks through the front door, smiling in his confident way at the table of tipsy women. "Good evening, girls."

"Hi, Henry!" The way in which they all greet my ex-boyfriend reheats my blood enough so I crouch behind the counter, frantically grabbing and stuffing my things in the crates at random.

"How was the shower?" He strolls over and kisses Nikki on the lips while she reaches up and ruffles his hair with the ringed hand.

"Good. We're getting all kinds of cool stuff."

"Great. Do you need anything?"

"No. Are you going out again or staying here?"

"I'm staying. There's a game on at eight that I want to watch. I'll go to the bedroom."

Candace interrupts them. "Henry, before you go watch your game, can you give Sadie a hand putting her things back in her car? Sadie, this is the groom, Henry. Henry, Sadie, our Coddled Cuisine consultant."

My knees are locked in a bent position behind the counter. I have to stand and face him now. Very slowly, equally painfully, I rise and meet his eyes as my head passes the edge of the counter. His expression shifts from mild interest to wide-eyed horror and he looks quickly at Candace and Nikki.

Candace nods at him and Nikki has returned her attention to her girlfriends. "Nice to meet you?" he croaks.

"Likewise, I'm sure," I reply. Quickly I move to stack the chopper and serving pieces into the last empty crate and survey the kitchen. Fairly clean. They won't know which mess was mine and which was theirs in the end, anyway. I dump the remaining appetizers onto a glass platter covered in pastel hearts and umbrellas and set the last serving dish on top of the heap of dishes.

"Go help Sadie before you get too comfortable." Candace prods, and Henry slowly walks towards me.

"Just grab those two crates over there." I point to the two by the stove and I balance the other two on top of one another and lift them as I stand. "Congratulations again, Nikki. Good luck with everything. Candace, I'll call you tomorrow and we can go over the orders then, okay?"

"Sounds great. Good night." I'm dismissed with a wave from Candace and ignored by the bride-to-be. I head for the front door, aching for the fresh air, freedom, and getting the hell out of here.

Henry is on my tail while I stride down the sidewalk to my parked car. I hear his size nine sneakers jogging across the concrete behind me. "Sadie? I never expected—"

"Me either," I interrupt him, my face hot with anger and humiliation. I reach my car and fumble for my keys, dropping them in the gutter. I set the crates down on the ground and pick up the keys, my hands shake so much and I can't stop them. Finally I get my car door unlocked, conscious of Henry standing three feet away, holding the rest of my new business venture in his arms. The irony of the scene does not escape me.

"Sadie." His voice is gravelly and I look up, confused by the expression in his eyes.

"What?"

"I fucked up. I'm so sorry. I made the biggest mistake of my life."

"How's that?" I get the right key pulled from the ring and jam it into the lock. The clunk of the door opening sends a shot of relief through my nerves.

"I don't know what I was thinking. You're on my mind constantly. I think about you all the time. I miss you." He steps toward me and we're less than a foot apart.

I keep stacking the crates into the passenger side and reach through to unlock the back door.

"Do you think…"He continues while I turn around, grabbing the top crate from him and setting it into the back seat. "Can you ever consider…" I grab the second crate from him, avoiding eye contact, and slide it in next to the first. I shut the door firmly and turn to walk around to the other side of the car when he grabs me by the shoulders. "Sadie. You have to look at me." I look up at him and he leans forward, kissing me like he owns me.

For a moment, I believe him. A fantasy of him getting in the car with me, coming home with me and starting over for good this time, races through my mind and I'm almost convinced of his sincerity. Then I push him away, my body faster than my mind.

"You're engaged, Henry. You're getting married in two months. That's not the behavior of a man still in love with me." I barely get the words out of my mouth, it's so dry.

He reaches for my shoulders again and I push his hands away. I step back and slide against the car—Henry's standing too close to me. I'm about to say, "We're over," when I spot Nikki watching from the front porch and I yell, "Get fucked, Henry. Not Prince Charming here, is he, Nikki?"

Ignoring Nikki's shrieks, I get behind the wheel of my car and shove the key in the ignition. He's leaning on the passenger side, looking through the window at me in the fading grey light of the evening. Turning the key with my right hand, I hit the power locks with my left hand hard enough to make my palm sting. Shifting into reverse with the crunching grinding of gears, I back out, oblivious to any traffic and other people.

By the time I'm almost home, I turn onto a side street and park on the edge of the road. Killing the engine, I lean my forehead into the hard plastic of the steering wheel and cry in anguish until my eyes swell to slits and the lap of my jeans are soaked through with tears.

# Chapter Thirty-Three

**"Coddled Cuisine offers many opportunities for advancement"**
—*Coddled Cuisine recruitment brochure*

I call in sick to Lottie's voice mail at four in the morning before laying back down on my soggy pillow. My head aches dully and my stomach feels all knotted up. This, coupled with a queasiness that stretches from my toes to my hair, has the odd sensation of a hangover, but without the fun of a night out. I close my eyes and the memory of Henry standing in front of me, asking for a second chance, fills my head so I open them and adjust to the darkness of the room.

It's so quiet and dark that I think I'd like to never leave. I pull my arms tightly around my chest and sink into the heaving sobs once more. Abandoning all sense and logic, I wallow in memories of Henry, better days, and my dried out tear ducts manage to eke out a few more drops. He was my first love—so kind and thoughtful, he brought me flowers and always picked up the tab when we went out to eat. Sex with Henry was satisfying; I could never get enough of him. He knew exactly the right moment and movement of his hips to make me orgasm. I knew that he loved broiled haddock, hated westerns, and secretly listened to rap music. How could he abandon me for that too-tan, too-obvious, ditzy bitch?

I settle back into the couch, my eyes blindfolded by an icy wet washcloth, when the phone rings. "Hello?" I struggle to keep the cloth over my eyes as I sit up to answer it.

"Sadie?"

"Hi, Evelyn." I drop back into the pillows with a sigh.

"Lottie said you called in sick today. Is everything all right?" Evelyn asks.

I want to tell her, but then I think about Todd. It doesn't matter. "I'll be okay. Must've been something I ate. I was throwing up all night. To be honest, I feel much better now, but I wasn't too sure when I called in this morning."

"Oh dear, you didn't eat at that Mexican place again, did you?"

"No, I, uh, I ate some bad pasta salad. Must've been too old, I guess."

"I see. Just thought you'd like to know Ron ran a repeat show today. He told Dean it would be wiser in light of your absence to postpone until tomorrow."

"He did?" My spirits perk up at this vote of confidence coming from Ron. "Was Dean mad?"

"No, he left early as usual. But what does it say that Ron won't run a show without you here?"

"It says something."

"It does. Get some rest, dear, and we'll talk tomorrow."

"Okay. Thanks for checking in on me, Evelyn."

"What are friends for?" She hangs up and I smile a little. Ron made them run a repeat show. How about that? I return to the bathroom to see if the washcloth improved the look of my face any and it seems to have a little bit. I dab a little concealer on my chin and forehead, add mascara and a peachy lip gloss.

Back in my bedroom I pull on underwear, jeans, and a sweatshirt. I cover my damp hair with a baseball cap and lace up my sneakers. After breakfast I'll call Candace and close out that chapter of my life once and for all.

Heading over to Bakers Too, I consider a visit to Kara at the gallery and decide against it. I don't feel like reliving last night with anyone. I want to be anonymous today.

Back at my apartment mid-afternoon, I flip on a soap opera while thumbing through my mail. Three catalogs, the phone bill, and something from Coddled Cuisine. I open that envelope first and jump to my feet when I read the amount on the check. I walk around the coffee table twice and sit down. I jump up again and grab the phone, dialing quickly and waiting for Jane to pick up. "Hello?"

"Hello?" I don't recognize the voice.

"Is this Sadie?"

"Yes, who is this?"

"Kimberly Carlyle."

"Kimberly?" My voice rises to a very unflattering pitch. Which number did I actually dial?

"Yes," she says slowly, waiting for me to gather my wits.

"I was dialing out," I explain. "I was calling my sister. I didn't expect to hear your voice on the line."

"Some coincidence," she agrees coolly and pauses. "Did I catch you at a good time?"

"What? Oh, sure. Yeah. What's up?" I sound like a total dumbass.

"Things have come up and I have an opportunity for you to consider."

"Uh-huh?" Does she want me to do one of her parties?

"I'm going to have to resign as district manager for Coddled Cuisine, and, after much consideration, I would like you to take over the reins, so to speak."

"Me? I hardly have any experience!" She has to be kidding.

"No one else with experience had any interest in taking over the position," she tells me. I'm vaguely insulted that I was her last call, but still flattered she'd consider me anyway.

"I—what do you have to do?"

"Mainly coordinate between the company headquarters and the reps in the area. You're the go-between for both sides. You train new reps, take care of the monthly meeting, and hold everyone accountable on this end. You earn a stipend directly from Coddled Cuisine for doing this," she adds.

"What kind of a stipend?"

"Three-hundred dollars a month."

"I'm going to have to get back to you." This is too good to be true!

"I have to know your answer by ten tomorrow. I have to catch a flight and I'd really like to get you the files and things you'll need if you agree to do this."

"Okay, I'll call you back." I hear a man's voice speaking to her in the background and suddenly the metallic hum of the dial tone fills my right ear. Three-hundred dollars a month! I pick up my first commission check and kick back on my couch, my brain racing through the possibilities. I could afford to work part-time and, for the first time in my life, be flush from month-to-month. I could afford a new wardrobe, a vacation, and spa treatments! Department store perfume! Matching bras and panties! Delirious with financial power, I clap my hands and laugh.

Five minutes pass before I'm able to consider the drawbacks of this opportunity. Sure, it will take some time out of my life, what though? An afternoon during the weekend? An evening once a month? I can't really come up with any other disadvantages, so I call Kimberly back right away.

A man picks up and I ask for Kimberly. "Just a moment," I hear scuffling and then her voice on the other end.

"Hello?"

"Kimberly, this is Sadie. I'll do it. I just have one question."

"Wonderful. What?"

"Is this a temporary arrangement or forever?"

"It's for as long as you want. How do I get to your place?"

"Okay," I give her directions and restack my mail before she gets here. I call Jane again while I wait.

I'm just finishing up telling her the news when I see Kimberly's car pull up across the street. "She's here so I have to go."

"I'm so excited for you, Sadie! I'll call soon."

I hang up and head down the stairs to meet Kimberly at the front door. "Hi."

"Take this. I'll go and get the rest of it." She shoves a huge and heavy cardboard box into my arms. I lean against the front door to keep it open while she jogs back across the street to her car and hefts another huge box out of the trunk.

She follows me wordlessly up to my apartment and, once inside, sets the box on the couch and opens the flaps. Inside, I see all kinds of Coddled Cuisine products: the trendy square serving plates I ate off of just a week ago, spatulas, knives, serving utensils, pots, and skillets. "What's all this?"

"As a bonus, from me to you as you begin this new venture, you can have all my Coddled Cuisine stuff. It's almost new, and you can use it when training or doing your own parties."

"Really?" She's suspiciously friendly and benevolent.

"Yes, you'll find most of the Coddled Cuisine line in here. Obviously I got much of this at a discount or for free. Anyway, here you go!" She smiles falsely at me. The entire thing strikes me as weird.

"Why are you doing this, Kimberly? What's going on here?"

"Just doing a little—let's call it a lifestyle makeover. I have to go now. The files, extra training DVDs, order forms, introductory material, basically anything you might ever need are still down in my car, if you'll come down and get them?"

"Sure."

She pauses and looks around my apartment as though seeing it for the first time. "You know, this reminds me of the dormitory I lived in when I was in college. I couldn't stand living in such a cramped room. Decent housing must be harder to find than I thought."

"Yeah," I reply. She is still evil and catty and I wish her perfect blonde-streaked hair would fall out in clumps. I silently follow her down the stairs and out to her car, where she hands me a binder neatly organized with dividers and typed labels.

"Good luck!" Her smile is friendly enough, but the way she sweeps her eyes up and down my jeans and sneakers lets me know that I'm not quite up to snuff in her book, and probably never will be.

I am now my own boss. Sort of. I don't have Kimberly to answer to, just the corporate people located in another state. And even better, I never have to deal with Kimberly again and feel so damn inferior. I sprint up the steps and charge back into my apartment to unpack all my new dishes and cookware.

The afternoon passes quickly while I read through the binder and put away my lovely serving platter, pitchers, and utensils. I'm almost finished when I remember Nikki and Henry. I tally the order forms and crunch a few numbers alongside the spring catalog before calling Candace.

"Hello, Candace?"

"Yes?"

"This is Sadie Davis. I have everything ready to call in. I just need to go over a few questions with you."

"How much free stuff did we get?" From the tone of her voice, I can't tell whether the wedding is cancelled or not.

"You earned two free products and two half-price catalog items. What other two items would you like to order then?"

"How about the Hostess Party Platter?"

"Which color would you prefer?"

Candace thinks a moment and then answers. "Black. We'll take the canister set, too. Also in black."

"Obviously you'll use the free product credit for the platter and the skillet set, leaving you with the chopper and canisters at half-off," I jab at my calculator and get a total for her. "Okay, with shipping and handling, your order comes to eighty dollars flat. You'll get everything within ten working days. If you have any problems with this, call and let me know."

"I will."

"Should I have it shipped to your address?"

"Yes, Nikki's so busy you know, I hate to have her bothered by this."

"Okay, it'll be shipped to you. Thank you so much for your order, Candace."

"Sure, thank you! Buh-bye!"

"Buh-bye," I repeat and hang up. I'll e-mail the entire order to corporate tomorrow after the show. Meanwhile, to get the terrible taste of Candace, Nikki, and Henry out of my mouth, I head out again. A little therapeutic stroll down by the lake is exactly what I need right now.

# Chapter Thirty-Four

**"Maintaining good records is very important"**
*—Coddled Cuisine training manual*

I settle in for an evening of microwave popcorn and Thursday night TV. The mountain of laundry can wait until later. I hate going to the laundromat at night—it's always so crowded and dim and creepy, and going during the weekend is such a total waste of free time. I'll drive to work one day next week and take care of it on my lunch hour. Reaching for the remote, I turn up the volume to hear the very end of the news, hoping for a weather report.

"And now for our breaking story. Northern Papers CEO Bill Carlyle was reported missing today after federal investigators attempted an arrest late last night at his home. Charges of embezzlement are pending against him and his wife, Kimberly Carlyle."

Gasping, I lean forward to see the photograph from Kimberly's refrigerator take up my television screen: a picture of the two of them, tanned and laughing, leaning back against a seat on a boat.

"Investigators suspect they have left the country. Anyone with information that may lead to their arrest can call the Hot Tips Hotline at 555-5768 or 1-800-555-TIPS. And now to our on-the-scene reporter, Jenny Spears."

The picture changes to a petite brunette standing outside a concrete building.

"Thanks, Tom. The mood here today at Northern Papers was somber as employees learned that pensions, 401Ks, stocks, and benefits all comprised a paper trail of fraud and deceit as their money went directly into their employer's pockets. Here's Tim Goodman, a foreman, to tell us more. Tim, how was Bill Carlyle perceived by his employees?"

"Everyone pretty much felt the same way about him: he was a decent guy. He'd give you time off if you needed and seemed generous. I'd say he was well-liked."

"Yet he stole significant amounts of money from his workers. Tell us, what were people saying today about Bill Carlyle?"

The bearded man in the flannel shirt looks about ready to cry. "If they ever catch that son of a bitch, I'll be in the front row to watch his conviction, and then I'll stand right outside the prison gates to watch him get bussed in."

The news reporter's face fills the screen again. "As you can see, tensions are running high at the plant, and we've recently learned that operations may shut down temporarily as a series of unpaid creditors also stand in the wings looking for retribution. Back to you, Tom."

I turn the volume down and stare into space, stunned. That's why Kimberly was in such a generous mood; she has no use for a cupboard full of Coddled Cuisine products overseas. But why bother making sure any of it was accounted for? Why didn't she leave the Coddled Cuisine stuff behind like her husband did with his own, much larger interests? I get the binder and look through it for clues. Maybe there's a hidden message so I can find her and then collect a reward for turning them in. I page through the entire thing and discover nothing of interest to anyone besides a Coddled Cuisine consultant or manager. Did she say anything useful, revealing that I might turn over to the police? I replay the last conversations we had and conclude that Kimberly shared nothing at all, other than "things have come up" which can mean just about anything.

I picture her on the lam, no doubt someplace tropical and luxurious, living the life of white linen on the beach with gorgeous palm trees swaying in the ocean breeze. And Bill, laundering his stolen money through a series of untraceable accounts, like something from a John Grisham novel. How does a person leave behind everything they know and start over completely? If they're wanted by the FBI, I'm sure they have no plans of getting in contact with anyone anytime soon. Still, why was she so meticulous about handing over Coddled Cuisine management? Very strange, no doubt about it.

I thumb through the binder once more, admiring the neat tabs with typed categories: *Catalogs*, *Sales Reps*, and *Promotions*. Lucky me to inherit this, anyway. Too bad I couldn't get my hands on her wardrobe and jewelry.

The phone rings, my shoulders jolt skyward, and I pick it up nervously, trying to calm down. Why am I feeling nervous? I half expect the person on the other line to be a federal agent, ready to pull me in for questioning.

"Sadie? It's Sydney. Oh my gosh! Have you seen or heard the news yet?"

"Just now, as a matter of fact." I sit down, relieved it's only Sydney.

"I can't believe it! To steal all of that money and leave town. It's like out of a movie or something. You don't think people you *know* are capable of doing things like this!"

"I know exactly what you mean."

"Did you see the photo they're showing on the news of her and Bill on the boat? I can't believe that I was pointing that out to you not even a week ago!"

"I had no idea this was going to happen."

"She called me two days ago to see if I would take over the district manager stuff, but I didn't ask why. She's not the sort of person you feel comfortable asking a lot of questions around."

"I hear you." I flip the binder open again to the first page.

"Obviously I was flattered. I mean, I'm new at this. But there's no way I could take on that responsibility. Not with my kids and coaching soccer and running to practice and school concerts and all that." Sydney sounds wistful.

"Um-hum." Does she know I took it over?

"Do you know who ended up agreeing to do it?"

"Me."

"You?" She recovers by politely adding, "That's great! I mean, wow, you're really jumping in with both feet, aren't you?"

I reply, "Well, I guess no one else was willing or had the time. She said it wasn't too much extra work."

"I'm sure you'll do a fine job. I guess you'll have to get everyone together as some kind of damage control and officially take over."

I hadn't thought about that, but she's probably right. "Maybe I could just mail out a letter, you know, explaining that I'm taking over and know nothing and then we'll run things as usual at the next meeting, only at my place instead of hers," I picture the gorgeous house now empty, the gracious backyard falling away from the kitchen windows in waves of luscious shades of green.

"That would probably work. I have to run, Claudia has to be picked up from her piano lesson and I need to pick up a prescription at the pharmacy. I'll talk to you soon!"

"Okay, bye. Thanks for calling."

"You bet! Bye."

I hang up and feel both a little sick and a little happy. Knowing that Sydney was asked and turned it down makes me feel better. At least no one will think I'm some power-hungry Coddled Cuisine dictator trying to take over the world. But to think that everything seemed so normal just a short while ago and now it's all over the evening news really slugs a gal in the gut. Slowly, I put the binder on my desk and head to bed, suddenly too exhausted to watch television, sort laundry, or do much else besides close my eyes and escape into sleep.

# Chapter Thirty-Five

**"Doing your first show solo"**
*—Coddled Cuisine training manual*

I heft my bags of dirty laundry into the back of my car and double-check my wallet for change. Between parking downtown and plugging the washers and dryers, I'll need a lot of quarters today. The birds chirp loudly as I walk around to get into my car, but the street is so still. Do only the birds and I feel springtime coming at last? I adjust my rear view mirror and turn the key. Time to get to work and get my guest (book critic Diane Smead to discuss summer reading lists) on the line.

Parking downtown is absolutely awful—the lots fill up quickly and cost a small fortune. I pay the attendant ten dollars, knowing I'll be back to park again mid-afternoon and end up paying another ten for the same spot. Ugh. Unfortunately, unlike some large corporate offices I've heard about, public radio stations do not offer their employees an on-site laundry service.

Already the heat of the day vents past my legs, the concrete is starting to absorb the warmer nighttime weather, a sure sign that spring is here. Good, it'll make talking summer reading lists with Diane Smead that much easier.

I bustle past Lottie, who barely looks up from *Working Mother* magazine, and I stifle a giggle (she's never working any time I see her behind that front desk). I'm almost to my office to grab the file for today's show when Ron catches up to me. Crap. I had hoped he was chasing down someone else.

"Sadie!"

"Good morning, Ron," I take a safe step back to avoid the toxicity of his breath.

"Dean won't be in today, some crisis in his family last night. Not sure if I can give out the details yet, but…"

My mind races ahead of his words. We did a rerun show yesterday because of my crisis, what could we run today? School funding? Juvenile crime? Urban sprawl? My thoughts are interrupted by Ron staring at me, clearly waiting for a response. "Excuse me? I'm sorry, I was thinking"

"I said, you'll go on as host today with your planned guest."

"Really?" My voice cracks like a twelve year old boy's. "I mean, are you sure?"

Ron scowls at me, his brows bristling above his beady eyes like two grey caterpillars. "Fishing for my confidence? Go now, get your guest on the air!" He stomps away, leaving me gape-mouthed and elated. A good guest, one of my favorite annual shows, and *I* get to be the host! I run to get the file. Anything on my computer can wait until later; I have a show to run!

While I get Diane on the phone, I take deep, meditative breaths to achieve a sense of calm and get my tongue under control. I don't want to be a babbling idiot like some people on the air. Here's my big opportunity to prove myself to Ron and to the world at large. Diane's smooth voice interrupts my tangle of excited thoughts.

"Sadie Davis, from *Idea Exchange*. Are you all set for today's show?"

"Of course, I love doing this program," she tells me with her trademark mellow enthusiasm.

"Okay, there will be one small change today," I go on to explain that I'll be the host and she seems amenable to the idea.

I do the show the way I'd want it done, no replay of yesterday's broadcast. The introduction to Diane goes without a hitch and I even shine a few times when we talk about books I've either heard of or read about recently. An hour and a half later, I glide down the hall back to my office, positive that I'm standing a good six inches taller than normal. After the show Diane actually says, "Great show, Sadie. I really enjoyed our hour together. You have a real talent for this business and I hope it doesn't remain untapped." I only wish I'd gotten *that* on tape to replay over and over again.

All morning I check my e-mail to read accolades that I'm sure people will send. I end up deleting advertisements for weight loss pills, a sale at The Gap, and something called Viadron. Evelyn stops by to congratulate me on the show and to ask about a rumor she heard through the family grapevine about her nephew coming to Madison to visit a new young lady friend.

I blush. "He's, um, coming to town next weekend."

"Oh ho! And he won't be staying at old Aunt Evelyn's place this time around?"

"Actually, I don't know. We never talked about it."

She shoots me a look and nods sagely, "I have a hard time believing he'd stay at our place to sleep alone when," she pauses meaningfully, "there are other options."

"EVELYN!"

"You know, dear, I was young once too. And just because I'm old doesn't mean I don't recall the meaning of fun."

"Don't you have some work to do or something?"

"Actually, I do. But watching you squirm and blush is entertaining."

"Out, Evelyn!" I point to the door. I'll positively die of embarrassment if she keeps talking like this to me.

"Okay, I can take a hint." Winking, she leaves and I sit down again at my desk to fritter away another unproductive hour glowing in the aftermath of my first show ever and thinking of next weekend with Todd.

A small metallic chime signals a new e-mail and I read the subject line, "Congratulations." It's from my mom. I open it, ready to bask in her approval and praise:

> Dear Sadie,
> Jane told me last night about your exciting news. How very proud I am of you to become the new district manager of Coddled Cuisine. I'm sure you'll do a

fabulous job and discover every sort of success in this new venture.
Love, Mom

I file her message, disappointed. Coddled Cuisine disappeared from my memory in the past couple hours of my life. In fact, I don't even know that I want to keep doing it if I have an exciting new career as show host ahead of me. I return half-heartedly to search for a guest to discuss the newest low-carb diet craze. Scrolling down the page, I reject hit after hit when the phone rings. "Hello, Sadie Davis here."

"I heard a familiar voice this morning!"

Jane! "Did you hear my show?"

"Honey, we all did! Erich called me on his way to work this morning, so the kids and I tuned in. The kids got to school late today. I told the school secretary that their aunt was making an important guest celebrity appearance and they didn't want to miss it."

"You did not."

"Did so. In fact, she mentioned something about getting your autograph."

"Funny. You are very, very funny. So, how was I?" Jane will give me an honest assessment. Okay, slightly biased as she despises Dean as much as I do, but who cares?

"Not bad, not bad at all."

"Better than the, er, the current host?"

"I think Olivia's pet rabbit could outdo Dean on the microphone."

"Good point."

"No honey, you were very good. I could tell at the beginning you were a little nervous, but that's probably just because I know you so well. I'm sure no one else could tell. You knew your subject well—that was obvious."

"I hope Ron thinks I did all right."

"How can't he? Besides, wouldn't you think it's a huge vote of confidence that he had you do the show? Anyway, why *did* you do the show today?"

"Apparently Dean's in the middle of some sort of family crisis. I'm not exactly sure what. Ron just sprung this on me this morning."

"I wondered why I hadn't gotten a phone call from you telling me to tune in."

"It all happened so fast."

"Will you be doing Monday's show?"

"I don't know, I really don't know. I haven't even talked to Ron since I got off-air. Damn, it feels so cool to say that!"

Jane laughs. "I'll have to hold an intervention when you start talking about the size of your trailer and needing fresh Beluga every day."

My first fan phone call is interrupted by Ron appearing in my doorway like a scary little shadow. "I have to go. I'll call you later, okay?"

"Okay. Congratulations again, Sadie."

"Thanks."

I offer up an explanation after I hang up. "My sister. She heard me on the radio this morning and wanted to congratulate me."

"That's nice. Okay, next week's line-up looks pretty good. I want to go over the Pakistan one with you later today to clarify a few things."

"All right. Did you have a specific time in mind?"

"Stop by my office when you see the door open." He pauses a moment. "Not a bad job this morning, Sadie. You did well pinch hitting for us today." Without further comment he turns and leaves. I guess I'll have to accept that as high praise. I've never received anything more complimentary than that from him before, anyway.

At lunch it feels very unglamorous to haul my five loads of laundry into Kleen Korner Laundromat. I plug the machines with quarters, punching the metal sleeves to start the cycles. I try to think of a single virtue of using a laundromat instead of having my own laundry room— the only thing I can come up with is running as many loads as I want at once, rather than having to change loads in and out of one machine. I guess, in a way this is a time saver, but I look around at the orange plastic chairs and the positively grimy looking stacks of magazines laying about. The ambience is definitely lacking. The only other person in here is a college kid, dressed in plaid tight jeans and sporting a frizzled goatee—maybe he's Francis's younger brother. I call Molly while I wait to move everything to the dryers.

She picks up on the third ring. "I have class in about twenty minutes. I just finished lunch and I'm about to head over there. What's up?" Papers shuffle and a door slams in the background.

"Guess who got to host *Idea Exchange* this morning?" I ask, grinning.

"Someone other than Dean LaCockroach?"

"Someone like me!" I stack my quarters for the dryers on the table in front of me.

"No way! Fantastic! How did that happen? What was your topic? How did it go?"

The beauty of an intellectual pal like Molly is getting to talk about my job in a meaningful way. I have her full attention while I describe the day's events and tell her every detail about the show.

"Sadie, that's fabulous. Hopefully Ron will mine your talent and replace that automaton behind the microphone. I've got to go to class now, but let's get together to celebrate."

"I'd love that, not that I necessarily need a special occasion to go out or anything."

"How does tomorrow night work for you?"

"Great."

"How about Bluephies at seven? I'll call Kara, too."

"Perfect."

After I hang up, I start removing my wet clothes from the washing machines when two women and five young children come in and take over the laundromat as if it's their living room. I trip four times over the same wagon full of toys as I make my way between the line of washing machines and the wall of dryers. I barely have the last washing machine lid shut when one of the women grabs it and slams it open to stuff it full of her clothes. Thank God I'm half done or I'd go crazy sharing this space with these people!

I sit down across from my dryers and try to concentrate on my good morning, Todd's visit, and how soon until

I can afford a condo with my own washer and dryer. Who cares how many times I'd have to go and change loads—at least I'd be in the privacy of my own space and not have to share my time with strangers. One of the boys pelts me in the head with some sort of foam missile and it takes all my restraint not to chuck it back at him. Instead, I remove the projectile from my hair and force a smile at him. "Here you go. Be careful next time, you could really hurt someone."

The women ignore me. They're busy watching Ellen DeGeneres on the television mounted and chained to the back wall. Goatee guy stuffs the last of his wardrobe into a huge military issue duffel and tosses it onto his shoulder in one smooth motion. He steps over the wagon and through the two boys playing war and pauses while pushing open the glass door leading out to the street. The look he sends me is a mixture of sympathy and what I believe is pity. I nod miserably in response.

# Chapter Thirty-Six

**"Self-employment offers many benefits"**
*—Coddled Cuisine recruitment brochure*

Saturday night I arrive at Bluephies and easily find Molly and Kara among the other customers. Seven is early by Madison standards, people don't usually go out for dinner until eight. "Hey, ladies!"

"Hey, Sadie Davis, girl talk show host!" Kara greets me with a wave.

"Where's Elizabeth tonight?"

"She's visiting her parents this weekend. Last minute sort of thing. She found a ticket online for three-hundred dollars and decided to go." Kara shrugs at this. As far as I know, Kara's never met Elizabeth's family. I don't know if there is any openness about their relationship or not, and I've never asked about it.

"Do they know about you and her?" I ask.

"Actually, they do. I met them about a year and a half ago, fantastic people. She comes from a very classically upper middle-class household. They golf. They eat at their country club every Friday night. They think it's cute that we're gay." She rolls her eyes and laughs. Only to Kara is people's social status immediately visible. She could write a book on the subject—she claims it's a gift, like knowing if a person's straight or gay.

"I see. So, you're single this weekend?"

"Yep, wearing nothing but my underwear while I sit on my couch belching and scratching myself."

Molly laughs. "Is that how you do it? I always thought you had to wear a stained T-shirt with a beer logo across the chest."

"That's just when company comes over."

The waitress comes to take my order and I survey the table to see where we're at tonight. Wine, cocktail, "I'll have a vodka tonic please, with a lemon."

As the waitress leaves, I look at Molly, no lipstick and wearing her glasses. "Where's Francis tonight?"

Kara widens her eyes at me and I sense her trying unsuccessfully to send me a mental message. Molly looks down at her drink and swishes the straw in little circles, making the soda fizz in bubbles to the surface before popping. I sneak a look at Kara and widen my eyes. How am I supposed to know what's going on with Francis?

"Do you want to tell her, or should I?" Kara finally says.

"I don't care. I can tell her."

"Tell me what?" I look from Kara's probing expression to Molly's which is unreadable since she's still staring at her drink. Kara shakes her head and sighs. "Apparently Francis is a fraud."

"Don't say it like that."

"What would you call it then?" Kara asks Molly. "He's a high school dropout from Lomira, working as a barista to support his girlfriend and their two kids. He's never been out of Wisconsin, to anyone's knowledge, and his sole claim to fame is holding down a job at McDonald's for five whole months before getting fired for stealing from the cash register."

"Molly! Is this true?"

Still looking down, she nods.

I repress an inexplicable urge to giggle at this story, it's so ridiculous. "How did you find this out? I mean, when did this happen? I had no idea!"

Kara looks again at Molly. "Do you want to tell her, or should I?

"You seem to be doing a fine job, don't let me stop you."

"I don't want you pissed at me."

I look from Kara to Molly. Would one of them just finish the damn story and stop letting me hang in the middle?

After a minute of silence, the waitress appears with my drink. When she leaves I speak up. "Someone should tell me the rest of the story. I feel like I got to watch the first half of a movie and then the projector broke."

"Okay, I'll tell her." Molly glares at Kara before turning to look at me. "I was talking with one of my students after class the other day about this coffee shop. I said I'd been there before and that I was going out with the new manager. She asked if it was Francis Mohen and I told her it was. Then she told me he was from her hometown. Apparently, he was in her graduating class and she told me she hadn't known he had broken up with his girlfriend. She asked which of them had the kids. I told her I didn't know about a girlfriend and kids. It turns out he got his girlfriend pregnant his senior year, dropped out of high school, and has held down a string of part-time jobs ever since. I guess he's been posing as a student for the last couple of years. Becky, she's my grad student, ran into him at a party and thought it was weird when one of her friends referred to him as a psych major since she knew he hadn't even completed his GED. So she asked around and learned that he just shows up at all the college parties and acts like he goes to school over at Edgewood."

"No way!" I'm completely shocked by this.

"So anyway, Becky tells me that his girlfriend and he were just together a month ago at a bar in downtown Lomira when she went home for spring break. I thought that we were together a month ago over spring break. To make a long story short, I went to the coffee shop and asked him if any of this was true. I knew it was, but I wanted to see his face and hear what he had to say about it in person."

"And?" I glance at Kara, who is nodding along with the entire story as if she'd authored it herself.

"At first he denied it. Then he started crying and carrying on, saying when he met me he just couldn't help himself. He wanted to be the sort of person he knew I'd fall in love with, which is why he lied." Molly trails off dully and takes a huge swallow of her beer.

"This is like a bad movie on *Lifetime*! What a total jack-ass!" I exclaim.

"Yep. I pick 'em, don't I?" Molly's expression is grim and I have to agree with her. First Scott and then Francis; she's so unlucky with love that I cringe thinking about it.

"Now what?"

"I feel like an idiot. Like the last time. I'm grateful that I didn't bring him to any of Kara's dinner parties or introduce him to Ben."

"Why's that?"

"I know Ben thinks I'm a huge freak. He'd laugh his ass off if he had met Francis and then heard about this."

"Molly," Kara begins and Molly shakes her head at her.

"Molly." This time she looks up at me. "We don't think you're a freak. Anyone can be lied to. Besides, look at me! I seem to recall a date I went on not so long ago when the guy ended up in the arms of the guy intended for you!"

She starts to smile, then her mouth gets a little wider and her shoulders start shaking up and down underneath her peasant blouse. Finally, the laughter takes over. "You know, you're absolutely right! You're as much a loser as me! And that was almost all Kara's fault!"

Kara sits back and shakes her head, rolling her eyes. "You two are the worst leeches I've ever met. Taking advantage of your friend in crisis…"

Molly wipes the tears from the corners of her eyes, takes off her glasses and sets them next to her drink. "I'm sorry, the whole situation *is* quite funny. I mean, have you ever known two straight women with such bad luck? It's enough to make a girl start to think—" She looks around the bar and Kara holds up her hand.

"Don't even think it. Don't say it and don't think it."

We're still giggling over Francis and Adam and Scott, and after five drinks and a delicious black bean and goat cheese enchilada, I tell them about Henry and his fiancé and the Coddled Cuisine party. We're roaring, sloppy drunk. Bluephies is crowded with women who cannot possibly appreciate the plight of the straight gal, with the exception of a few straight couples who maybe can, when Ben shows up, freshly showered and looking tired around the eyes.

"Ladies, can I join your party? Although I think I've got some catching up to do before I'm at the same point as you." He points at our empty glasses crowding the table.

"Ben!" I stand, flinging my arms around his neck. "The one bad man we can accept into our company!"

"To Ben!" Kara raises her wineglass in salute and Molly toasts him, too.

"Well, this was worth coming down for." He grins and gestures for the waitress. "I'll have a gin martini, and can you please clear some of this away?"

The waitress obliges while he pulls up a spare chair and leans forward, elbows splayed across the table. "What's new tonight?"

"Did you do it?"

"Do what?" I ask Kara. What on earth is she talking about? I look over at Ben, who frowns and shakes his head.

"What? I'm just asking."

"It's done."

"What's done?" I hate feeling left out, like there's a whole conversation going on over and above me that I'm not good enough to be let in on.

"Nothing," Ben says curtly.

"He had Francis fired." Kara announces this with a triumphant smile.

"What?" Molly nearly tips her glass over as she looks from one to the other in shock.

"Ben knows the owner and he talked with her and had Francis fired."

"Well—you can't just do that!" Molly sputters. "I mean, he's a jerk and everything, but you can't just fire someone for *that*."

"You're right, you can't," Ben agrees.

"Well then…Why?"

"Evidently there's been money missing from the till. And with a more complete understanding of his employment history, it was easy enough to make the connections."

"But, Ben! He has two kids! He can't get fired! How will he feed them?"

Ben looks at Molly in amazement. "I thought this would make you happy."

"Well, it doesn't. I mean, just because he's a total rat doesn't mean he deserves to get fired!"

"He's also a thief," Ben says quietly. "I think it's fair for Joanie to fire him for that."

Molly shakes her head fiercely. "You know what? Do me a huge favor, just stay out of my business in the future." She stands unsteadily and narrows her eyes at us.

"Excuse me." She heads for the ladies' room as I watch Ben and Kara look at each other in dismay.

"What!?" Again, this feeling of being completely left out.

"Nothing." Ben shakes his head and the waitress appears with our round of drinks. He pulls out his wallet and hands her a twenty. "Keep it."

"Thanks!"

Taking a huge swallow from his martini, Ben looks at the glass thoughtfully and then sets it down and runs both hands through his hair, rumpling it along the way. "Women! Can't live with them and can't leave them by the curb."

"Well, technically you can," I tell him.

"Huh?"

"You let me live with you once. That proves you can live with them," I remind him. "Don't mind Molly, she's just very sensitive." I always feel like a bridge between them. Ben's so shallow and handsome and male while Molly is so deep and profound and just everything opposite. I don't even think they'd be at the same table if it weren't for me.

"She'll be fine," Kara agrees. "God, I think I'm actually getting drunk tonight!"

I burst out laughing—I'm right there with her.

When Molly returns from the bathroom, a tense but acceptable peace resumes at our table. We switch gears from talking about men and love and sex to discussing important issues, like how Ben's new cook is working out, my hopes to replace Dean on *Idea Exchange*, and what the hell the chick with the green hair is thinking, wearing clogs with five-inch heels like that.

At bar time I stumble out behind Kara and she flags down a cab. I'll stay with her tonight—the guest bedroom there is nicer than my own bedroom at my place. In the messy hustle of the crowd, we lose sight of Molly. I'll call her in the morning. She'll be fine.

"To the condo!" Kara cries after we collapse in the back seat of the cab.

"To the condo!" I echo, and we giggle again at the hysteria of it all.

# Chapter Thirty-Seven

**"It's great to have a second career"**
*—Coddled Cuisine recruitment brochure*

On Monday, Dean's sitting in his chair, looking healthy and capable. Clearly my hopes were high and a dull ache in my gut spreads and clenches tightly. "Good morning, Dean."

"I hear you filled in as substitute for me on Friday. Good for you to take a shot at the mike. Not as easy as it looks, is it?"

"No, no it's not." I mumble and drag out the introductory information on Judge Erikson.

"I hope everything's okay with your family." I say this more out of politeness than actually caring about his personal life.

"My sister had surgery on Friday. She went into labor a month early. I went to the hospital to take a look at my new nephew."

"I didn't know you had a sister." This information makes Dean seem slightly more human, tolerable even. "Is everyone healthy?"

"An eight pounder, big boy. Can't believe she squeezed it out."

"What did she name him?"

"Skyler Dean Hennes. The Dean part is after me, his godfather."

Oh brother. "Okay, today's show is about alternative sentencing. Judge Erikson is from Dane County and has twenty years of experience."

The show actually goes fine, which pisses me off. I fantasized that Dean would completely screw it up and Ron would come running to beg me to take over his job. But of course, no such luck. At my desk I try to bend my brain around some happy thoughts to get out of my funk. Todd's upcoming visit cheers me up enough to look over a pile of messages to return, including two from Dean marked "urgent," which he had no problem forgetting to tell me about when we were together for the past two hours.

Todd's coming to town Thursday night. I have to take Friday off. I'm the new district manager of Coddled Cuisine. These are good things. I should feel happy.

In the afternoon I meet with Dean to go over tomorrow's program. "Dean, you sent me two e-mails labeled "urgent" and said to call you back. I didn't find attachments or anything, so I'm sort of at a loss to know what was so urgent—"

My inquiry is rewarded with a classically blank expression and a shrug. "No idea. Nope, sorry. Okay then, tomorrow's show is on tribal gambling. What's the spin on it? How to beat the odds at the slots?"

"No. It's how the gambling contracts should be negotiated, by the governor or the entire legislature. What the current limits of power are and what can we hope to retain, lose, or gain in future gaming agreements."

"Am I talking to one of the Indians? A chief?"

"Um, no. You'll be discussing this with Dr. Flankston, a professor of Indian affairs and political science at UW."

"I think it'd be more fun to talk to one of the Indians. You know, ask them how they rig the slots to never pay out. How many busses of old people come through in a week. A real behind-the-scenes look at the casino business."

Breathe in, breath out. Patience, Sadie, patience. "That is an interesting concept, but we're committed to Dr. Flankston and the current agenda for tomorrow's show." *Never mind that this is* Idea Exchange, *not some stupid tabloid show. Never mind that you have done absolutely zero of the prep work for this to happen, asshole. It's so easy to change the whole show when you have not a shred of a clue of how of create one. It's so easy to judge my work when you've never tried it your-self.* "Maybe you can line up a guest for a future show to discuss that."

"I thought that was your job."

"Well it is, but—" I see where this is headed. "I'll look into it."

"Good. Okay then, gaming is the topic for tomorrow. Dr. Flagship."

"Dr. Flankston." It's going to be a long afternoon.

# Chapter Thirty-Eight

**"Coddled Cuisine offers their
consultants many benefits"**
*—Coddled Cuisine recruitment brochure*

A. Martinson's mailbox label has changed. It now reads
D. Angeleaux. Hmmm. Hadn't realized he moved.
Maybe he moved in with Irving, the accountant. I pull a
huge envelope out of my mailbox and look at the return
address: Coddled Cuisine. Upstairs, I rip into it before
I even kick my shoes off. A stack of summer catalogs
and several sheets of perforated recipe cards fall into my
lap. The letter welcomes me as a new member of the
Coddled Cuisine team and outlines some of the benefits
I'll receive as district manager. I look at the attached
check. I'm getting paid already? I haven't done anything
yet! The next page offers up the biggest surprise: gift
cards for nationally franchised stores.

> Our gift to you.
> Coddle yourself so you can coddle others.

Wow! My mood rises at this unexpected bonus.

After feasting on microwave pepperoni Pizza Rolls and diet soda, I hunker down to write my first official correspondence as Coddled Cuisine district manager.

> Due to the sudden departure of our district manager, Kimberly Carlyle...

I lean back to savor my tact and diplomacy.

> It is with great excitement that I step into her shoes as district manager for Coddled Cuisine.
> To discuss June's agenda, I invite you to Fifteen Orchard Avenue Madison, Wisconsin at seven o'clock on Wednesday, June Eighth.

Okay, what else? Parking.

> Since I live downtown, parking is some-times difficult. You'll find two public ramps within walking distance. Otherwise you may get fortunate enough to find a spot on the street.

Including a map of the area might be a good idea.

> Please call me at 555-1707 with questions.
> I look forward to seeing you on the eighth!
> Sadie Davis.

Now I only have to figure out what I'm supposed to discuss. I fold the letter and put it in my purse to type up at work and notice the blinking red light on my answering machine. I push play, hoping it's not Todd calling to cancel this weekend.

"Sadie? This is Molly. Call me when you get home." Her voice sounds choked. I hear the rest of my messages before returning her call.

"This is Coreen Nesblum." A sing-song voice fills the room. "I was at Evelyn's Coddled Cuisine party and I'd like to book one of my own. My number is 555-1626." Now that's a good message.

"Sadie, this is Mom. Jane told me about your show on Friday. How lovely for you! Call me back and tell me all about it."

I call Coreen and book a show for early June, happy to see my side job is living up to its promise of at least one show a week. Then I dial Molly's number. "Molly?"

"Can we get together sometime this week?" She sounds odd, not sad but very strange.

"Sure, what's up?"

"Nothing to worry about, I just want to talk to you about something. It's nothing bad."

"How does tomorrow night look?"

"Let's meet at Kabul at six."

Kabul of spilled food and Adam Martinson. Why not? "Perfect. See you then."

After I hang up with her the phone rings again.

"Sadie, this is Gretchen Vosters. I have a favor to ask of you."

"Sure, Gretchen, what is it?" I scrunch up my face in an effort to place her, one of the two middle-aged women who sell Coddled Cuisine.

"I took over the bulk of Kimberly's parties but something came up and I can't do the one next Monday night. Any chance you're free?"

"I'd be happy to do it."

"Super." She gives me the address and phone number of the hostess and I thank her three times before getting off the phone. "Sadie, get over it. We do this all the time. Believe me, I'll return the favor soon enough."

Amazing how a person's mood can shift so quickly from funky to good again. I whistle while I get ready for bed, scrub my face (still pale from Saturday night's excesses) and slip into pajamas. The sky is still bright when I turn on the TV and snuggle down into my couch. I should take a walk or do something outside to celebrate this warmer weather, but right now it's enough to just sit here, letting Todd and Coddled Cuisine take over my brainwaves. Tomorrow I'll exercise, clean my apartment, and shop for groceries. Tonight, I'll just finish my recovery and rest my still-achy muscles.

# Chapter Thirty-Nine

**"Consultants avoid office politics
by working from home"**
*—Coddled Cuisine recruitment brochure*

First thing after the show I put in my request for Friday off. I'm breathing regularly now, thanks to the guest who took over the program and answered the callers' questions without giving Dean much chance to editorialize on-air. He still kept trying to change the direction of the intended conversation, asking Dr. Flankston if he *really* thought the tribes were profiting in gaming and whether he could offer up any tips on how gamblers could beat the odds. Dean's always been a closet conspiracy theorist. Dr. Flankston was appropriately gracious and charming and deflected his questions with finesse. I want to call him after the show to apologize for Dean.

Ron waves me into his office with his free hand, gripping the telephone receiver to his ear with the other. "Yah, yah, yah, that sounds great. I'll get back to you on that. Listen, someone's in my office just now. We'll talk more later." He hangs up and looks at me. "Sadie?"

"Ron, I need to take Friday off."

"Who do you have booked as a guest?"

"A political scientist from the Capitol. He's supposed to talk about reinstituting the draft."

"Do you think this is something Dean can handle alone?"

"I normally prepare the questions very thoroughly, and Andrew has been on other programs before, so he is an old pro at the interview scene."

"Any chance you can book him for a different date?"

"I guess so. What would we do instead? Rerun a program?"

"Let's switch our June call-in date with this guy."

"I guess we can do that. I'll call Andrew and see if it'll work."

I turn to leave when Ron calls me back. I look at him and see he's scowling.

"Are you happy working with Dean?"

My chance. My big opportunity to level with Ron. This could be damaging or save me from further frustration. If I say I'm happy, I stay in the same spot I've been in for the last two years. If I say I'd like a change, maybe he has a different job for me. Maybe he's looking for a new show host! What do I do? "Ron, to be frank, he's not exactly the easiest to work with." I decide to go all out. "It was actually easier to host the show myself the other day."

"I see. You can go now."

What just happened? I feel less confident the more I think about it and by lunchtime my stomach is churning with the possibility that I might get fired. I should've told him I was happy. I should've said all good things. Damn it. Why can't I just keep my big stupid mouth shut?

I find Evelyn in the break room eating lunch with Delaine. "Hi, girls."

Evelyn smiles warmly at me while Delaine mumbles a greeting around a bite of her sandwich.

"I understand Todd's coming to town on Friday night. Any chance I'll get to see my favorite nephew?"

"I don't see why not. What do you and Dan have going on this weekend?"

"Not much. We're having dinner with some friends on Friday night. Would you like to drop by on Saturday sometime? We could grill out or something."

"I'd like that. He will, too." It'll be weird but nice to get together with another couple. This is what couples do. It makes you official in your togetherness and it gives you a chance to sort of compare your relationship to someone else's. Besides, I'm not exactly sure Todd is ready for a night out with Kara and Elizabeth and I don't know too many other couples of the unmarried sort.

"Great. Let's plan on four on Saturday, give me a call if that won't work out. Dan and I will both be anxious to hear how his interview goes, anyway."

"What interview?"

Delaine is now looking from Evelyn to me with an expression of pure confusion. "Who is Todd?"

"My nephew. I set him and Sadie up on a blind date a month or so ago."

"Really? What's he like?" Delaine bites another chunk off of her sandwich and looks at me longingly. I realized long ago how my single status makes me fascinating to those who have been married for decades. They get to live vicariously through me. Only the trouble is I don't give them a whole lot to work with—my love life is usually about as barren as the Sahara.

"He roller skates and does magic tricks. He prefers the company of older women, enjoys a stiff drink, and playing *Ms. Pac-Man*." I smile and add, "Good sense of humor, too."

"And otherwise?" Delaine prompts with unabashed curiosity and I blush dark red mostly because Evelyn is sitting right there.

"What do you mean?" I ask.

For two old women, Delaine and Evelyn can give the nastiest laughs I've ever heard. I'm no prude, but their minds are beyond the deepest sewers. "A blushing girl who refuses to dish details. I think your nephew is doing just fine where it matters, Evelyn."

"I'm assuming it's the O'Leary side of the family that gives him such gifts!" Evelyn brags back to her.

"Enough, you two." I'm beginning to wish I'd stayed in my office for lunch.

When they calm down, Evelyn gets serious again. "Did you hear about Bernadette?"

"What about her?"

Delaine's nodding along so I assume she already knows what Evelyn is about to tell me. "Jill Carlson is leaving."

Jill is Bernadette's on-air producer. Basically, she does for Bernadette what I do for Dean, but on an entirely different level. For one thing, it's a collaborative position. Bernadette suggests ideas for shows and does a lot of the leg work preparing for the programs herself. I've never heard of Jill having to write out entire lists of questions for the show or tutor Bernadette on current affairs. "Where's she going?" I can't imagine anywhere more desirable than where she is right now.

"Her husband got a job with Boston College, they're moving out there this summer after he finishes his classes here."

"Even more exciting, I guess she's got some choice job interviews lined up out there already. Apparently she knows someone who knows Dick Gordon," Delaine chimes in.

"Shut up!" This is unbelievable.

"I know."

"So who's taking over for Jill?" The beginning of a tiny flame of hope warms the center of my chest. "Are they posting the job?"

"I know Bernadette has talked with Ron since Jill made her announcement yesterday and I have it on pretty good authority that she has someone in mind to replace her."

"Who?" Oh God, please, please, please, let it be *me*. To work alongside someone as classy and intelligent and *wonderful* as Bernadette would be—

Evelyn answers my question with a wink and a tiny smile. "I'm not at liberty to say just yet."

"Really." I half-whisper this.

Delaine grins and Evelyn nods her head. Maybe I didn't royally screw up my future at the station after all. I wanted to tell Evelyn all about my conversation with Ron, but now it feels presumptuous and sort of embarrassing to bring it up at all, so I don't. Instead I smile and go over to the vending machine to buy a bag of microwave popcorn and diet soda for lunch. To get pulled from Dean's show to work for Bernadette's! Not only would that be incredible, it would prove what an incompetent jackass Dean is when they try to find someone to replace me! It's really hard to suppress the urge to giggle and skip all the way back to my office.

I'm sitting at a side table in Kabul when Molly shows up, wearing her contacts and lipstick. I can't shake the foreboding that she is back with Francis, if only to irritate Ben. She smiles and waves as she crosses the restaurant.

"What's up?" I ask her after I settle into the seat across from her.

"I should ask you that question first. *You* have a twinkle in your eye."

"I can't help it." I burst out with every detail about my meeting with Ron and what I learned from Evelyn at lunch. "I know it's premature, but I really can't imagine who she could pick to replace Jill. I always thought she liked me and it would be an absolute dream to work on her show."

"That'd be great." Molly's face is serious. "But what if, and I'm only trying to prepare you for the worst, what if she has someone else in mind?"

"Who else could it possibly be though?" The thought hadn't occurred to me. Molly isn't an unfaithful friend, but sometimes her realism really pisses me off.

"I don't know. I'd hate to see you get your hopes up and then have it not work out, that's all."

"I know," I mutter bitterly. "I'm just so sick and tired of holding Dean's paw and pulling him along."

"I know. I hope it's you. You completely deserve it."

"Thanks."

We're silent for a minute while she swirls the ice in her water glass. I feel mutinous and guilty for feeling mutinous towards her at the same time. Then I remember.

"What did you want to talk to me about?"

Silence. She drinks out of her water glass and looks at me, out the window, and back at me again. "I don't really know how to tell you this," she begins.

"Listen, if it's about getting back together with Francis, I'm not going to judge you."

"No." She smiles. "It's not that. God, what kind of an idiot do you think I am? I'm a little pathetic, but I didn't think I was that bad."

"Oh, I'm sorry. I just thought—"

"It's about Ben."

I knew it. I'm going to have to choose between them. I'll just keep them separate as friends. How often are the four of us really together anyway?

"We slept together Saturday night."

I drop my water glass with a cold and wet thud and the wetness streams off the table and soaks my lap while I absorb this shocking bit of news.

"*You what?*" My voice is screechy and I clear my throat. "I mean, come again?"

Her words rush out at me in a flood. "He drove me back to his place at bar time. I came out of the bathroom and you and Kara must've already left. I don't know, it was really crowded and he offered me a drive home. When we reached his place I turned to ask him if he forgot where I lived. Then he parked the car, turned to me and told me he was sorry about Francis and everything, but he only did it because he loves me. And then he leaned over and kissed me. And, well, one thing led to another and before I knew it I was laying on his bed. Where many women have gone before." She cringes. "And it was the most amazing sex I think I've ever had."

"Holy shit!"

"I know."

The waiter comes to mop up the water from the table and replace my water glass, giving me time to construct what I hope is a sensitive response before I speak again.

"So is this a one-time thing or…"

"I don't think so."

"Really? Ben is the king of the pigpen, the most repulsive ladies' man around. You hold him in the lowest levels of contempt. What makes you say that?" I pat myself on the back mentally for such a diplomatic response.

She smiles for a few seconds before continuing. "As it happens, there have been a number of misunderstandings in the past. A lot of his mocking has come from his insecurity around me. A lot of the women he's brought around have been mostly for show, to maintain his image."

"What about the one he brought to Kara's dinner party?"

"Rhonda? That was their last date I guess. He hasn't gone out with anyone since that night." Molly shrugs.

"I'm happy for you. I think. You're really positive this wasn't just Ben getting himself a piece of ass with you because all the other women around were gay?"

"Sadie!"

"Just kidding. Kind of."

"I know it's weird, but it really feels right. I don't know how else to explain it. And I wanted you to know first out of anybody else since you did introduce us, technically, and you are one of my closest friends."

"Molly, I'm truly happy for you! I am. I hope it works out exactly the way you want. My two buddies, together as a couple. I'm not sure how I feel about this, but I'm sure I'll get used to it over time." A pang of loneliness strikes me. I'm the last single person standing if this thing with Todd doesn't work out. And I don't want to make it work out just so I'm not alone. "I'm just miserably jealous right now. You still have to dish, even though I know him."

"Are you sure? I don't want you to be uncomfortable."

"It's Ben, Molly. Anyone else I admit I'd be uncomfortable. But it's Ben. So dish."

# Chapter Forty

**"Read how Coddled Cuisine has
helped make dreams come true"**
*—Coddled Cuisine recruitment brochure*

By Thursday I'm completely on edge, anxious to see
Todd, nervous and impatient to hear about Bernadette's
new on-air producer, and so damn weary of Dean being
such a pompous ass. At the end of the show he turns to
me. "I guess I'll see you tomorrow."

"Monday."

"Excuse me?"

"You'll see me on Monday. I'm taking tomorrow off.
I've told you that every day this week. You're doing the
June call-in show tomorrow."

"Monday then." He snaps before stomping off in
the direction of Ron's office and I head to the ladies'
room. Looking in the mirror I run down my to-do list.
I scheduled a haircut at noon and I've perfumed and
powdered and prettied myself to the best of my ability.
My apartment's spotless, and I discreetly stowed all

embarrassing feminine hygiene products, and double-checked my bedroom for dirty underwear or anything else that would make me look weird or strange to Todd. I'm so nervous I could puke. Nervous and excited. This weekend will show where we're headed—if anywhere—together. I tell my reflection, "Girl, just get him."

Back at my desk I check the local news. The Carlyles have been pushed into the back pages of the newspapers by now, but they're still at large. The accountants and federal authorities announced an estimate of their haul, about eight million bucks. It's chilling to think I sat in the home of such evil, greedy people.

Just when I'm about to print out my Coddled Cuisine invitations, Ron appears in my doorway. "Got a minute?"

"What's up?" I minimize the file so he can't see I'm doing one company's work on another company's time.

"We have to discuss something. Come with me to the conference room."

The conference room is used primarily for firing, interviewing, and the occasional large staff meeting. A dusty space monopolized by a huge oval table and gigantic wheeled office chairs, all nicer than the ones we sit on every day—an arrangement that has never made any sense to me. I follow Ron down the hall, perspiration cold and clammy in my armpits. I fear the worst.

He gestures for me to sit next to him and then wraps his gnarled fingers together on the table before him. "As you know, we're doing some restructuring around here."

"Uh-huh."

He looks at the clock and then at the door where Bernadette appears on cue. "Hi, Ron. Hi, Sadie." She sits on the other side of Ron and smiles at me. "Sorry I'm late."

"No problem. We just started. As I was saying, we're making a few staffing changes and within this we have an opportunity for you, Sadie."

Is this it?

"As you've heard, Bernadette's on-air producer, Jill, is leaving us. We need to replace this position urgently, as Bernadette's show is one of our better-rated slots. It's also a two-hour slot, as opposed to the one-hour *Idea Exchange* gets. The focus of the shows is completely different as well. *Idea Exchange* is generally about local and state issues, while Bernadette's show encompasses the arts, politics, and general popular culture. We'd like to offer you Jill's position—"

"Yes!"

"But you'll need to understand—"

Bernadette beams at me and I feel like I'm in the presence of my very own elegant and sophisticated fairy godmother. "I'd feel privileged to work on this show."

"The pay cut won't be an issue then?"

I gawk at him, blood racing from my head. My salary already has to be supplemented by Coddled Cuisine! Then Ron's lips stretch in what first appears as a grimace until I realize this is his attempt at humor. Relaxing, I nod. "Shouldn't be too much of an issue, I hope."

"Actually, you'll stand to make more than you do now." Ron pulls out a tattered calendar. "I have to find your replacement for *Idea Exchange*, so you can't start until that takes place. Fortunately, Jill gave us a month's notice, so we have some time to do that. I'll let you and Bernadette hash out the details and I'll talk to Dean."

"Thank you so much!" I stand and shake Ron's right hand vigorously. "I look forward to doing this. I really do."

Ron nods and grunts twice before pulling his hand back and heading out the door. I turn to look at Bernadette. "I'm so excited to work with you!"

"Me too. This will be an excellent match."

I'm floating by her confident praise.


Glorious Friday, at last! I wake up to sunshine and immediately begin the anxious fussing around my apartment. I soak long in the tub and my face tightens under a mud mask. Nothing will go wrong this weekend because I am a woman who prepared.

Later I wipe steam off the bathroom mirror and am gratified to see only one very small red blemish on my face. It's by my hairline so it's hardly noticeable.

In the grocery store I carefully double-check my shopping list. I've selected some of the recipes from *Coddled Cuisine's Best of 2010* cookbook, one of Kimberly's leftovers. Appetizers seem romantic, so I'm going with the Cheesy Crab Canapés once more. A smothered steak recipe alongside a salad and a really nice loaf of bread, topped off with a triple-berry shortcake for dessert. If the way to a man's heart is through his stomach, Todd MacGynn better look out—I've got all the tools the experts use! Egg casserole for breakfast Saturday, then we'll go out for lunch, and to Evelyn's for dinner where I'll bring Coddled Cuisine's Sensational Spuds and Six-

Layer Summer Salad. At the check-out the total is more than my grocery bill for an entire month, but I can write most of it off as cooking practice.

Four hours later my phone rings. It's Todd.

"I'm coming into Madison right now and there's some accident up ahead. I'm about a half mile south of the highway eighteen exit. Should I try to get off there?"

"Yeah." I direct him to downtown and glance at the clock. He'll be here in about a half hour and my kitchen is trashed. I hang up with him and continue washing my way through the piles of dishes. This is why I'd rather eat out. I can never anticipate the mess cooking will make and I hate having to clean it up. Empty cartons and bags litter the floor. My wastebasket has more volume in it than the serving dishes stacked in the fridge.

I'm tying off the top of a garbage bag when the buzzer goes off. What the hell? It's only been twenty minutes! I push my hair out of my eyes and head to the intercom.

"Hello?" Please be a neighbor, mailman, anyone but Todd!

"I'm here! Found a shortcut!" Todd's voice announces triumphantly.

"Great, come right up. Take the stairs on the left."

Running to the bathroom, I repair the damage a hot, sweaty kitchen has done to both my hair and make-up and I flip my shirt off and stuff it into the hamper. Pulling on a clean shirt, I notice it's inside out. My heart is racing. I inhale deeply to calm down. I put the shirt over my head and go back to the mirror to fix my hair again. Will he still be sexy and wonderful? Sometimes when you see a person again in familiar turf all the magic disappears. I worry. A knock at the door interrupts my sudden panic. I'm unreasonably pissed at him. It's not his fault that he's here on time. It's my fault for never being able to get my act together. I breathe deeply and open the door.

"Sadie, you look fantastic! What smells so good?" Todd leans forward and inhales deeply while handing me a bouquet of daisies wrapped in polka-dotted paper.

"Come in. I just got done making dinner. Thanks, I'll find a vase for these."

"Home cooking? Wow, if I knew you could cook I'd have visited sooner."

Todd stands in the middle of my living room and suddenly seems larger than life. The room shrinks around his broad shoulders and blazing goatee. I look at his scuffed work boots and well-traveled duffel and I know for certain that I want this to work.

Dragging me into his arms, he presses his lips against mine and I know perfect longing and contentment in the same instant.

After gorging ourselves on steak, bread, and generous helpings of shortcake, Todd leans back and stretches his arms wide. "I haven't felt this stuffed since Thanksgiving last year."

"Whose cooking was responsible for that?"

"My mom's. She's an awesome cook." He pauses and then leans forward, bowing his head toward me. "Want to meet her sometime?"

Joy surges upward past my lungs and pushes into my throat. "She's Evelyn's sister, right?" My voice cracks.

"Yep, Evelyn's baby sister."

"I'd love to meet your mom. We could exchange recipes."

Todd grins and nods. "And she can show you all the embarrassing pictures of my childhood."

"Sounds like a blast."

"My parents will be relieved to meet you, you know."

"Why's that?"

"I've never brought anyone home to meet them before. Not since high school anyway, and that didn't really count as my prom date lived down the road and our folks had been friends since before we were born."

"Oh."

"I think they're worried I'm gay."

I suppress my giggles at the thought. "Why on earth would they think that? You're a country bachelor, for God's sake!"

"Yeah, but magicians, you know. Siegfried and Roy. David Copperfield..."

"David Copperfield?" I ask incredulously.

"Oh come on, he's engaged for a decade to a supermodel but they never marry?"

"Maybe *she's* gay."

"Yeah, any guy interested in entertainment is automatically suspected: artists, dancers, actors. Even magicians." He reaches across the table and takes my hand.

"You're right. That is true." Our faces move closer for another kiss and he rubs his thumb across my knuckles.

A shrill cell phone tone fills the air and Todd leaps out of his chair. "That's me! I'll be right back. Can I take this in your bedroom?"

"Sure." He hurries to grab his phone off the coffee table and closes the bedroom door behind him. What kind of phone call does he need to take in private? I strain my ears to hear what he's saying on his end.

I can't make out anything he's saying, so I stand and begin to clear the table. I'll just ask him who called when he comes back out.

I'm filling the sink with soapy water when Todd appears in the doorway. In two steps he crosses the distance between us and lifts me into a gigantic bear hug, spinning me around, and flinging soapy water everywhere.

"What's going on?"

He sets me down and looks at me solemnly. "Sadie, are you ready to move out of a long-distance relationship?"

"Wh—?"

His lips stretch into a huge smile. "I mean it. I promise I'll take you out every Friday night if you'll let me."

"What do you mean? How can you?"

He starts to chuckle and hugs me again.

"What?"

"That was the head of the Comparative Biomedical Sciences program at the University. They've offered me a job."

"There? I mean, here?"

"Yeah, here. A position as a lecturer and to head up some of their research projects over at the School of Veterinary Science."

"Holy shit! No kidding!"

"Yep." Todd leans back against the stove and crosses his arms. "I'm trading in my practice in Neillsville for a big-city job in the Ivory Tower."

I'm speechless.

"We can become one of those short-distance relationships, if you want."

"I guess you're right," I murmur.

"If that's what you want, Sadie."

I don't have to answer with words. I cross the three and a half feet of kitchen tile between us and wrap my arms around his neck. Kissing this goateed man is becoming one of my favorite things to do.

After rolling out of Todd's arms Saturday morning, I brush my teeth and check my hair. In college I had a friend who got up in the middle of the night at her boyfriend's place to completely redo her make-up and hair so she'd look flawless first thing in the morning. I only aspire to eliminate morning breath and enormous cowlicks.

The egg bake is in the oven and the coffee maker gurgles steadily when Todd joins me. "Good morning," he yawns.

"Good morning to you, too."

"Guess you can be a morning person when you don't drink whiskey," he teases. I love how his eyes sparkle when he smiles at me.

"Guess you can sleep in when you've had a good work out the night before."

"Guess so. Mmm. More home cooking?"

"You bet. Compliments of Coddled Cuisine."

"I could get used to this." Todd sits next to me on the couch and I snuggle into his side for a moment, enjoying the warmth of his body.

"Me too. I'll get you some coffee if you'd like."

He rumples his fingers through his hair and looks around the living room for a moment. "No newspaper?"

"I usually read at work."

"May I?" He gestures to the remote control.

I nod. How cool is it that he leaves the morning news on my favorite station? We drink our coffee together, and it feels like it's our seventieth Saturday morning together on my couch instead of our first.

"Congratulations, Todd!" Evelyn throws her arms around her nephew's shoulders and beams at me from her front stoop. "When do you move to Madison?" She drops her arms and motions us into her house.

"In two months. I'll start midsummer and that will give me enough time to hopefully find and train my replacement in Neillsville."

"Two months." Evelyn repeats. "Will you be okay with leaving your country home?"

"I think I'll try to rent it to my replacement. I could never sell Gran's place. Besides, this isn't a permanent position."

"Yet." Even I'm surprised that I interject this comment. Whoa, Sadie! Slow it down!

"Right." Todd's grin assures me that maybe I'm not a complete nutcase.

"And you've brought potatoes," Evelyn gushes. "Sadie's becoming Miss Becky Home-Ecky."

"I have all kinds of untapped potential." I tell her.

"That you do, dear. That you do."

We follow Evelyn through the kitchen and into the backyard where Evelyn's husband is firing up the grill. He salutes us with his spatula and I inhale the sharp odor of charcoal and lighter fluid. Who'd ever guess I'd spend my Saturday night in love, on a double date of sorts?

## Chapter Forty-One

**"Coddled Cuisine offers you freedom, friendships, and pride"**
*—Coddled Cuisine benefits brochure*

I don't mind going to work Monday morning. The end of my time as Dean's personal slave is in sight. Todd and I have a real future together, and I'm going to Neillsville to visit him in two weeks. I've made such strides up the Coddled Cuisine corporate ladder that I put Donald Trump to shame. Even the weather agrees with my mood this morning—it's one of those balmy May days when it'll reach eighty by noon, and every college kid'll be stretched out on the lawn by the lakeshore. A school bus lurches past as I wait to cross University Avenue. I wave to a little girl who is looking out the window, her nose smushed against the glass. She holds her hand up and wiggles her fingers back at me.

"Good morning, Lottie." I pat the top of her computer as I pass her desk. "Are you all ready for that new baby?"

"Just have to get that wipes warmer off of eBay and I'll be all set."

"Good for you."

I stop by Evelyn's office to leave a bagel and coffee from Bakers Too on her desk. Using a magic marker, I sign my name on the napkin.

Today our guest is Lauren Carter, an activist for women's rights slated to discuss the Supreme Court's influence on reproductive rights. Dean has Lauren's biography and a brief background of how reproduction landed in the courts. We reviewed it yesterday in his office and he whined and pontificated the entire time. "We're put on this earth to procreate. If you don't want babies, then you shouldn't have sex." His narrow view of women's health issues is a reason why we don't bring in a speaker like Lauren very often.

"Ready to discuss condoms?" Dean asks when he comes in the studio.

I ignore his juvenile commentary and get Lauren on the line. She's an experienced speaker—hell, she's addressed Congress before—so I'm not worried about her. I'm not concerned about Dean, either. If he sinks or swims, it makes no difference to my career.

"Okay, Dean. Lauren's ready."

"Good morning, you're listening to *Idea Exchange*. I'm Dean LaRoche and our guest this morning is Laura Carter, a liberal woman activist."

"The name is *Lauren* Carter, Dean. Yes, I'm a women's rights activist. Thank you for having me on your show this morning."

"Right. So it says here, *Laura*, that you support abortions and passing out condoms to teenagers."

"*Lauren*. Well, I prefer to say that I've taken an inerest in women's reproductive rights. It's interesting to note that in Wisconsin men have easier access to Viagra than women have for birth control pills—"

"Don't many religious groups see the Pill as a form of abortion?"

"No. Some religious groups view the Pill as against their doctrine, as it prevents conception, but it doesn't undo conception, Dean."

And so the banter continues until callers take over and Dean's interjections are limited to every three minutes or so. I cannot believe he's so rude on-air today.

After he's done insinuating that women should limit themselves to the home and family, my blood reaches boiling point. After today, my revenge on Dean will be complete with one simple move—rather one simple *non-*move.

The show wraps up with a few final zingers aimed at Lauren.

"Thanks for taking time to be with us this morning, *Laura*. I think it's safe to say that men and women have very different views on these topics."

Gracious to the end, Lauren replies, "Thank you, Dean, for having me on your show. I'd like to add—" Dean hangs up her line, cutting off her final remarks, and I vow to call her back to personally apologize.

I reach forward like I have a thousand times to switch us off-air. But this time I don't move the switch. My head is rushing and my face is hot, but I'm determined beneath my trembling.

"Dean, you were really rude to our guest today." I gulp for air.

"Sadie, you should leave the guest list to me in the future. I don't think our listeners support providing abortions as birth control."

"Dean, half of our listeners *are* women. Lauren's addressing reproductive health issues that directly affect them. Planned Parenthood is more about delivering pap smears and other routine exams to women who can't access them."

"If women wouldn't whore around, this wouldn't be an issue in the first place. There's absolutely no reason to fund these clinics."

"Are you saying that women shouldn't have basic reproductive rights? Shouldn't have basic freedoms? Or access to medical care?" I glance out the window and see Ron scowling through the glass and the phones lighting up like Christmas trees. A second later, Evelyn and Lottie join Ron in the hallway.

"I'm saying we'd have a lot fewer problems if women knew their place—at home, making and raising babies, like God intended!" Dean shouts this last line and slams the desk with his open hands. Ron crashes through the door at the same instant, all five feet of him directed at Dean.

"Out!" Ron yells.

I reach forward and switch us off-air.

"What?" Dean turns his head to look at Ron. He's probably never felt the full force of Ron's fury before.

"I SAID GET OUT!"

"Get out? Do you realize who I am?" Dean demands.

"Maybe you don't realize who *I* am." Ron's voice is low and menacing.

I never noticed before this moment how terrifying Dean's size was. And when he moves so slowly and deliberately, it makes his size even more threatening. He walks toward my desk. Each movement brings him closer to me and I feel my courage shrivel up at the edges. He looks down at the control panel and understands what I've done.

Ron's voice breaks the silence. "Dean, I said leave *now.*"

Dean takes one more step towards me and stops. My nose is level with his thighs. I don't want to look at him. I raise my gaze and stare back at him while my heart threatens to batter a hole through my chest. For the first time in two years, I recognize the complete contempt Dean has for me. He curls his upper lip and jerks his chin up. Then he turns and walks slowly out of the booth. I shrink two inches when I let out my breath. I hadn't realized I was holding it.

"Sadie."

I look up at Ron. Here it comes.

"Yes?"

"Go to your office. I'll talk with you later."

"Okay." I gather my things and head for the door in humiliation. I've been sent to my room like a child. Why did I push my luck? I was a month away from a dream job with Bernadette and I had to blow it. Now I'll have no job.

In my office I redial Lauren Carter to apologize. She's gracious and forgiving. I sense she's dealt with Dean's type before.

"Lauren, I hope you'll consider doing a show again in the future. I'm—I'm supposed to start working on a new show soon, and you'd really like this host." I stop talking, realizing that I might not work on any show soon after this morning.

"Don't worry, I'd be delighted to be a guest again. Thanks for calling me back."

After I hang up the phone, I sink into my chair and hold my head with my hands. Stupid. Idiot. Dumb. Moron. But oh, what scrumptious revenge.

I think about Dean's expression. Until today I had written him off as ignorant and clueless. But the combination of his empty brain with a total disregard for all my hard work for him makes me incredulous that I worked so hard for him.

Can I make a living off of Coddled Cuisine? Everyone I've talked to seems to think I can. I better be able to. After today, it's sure to be my only source of income.

"Sadie."

I look up at Ron and it takes all my willpower not to start groveling for mercy.

"That stunt you pulled today—" He stops and places his hands on my desk to lean forward. "You might as well pack your things right now if you plan to ever do that again." He turns and leaves my office.

"I won't have to working for Bernadette."

But I still have to face Dean until Bernadette can use me.

I don't see Dean for the rest of the day and no one knows where he is. Everyone is too busy congratulating me.

"You go, girl!" Delaine whispers as she passes me in the hall. Evelyn buys me lunch and reassures me of my job security. Lottie winks at me when I leave. Even *Wisconsin Outdoors Life* reporter Larry Smullen gives me a wider smile than usual. Apparently Dean isn't as popular as I've always thought.

I leave the office with tomorrow's guest confirmed. I'll get here early tomorrow and try to keep an open mind for whatever happens.

When I get home I hear Jane's voice leaving a message on the answering machine. I race to pick up the receiver.

"Jane!"

"Hey! I figured you would be out after work today, celebrating your emancipation from Dean LaCockroach."

"Not sure what's going to happen, actually. I'm just glad I still have a job."

"What do you mean?"

"I left him on-air on purpose. I set him up."

"You did?" Jane sounds amazed at this. "I would've figured his rude attitude on the show would get him fired."

I never thought about how he came off to the audience. "Really?"

"Oh my God, have you no idea of how he sounded today?"

"Honestly? He sounds so bad off-air that I always assumed everyone else knew it already and didn't mind."

"Stupid, yes. But he has never sounded so insulting. Getting the guest's name wrong—lying about her credentials—he was in rare form today."

"I guess so."

"So what happens tomorrow?"

"I don't know. That's the scary part. I don't start for Bernadette yet, but I don't think I have it in me to face Dean again."

"Presuming he's still employed there."

"Presuming that, of course."

"Want my advice?"

"Call in sick?" I ask hopefully.

"Show up and do what you've been hired to do. Nothing more. Nothing less."

"I knew that would be your advice," I grumble.

"Why did you ask?" Jane replies. "Got to go before all hell breaks loose here. Olivia lost the rabbit and Erich invited some co-workers for dinner."

"Have fun."

"I'll call you tomorrow."

I call Molly next. A girlfriend fix will cure my blues. I'm not sure whether to cry or get drunk.

"What are you doing tonight?"

"Ummm…something with you, right?"


Molly's my favorite friend in the world. We meet for a rousing celebration of my triumphant on-air revenge over pitchers of Killian's Red.

"I can't believe you pulled it off! At last!" Molly crashes her mug into mine for the fifteenth time tonight. "To women!"

"To beer!" I take a long swallow and the heavy dream-like feeling of too much alcohol starts to hit. "Uh, Molly? I think we better switch to soda here before things get ugly."

She laughs and finishes the rest of the beer in her mug. "I've got a better idea. Let's switch to *pizza* and soda and get the hell out of here."

Giggling and swaying slightly, we head down State Street in search of some food to sober us up. It strikes me as we sit down to order a large vegetarian stuffed pizza at Pizzeria Uno that I didn't even wonder if I could afford it this time. And when a group of handsome suits take the table next to ours, I don't even glance over twice.

Today I'm Sadie Davis, twenty-eight, half of a couple, and flush with cash and friends. I only wish I could steal Trump's line and tell Dean, "You're fired."

At one in the morning I'm stumbling up the steps of my apartment building when a shadow moves in the corner of the porch. Shit—just when life's going good for me, I'm going to get mugged. Too drunk to put up a good fight, I hold my purse out when the man walks towards me, arms outstretched.

Instead of holding a gun or a knife, he's holding a huge box with a bow on top.

"Todd? Oh my God, you scared me to death!"

"Where have you been all night? I've been waiting here since seven." He looks at me, taking in my blood-shot eyes and rumpled hair.

"Molly and I went to celebrate my emancipation from Dean—what're you doing here?"

"I caught your show this morning. I wanted to take you out tonight and celebrate your courage." He looks disappointed. "Guess I was too late to surprise you."

"No. I mean, yeah, you are for tonight. But come on up anyway." I fumble for my keys and let us in the building. "Do you have to head back tomorrow?"

"I do."

Damn. Here's Mr. Right, ready to take me out on the town as a surprise and I blew it by going out with Molly. Fuck.

In my apartment Todd presents me with the gift. "What's this?" I ask.

"A token of my affection. It's symbolic."

I read the card. "To Sadie—May you get thousands of points and always figure out the right move." I slide the ribbon off the box and tear away the gift wrap.

"I'll hook it up right now and we can play," Todd says.

An Atari 1200 and a *Ms. Pac-Man* game sit nestled in the tissue paper.

"Can we keep it at your place for now?" he asks.

"For now—until you move to town." I kiss him and he wraps his arms around me.

"Then where will we keep her?"

"Here still—same place you'll be." I set the box on the couch.

He lifts me up and carries me to the bedroom, whispering in my hair, "Let's set it up tomorrow."

# Epilogue

Six months later, Molly and Ben continue to annoy and adore one another alternately since he moved in with her and learned the definition of a clean bathroom, while she learned to appreciate the power of capitalism when presented with a one-carat diamond engagement ring. Kara took over their wedding plans because she says she'll never get to do this for herself as long as conservatives dominate Wisconsin's legislature.

Dean LaRoche got his walking papers from Ron when the third intern quit on him. Rumor has it he's doing a sports and weather report for an AM station near Rhinelander.

Bernadette's show continues to pull in fabulous ratings and there's talk of national syndication. We spend an hour every day post-show discussing our future fame and fortune, if it all works out.

Lottie had a girl, April Louise. Everyone got invitations to a scrapbooking party the following month, presumably to fund April's scrapbook. I declined.

At my ten-year class reunion, I learned from Jessica Lewiston that Henry did end up marrying Nikki and they're pregnant with their second child. I snicker at the thought of him changing diapers and giving up *SportsCenter* for *Sesame Street*. I showed up looking svelte and sexy in a black linen sheath dress that complemented my tan.

Unfortunately, Todd freckled and burned while we were in Hawaii. But he wowed the crowd at the annual Coddled Cuisine convention with magic tricks during the awards banquet. I'm still a district manager. I do one or two parties a week, handing over my excess shows to my newest recruit, Evelyn, who in exchange has taught me how to cook. She says it's the least she can do for her future niece.

My mom told me last weekend that she's proud of me. She really likes Todd, of course, because he plays Sheepshead, and Jane's kids adore him because he can do magic tricks. It's like having Uncle Bert around all the time.

Uncle Bert gave up his magic shop and now works on a cruise ship full-time, making swords and fish and swordfish vanish. Jane and Erich plan to take the kids on a cruise next Christmas to visit him.

The Carlyles are still at large. While I think about Kimberly sometimes, it's to marvel at how I've surpassed her in sophistication, confidence, and honesty.

Todd's in line for a permanent position at the University and has an old intern lined up to take over the Neillsville practice and rent his house. We put in an offer on a house three blocks away from the Carlyles' old neighborhood last week, the day after Todd got on one knee and pulled a blue velvet ring box from behind my left ear. "Every time I look at you I believe in magic, Sadie. Will you marry me?" The diamond looks stunning against my Hawaiian tan.